Visit our website at www.skyhorsepublishing.com.

10 9 8 7 6 5 4 3 2 1

Library of Congress Cataloging-in-Publication Data is available on file.

Cover artwork: "Chivalry" by Megan Euker
Cover design by APOTH Creative
Photo of front cover art and author by Jon-Patric Nelson
Photo of back cover art by Jay Knickerbocker

ISBN: 978-1-5107-7832-0
Ebook ISBN: 978-1-5107-7871-9

Printed in the United States of America

Dedications

In today's reality, where selfishness has been deemed virtuous and decency a crime, I dedicate this book to the chivalrous beings of humanity, our last hope.

Contents

Character and Terms List

Aakil	Sa'eeda's husband
Abbaa gudaa	Grandfather
Abby	Classmate of Ahmed
Adeera (Uncle Caleb)	Father's brother
Ahmed Selassie (Isa)	Ethiopian main character
Angela	Italian girl that frequented Koss
Arnie Schuman	Sixtyish man with white kinky hair; Bob Herman's manager
Bob Herman	Blonde man in his 30's, special projects manager; finds brown bag with manuscript on bus
Bobby "Bones" Calabrese	Classmate of Ahmed
Captain Ginsel	Attorney representing a US officer who made a fortune selling US equipment to the other side
Captain Kosel	Ginsel's client
Chuck	Guy at the race track
Colonel Drummond	Colonel to Ahmed
Corporal Clark (later Detective Clark)	Soldier with Ahmed
Corporal Gallo	Short, bald man with a hooked nose
Corporal Harms (later Detective Harms)	Short, thin, black soldier with glasses
Corporal Hurt	Drummond's assistant
Corporal Kamar	Arab soldier who refers to Ahmed as "Isa"
Corporal Kennedy (later Detective Jack Kennedy)	Soldier with Ahmed; a blonde-haired man with a US flag tattooed on his right forearm
Donny	Guard at GAM

Fatima	Ahmed's sister
Gaadha	Mother
Gael Veenstra	41-year old redhead, works at GAM
Gent America Media (GAM)	Media company Bob Herman works for
Halliburton	One of the world's largest providers of products and services for the ever-evolving needs of the energy industry
Hessna	Ahmed's favorite sister
Holt	Lanky, dark-skinned soldier with a thin mustache
Hussein	Ahmed's father (Abbaa)
Jafaar	Ahmed's cousin
Jennifer	Young blonde woman at GAM
Kamar	Arab soldier
KBR	Private defense and intelligence company
Larry	Large, dark-skinned guy, answers door for Sister Brenda
Lou Mell	Works with Bob Herman
Lucia	Petite, mixed-race beauty
Mark Koss	70-year old man, owner of Gent America Media
Mengistu Haile Mariam	Ethiopian chairman
Mr. Thomas	Ahmed's school teacher
Muhammad	Ahmed's brother
Nadine	Heroine addict that Koss frequented
nama goota	A chivalrous man
Phillips	Head of corporate sales at GAM
Sa'eeda	Ahmed's cousin in Ethiopia
Saa and Sabira	Sa'eeda and Aakil's daughters
Selton	Bestselling author at Gent America Media
Senator Feinvine	Senator
Shelby Warren	Attorney
Sister Brenda	Nun
tahajjud	Evening prayer
Ted Basle	60ish, works for Gent America Media as the "utility man" who gets the job done

Teru	Light-skinned Ethiopian woman in NY who taught Ahmed English
Tommy	Sister Brenda's brother
Tony Baroni	Classmate of Ahmed
Tony Russo	Lucia's former boxer boyfriend
Van	Guy at the race track
Wako (Eessuma)	Mother's brother

PART I

Chapter 1

Oromo

Ahmed Selassie had dark brown eyes and light brown hair and was the youngest of four. Muhammad, Fatima, and then before Ahmed came his favorite sister, Hessna. His family lived in Harar, an ancient, walled, Ethiopian city of 150,000, five hundred kilometers from the capital, Addis Ababa, in the state of Oromia. At 1,885 meters above sea level, Harar is titled the "City of Saints" and is the fourth holiest place of Islam. Prophets assuredly enjoyed the climate; the average high temperatures are in the upper seventies and low temperatures in the mid-fifties, throughout the year.

Ahmed's Abbaa (father), Hussein, was a wise, knowledgeable, and trusted merchant who spoke eleven languages. The state of Oromia produces cotton, every type of grain, potato, mango, avocado, banana, lemon, pineapple, peach, onion, garlic, coriander, ginger, okra, and many other varieties of vegetables. The region exports coffee, oil seeds, hides, and skins. Ninety percent of the inhabitants work in agriculture.

Ethiopia also has vast amounts of gold, silver, platinum, uranium, nickel, marble, and natural gas, but Ahmed's family concentrated on marketing agricultural products.

Ahmed was five years old. His family was leaving on vacation to visit Lake Basaka in Metehara. Haadha (mother) said that Lake Basaka was paradise on earth. Metehara is full of beautiful, rugged mountains and streams and wildlife, including hippopotamuses, crocodiles, lions, leopards, rhinoceros, buffalo, giraffes, wild ass, zebras, and elephants.

The area is also home to the nyala, ibex deer, the colobus monkey, and the red fox, Ethiopia's rodent-eating wolf. These animals are found nowhere else in the world but Oromia.

It was quickly becoming a family ritual, and in midsummer; Haadha and Abbaa prepared for days. Haadha boiled jars of fresh fruits and vegetables. Abbaa worked on the tents, bows and arrows, and fishing equipment. Unfortunately, Ahmed was sick with the flu.

3

Hoping that Ahmed would recover, the family postponed the trip a day. However, harvest would soon arrive and the family could wait no longer. They sadly departed without him. Ahmed was disappointed, but he also loved being with Abbaa Gudaa (grandfather), his father's father and a proud, patriotic man from Harar. Everyone seemed to love Abbaa Gudaa. Ahmed believed that Abbaa Gudaa was the most important man in Oromia.

Ahmed was different from any child Abbaa Gudaa had ever known. He was curious about everything. Ethiopia, with over one hundred million inhabitants and eighty distinct people and languages, was the perfect home for such a mind. The Ethiopians are a fascinating mixture of Arab, Asiatic, and African, with skin tones from very light to very dark.

Ethiopia, the second-most-populous nation in Africa, is a mysterious country, where all religions and races are tolerant of one another. Oromia, Ethiopia's largest region, is larger than Belgium, France, Italy, the Netherlands, and Switzerland combined.

Abbaa Gudaa, too, was secretly happy that his grandson would miss the family vacation. In the past, together, they had visited many of the hundreds of beautiful shrines and mosques that speckled Harar. Once Abbaa Gudaa brought Ahmed to the Harar Beer Bottling company. The owner loved Abbaa Gudaa and gave him tickets to the soccer game at the Harrar Birra Stadium.

The morning after the family left on vacation, Ahmed sat on Abbaa Gudaa's lap and listened to an old Harar story. His grandfather spoke with heart and expression, stopping along the way to make sure that Ahmed digested every word. Abbaa Gudaa told Ahmed that stories like this one would help mold Ahmed into a fine man.

Once upon a time, there was a very holy man. He lived in the city Addis Ababa, and every day he went to the mosque five times to pray. But the city was big, and there were many people in the streets. "This place is very noisy," the holy man thought. "I can't pray to God here. I must go to a quiet place, far away from the city." So the holy man went out of the city. He walked for a long time.

At last, he came to a high wall. There was an orchard of fruit trees on the other side of the wall. "This is a fine orchard, with many fruit trees," thought the holy man. "Those guavas and bananas look delicious, and I am very hungry." A stream of water was running out of the orchard. The holy man looked at it. "What's that yellow thing in the water?" he thought. "Oh, it's a guava. It's outside the orchard, and no one can see me. I will eat it." So the holy man took the guava out of the stream and ate it.

Soon it was time to pray, and the holy man began to wash himself in the stream. But then he began to think. "Why did I eat that guava?" he asked himself. "It wasn't mine.

It belonged to the owner of the orchard. I did a bad thing. I must go to the owner of the orchard, and I must tell him I am sorry." So the holy man found the gate of the orchard, and he went inside. The orchard was very big, with many guava and banana trees. In the middle of the orchard there was a big house.

The owner of the orchard was coming out of the house. The holy man went up to him. "Excuse me, sir. I want to tell you something," he said. "I found a guava in the stream outside your orchard. I was hungry and I ate it. But it was your guava. I was stealing it from you. Please forgive me." The owner of the orchard looked at him. "No," he said. "I can't forgive you. You did a bad thing. Now you must do something for me." "What must I do?" the holy man asked. "You must marry my daughter," said the owner of the orchard. "My daughter has no eyes and she cannot walk. But if you marry her, I will forgive you. If you do not marry her, I will not forgive you." The holy man was sad.

"This is a big price to pay for a small mistake," he thought, but he said to the owner, "Yes, I agree. I will marry your daughter. Let me see her now." "No," said the owner of the orchard. "First you must marry her. Then you can see her." So the holy man married the orchard owner's daughter. She was covered with a veil, and he could not see her. "Now," said the orchard owner. "My daughter is your wife. Take off the veil and look at her." The holy man took off his wife's veil. "Oh!" he said. "But—but you are beautiful! Are you blind? No, you can see! Are you lame? No, you can walk! But your father said, 'My daughter has no eyes and no legs.'"

The owner of the orchard smiled at him. "You did not understand me," he said. "This was my meaning. My daughter has no eyes for wicked things. She never looks at them. And she cannot walk in evil places. She always follows the path of goodness. I was looking for a holy man to be her husband, and now, my dear son-in-law, I have found one."

And from that day, the holy man lived with his wife and her father, and they were very happy.

Abbaa Gudaa finished the story, and they ate injera bread with vegetables. Ahmed fell fast asleep in Abbaa Gudaa's bed, which was in the room next to Ahmed's parents' room.

Ahmed woke to hear his Eessuma (mother's brother), Wako, and Abbaa Gudaa crying and screaming in an ancient Oromo dialect.

Ahmed understood only that darkness had the family in its grip. Soon the house was full of women, screaming, ripping their gowns, and pulling their hair out.

Ahmed lightly sauntered into the front room of the house. Women were washing the bodies of his mother and two sisters.

Ahmed ran to his sister Hessna. She had a gash on her head and her eyes were frozen open. Rigor mortis had set in on his mother's body, and an old woman was sitting on her arm forcing it to lie flat with the rest of her.

Two other packages were wrapped in white. Ahmed cried, sure that the wrapped bundles were his father and his brother Hussein. Abbaa Gudaa arrived from behind and carried Ahmed into the yard where men were singing verses of the Koran.

Abbaa Gudaa looked into Ahmed's face and cried. Ahmed hugged him with all his might, hoping that doing so would wake him from this horrible nightmare. His family's car had gone off a cliff on the way home from their vacation.

After a few moments hugging and kissing, Abbaa Gudaa placed Ahmed on the ground. The man next to Ahmed took his hand. Abbaa Gudaa took Ahmed's other hand and began singing. Ahmed did not know the words. But his babbling mixed with tears created depth and substance.

Ahmed understood that the men were singing to distract themselves from the pain. He sang with all his soul.

For six days of mourning the house was filled with friends and relatives.

At the end of the week, a huge ox was slaughtered, and the family and their friends had a great festival.

Women took turns raising Ahmed in the air. They sang to the salvation of his dead family. They sang for his rebirth without them.

At noon, lunch was served. After lunch, the women cleaned the house. The men distributed the Holy Koran. With passion and persistence, they completed the entire book. Around sundown, everyone ate a series of dishes made of local vegetables and spices, then drank tea. The women tidied the abode, and the banquet was over.

Ahmed's aunt and cousins came over each day to care for him and Abbaa Gudaa. Abbaa Gudaa wished that he had been on the trip. He no longer uttered a word. Ahmed understood; the loss was too much to pronounce. Ahmed, also, did not speak.

After a week, Abbaa Gudaa died.

It was 1981. Ahmed was six years old. He moved in with his aunt and uncle's family. One night while it was still dark, his aunt packed him a small suitcase. The women cried and hugged Ahmed. They then walked him to the bus stop in the center of Harar.

The bus arrived, and his relatives cried and kissed him again. Ahmed boarded the bus with his fifteen-year-old cousin Jafaar. Jafaar was light skinned with hazel eyes and jet-black hair.

The trip between Harar and Addis Ababa was exciting. Ahmed watched out the windows. He saw waterfalls, lakes, mountains, zebras, giraffes, monkeys, and elephants.

Every hour or so, the bus stopped at another town. Some passengers would get off and some would get on.

Ahmed and Jafaar ate the injera and vegetables that his aunts had prepared. There was an elderly man seated behind them who didn't bring food. Jafaar explained to Ahmed that it was their duty to share with him. Ahmed was certain that Jafaar would someday become a good man like their Abbaa Gudaa had been.

The bus erupted into applause as the tall buildings of Addis Ababa came into sight.

Everyone disembarked in the center of town. Ahmed and Jafaar had never seen anything like Addis Ababa. They walked about for a few hours. Finally, they took the train to the Bole International Airport, finding it incredibly difficult to believe how smooth and fast the railed bus traveled.

On the plane, Jafaar let Ahmed have his seat by the window. The takeoff was an experience Ahmed never wanted to forget.

Ahmed looked down. He tried to see if he could spot his house from the sky. He missed his family terribly, but the adventure that he was living numbed the pain. They landed in Frankfurt and then boarded another plane for New York.

At New York's JFK Airport, Ahmed's adeera (father's brother), Uncle Caleb, met them and took them into New York City by cab. Ahmed looked out the windows at the tall buildings, bridges, garbage, water, and people, all the time wondering what he was doing there.

Chapter 2

New York

Uncle Caleb was a fifty-five-year-old philosophy professor at New York University. He had arrived in the United States twenty-five years prior, in 1955, when he was thirty years old.

Ahmed looked up and down the street as they exited the cab. There was no sand and no dirt, just streets, sidewalks, and buildings. He carried his bag up the thirteen stairs to Uncle Caleb's apartment, not wanting or expecting assistance. Jafaar followed closely behind Ahmed but stood on the concrete landing staring at the new world until Uncle Caleb tapped him on his shoulder.

The house was brown, filled with leather, woodwork, tables, and chairs.

Uncle Caleb spoke perfect Oromo, perfect Arabic, Amharic (the official language of Ethiopia), Farsi (Persian spoken in most of Iran), Dari (spoken in Afghanistan), French, English, and Italian.

At 3:24 in the afternoon, Uncle Caleb rolled out a rug and he and Jafaar said Asr, their afternoon prayer. Ahmed, who had witnessed prayers thousands of times, sat on the large, ripped leather chair until they finished.

The following day, Uncle Caleb showed the boys a bit of New York. Everything that Ahmed saw fascinated him. Each new experience made him think of Abbaa Gudaa.

Ahmed sometimes saw his grandfather's gentle face in the trees, in the sky, in the bar of soap, and always as he lay in his bed. He stared into the dark and watched as Abbaa Gudaa walked with Hessna, Fatima, and Muhammed. Ahmed hoped to some-day be reunited with them. He often wondered if things would have turned out better had he not missed the vacation with his family.

After three days, Uncle Caleb, Jafaar, and Ahmed took a cab to the airport. Ahmed knew that Jafaar was leaving for home. He missed his cousin before Jafaar was even gone. Ahmed cried on the way to the airport, but didn't let anyone see.

Uncle Caleb was a quiet man, and when he did speak, he only spoke in English, a strange language, which Ahmed had difficulty understanding.

Ahmed did not want to disappoint. He studied every detail: eyes, lips, facial expression, arm and hand movement, and the tone of his uncle's voice.

Of course, they connected instantly. Uncle Caleb was also the son of Abbaa Gudaa. The blood that flowed through their veins was the same. The love that they shared surged from the same fountain.

On the fifth day, Teru, a light-skinned Ethiopian woman, came to stay at the house. Each morning, Uncle Caleb loaded a small leather case with books and left. Teru spoke Amharic and English. Uncle Caleb instructed her to teach Ahmed both languages, but to concentrate on English as Ahmed would soon begin school.

From the moment that Uncle Caleb left in the morning until he returned, ten to twelve hours later, Ahmed sat at the kitchen table surrounded by books. He gradually began writing the English alphabet and pronouncing English and Amharic words.

During breaks, Teru turned on the television. Ahmed watched Big Bird, Elmo, Ernie, Oscar the Grouch, Count von Count, the Cookie Monster, Bert, and Bruno the Trashman—all characters of *Sesame Street*.

Each evening, just before Uncle Caleb appeared, Teru cleared the table and assisted Ahmed to do *ghusl*, a full body wash.

Uncle Caleb would gently place his satchel on the table, nod at Ahmed, and sit for dinner. If it was prayer time, they waited and ate after.

This went on from the spring through the summer. One morning, Uncle gave Teru money and instructions. Ahmed and Teru went to stores and bought Ahmed clothes. It was good timing. None of the clothes Ahmed had brought from Ethiopia fit him any longer.

Teru explained to Ahmed in gentle Amharic that Monday he would go to PS 41 Greenwich Village School at 116 West 11th Street. She insisted that he memorize the house and school addresses.

Ahmed entered first grade. Thanks to Teru, Uncle Caleb, Big Bird, Count von Count, and some of the other *Sesame Street* characters, he excelled.

In the evening, Uncle Caleb read the Koran to Ahmed. Ahmed believed that it was the most that his Uncle Caleb ever spoke to anyone. Abbaa Gudaa was much different than his son Caleb, but Ahmed quickly also learned to love the soft, quiet ways of his Uncle Caleb.

Being a teacher of philosophy, Uncle's home was full of books, newspapers, and magazines. Ahmed delved through them whenever he had free time and read the *New York Times* each day when he arrived home from school.

It was October 23rd, 1983. Ahmed was in the third grade. He read about the Marine barracks bombing in the Beirut Airport:

It was the single deadliest day for US marines since the Battle of Iwo Jima. 241 US marines, 58 French troops, six civilians and two suicide drivers were killed. Over 120 people were wounded. The assailants used 21,000 pounds of TNT.

The story was painful to read, reminding Ahmed of the loss of his own family.

When Uncle Caleb arrived, he spoke quietly in Amharic to Teru about the bombing. Ahmed by now understood the language, but just as much, if not more, was communicated to him by the desolation in his uncle's voice.

Uncle, at the time, was instructing a Middle Eastern philosophy course, and several days after the Marine barracks bombing he was attacked by one of his students. Uncle Caleb limped, soberly entering the house. At dinner Ahmed focused on the pain in Uncle's face. Of course, Ahmed knew nothing of the fall down the stairs Uncle had suffered, pushed by an enraged student.

"Uncle, why did terrorists blow up the marine barracks?"

Uncle stared into the bookshelf and spoke after ten seconds. "Do you know the meaning of terrorists?"

"No, Uncle."

"My son, the Israeli army invaded Lebanon with our help." (Uncle most always spoke of himself as an American.) "Thousands have been killed, and many more lost their homes. No one called Israel and the US 'terrorists.'"

Ahmed stared at his uncle. "But why?"

"Because we have planes, bombs, soldiers with uniforms, and control of the media. Today, if you don't have a plane to kill people with, you are a terrorist."

"But Uncle, the people who bombed the barracks blew themselves up to murder innocent people."

Uncle Caleb grasped Ahmed with his painful eyes. "Yes, and six civilians were killed." He paused, "Ahmed, you lost your family two years ago."

Ahmed painfully reflected.

Uncle Caleb continued. "If your family was murdered by invaders and you retaliated, would you be a terrorist?"

Uncle dabbed his mouth with a napkin. The injera and vegetables on his plate were barely touched. Quiet took hold of the room.

Ahmed stared at his uncle's food. After almost a minute of silence, Ahmed slowly began eating his brown beans.

Uncle Caleb spoke. "Some call them terrorists, others patriots, and still others, martyrs."

Ahmed gazed, never remembering the presence of so much gray in his uncle's beard. Ahmed gently moved on his chair and glanced at Teru before again turning and focusing on his uncle Caleb.

"And Uncle, what do you think?"

His uncle nodded slightly, as if the world was going to notice his next words. "I think that men who are harmed become unjust."

Uncle noted Ahmed's intrigued facial expression, believing that he would someday be a fine man. "Eat, my son, there is enough sadness in the world."

Now, in fourth grade, many of Ahmed's schoolmates were Italians from the South Village. One afternoon, the math teacher, Mr. Thomas, asked Ahmed in front of the class who had stolen the calculator off of his desk. The closing bell rang, and the teacher warned Ahmed that he'd pick up the discussion on the following day.

The day before, on his way out of class, Ahmed saw Bobby "Bones" Calabrese snatch the calculator. Mr. Thomas was just as sure that Bobby stole the calculator as he was sure that Ahmed witnessed the theft. Ahmed went home and told Uncle Caleb about the situation.

Uncle listened intently and then measured his words before speaking.

"Certain leaders want to change society, but Islam, instead of turning us into a nation of snitches, rats, and informants, denigrating us to a low level of humanity, raises us to a heaven-high level of being, the ones who bless everyone and everything—in sight and out of sight."

Uncle Caleb eyed Ahmed firmly. "Islam raises us, not lowers us." Uncle paused, smiled, and lightly nodded his head. "No nephew of mine is a snitcher."

The following day, Ahmed was called by Mr. Thomas. The young man stood. The room was still as a rabbit not wanting to be spotted by a hunter.

"Mr. Ahmed Selassie, you are always the last person to leave the room. Now who stole the calculator off my desk Tuesday afternoon?"

Ahmed remained silent. Bobby Bones and his friends stared anxiously.

"Well, Mr. Selassie?"

Ahmed stared into Mr. Thomas's face. He had Uncle Caleb's support and even without it would probably still not be intimidated.

"Don't be afraid, Mr. Selassie. The school will protect you from these thugs."

Ahmed's soundless, calm, cool stare stunned the whole class. Mr. Thomas never felt such a loud *go fuck yourself* in his life—and he had gone through two divorces.

Abby, the skinny, redheaded girl of Dutch heritage, stared more than the others. She never paid much attention to the small, light-skinned, large-nosed boy from Ethiopia, but suddenly he seemed incredibly interesting.

"Mr. Selassie, if you do not tell me, you will be in grave trouble."

Thomas glanced over the riffraff before continuing. "Come now, don't be afraid," he said in an almost British accent. (Thomas was not English and had never even been in a United Kingdom country except for Canada, and that was when he was an infant.)

The swelling silence thickened like a bowl of forgotten oatmeal.

Tony Baroni whispered something inaudible to Ahmed.

"Anthony Baroni! What did you say?"

"Nuttin', I din't say nuttin'."

Thomas knew that Baroni would only be a waste of his time, and quickly darted his beads back to Ahmed, scrutinizing him as a hopeful law student would the first question on the law school exam.

"Selassie, I am losing my patience. I told you." Thomas cleared his throat. His voice dropped a few octaves before continuing. "You have nothing to be afraid of," the teacher said in a Darth Vader–like voice.

"I fear only Allah," Ahmed said quickly and firmly.

The battle line was drawn. The audience was at the edge of their seats.

Mr. Thomas heard clearly, but was hoping to bully Ahmed into changing his mind. "Speak up, boy! What did you say?" (Darth Vader had left his voice).

Ahmed replied calmly. "I said, I fear only Allah."

The room buzzed like a hundred hornets' nests.

"Silence!" Mr. Thomas screamed. At the same time, he slammed his fist on his desk and glared at Ahmed.

Ahmed's facial expression remained serenely constant.

Thomas had his fill of this boy's insolence. The angered teacher rushed toward Ahmed. Ahmed stood motionless, his face free of any emotion.

Thomas grabbed Ahmed's collar. "Get your books! You're going to the principal's office. He will make you talk!"

"He will not," Ahmed said steadily. "Allah raises. He does not lower us to be snitchers."

Thomas slapped Ahmed's face. Ahmed remained unmoved and gazed boldly. Thomas struck him again, took his hair, and banged his head on the desk.

"Hey!" Bones yelled, "Leave the kid alone! He didn't do nuttin'.'"

Thomas let go of Ahmed's hair. Ahmed slowly raised his head. His nose was bleeding. His bottom lip was torn by one of his teeth when his face was rammed into the wooden desk.

Thomas gazed. *Damned Ay-rabs*, he thought; he meant no harm and only mismeasured his actions because the boy had such a big nose. . . .

It was only then that he became frightened. He reached to touch Ahmed's lip. Blood was falling in drops, and stitches meant a police report.

Ahmed moved away, folding his lip into his mouth, sucking the blood down his throat. He liked the taste of his first wound for Allah; it would not be his last.

Mr. Thomas removed a handkerchief from his pocket and escorted Ahmed to the bathroom.

"I did not mean to do that to you, Ahmed," Mr. Thomas said smoothly. "That is the third calculator stolen this year. I know who did it. It was Bobby Bones and his band of Italian hoods."

Ahmed wasn't quite sure what Uncle Caleb would think about the incident. When Ahmed arrived home, Teru cleaned his cut lip.

Uncle Caleb walked in at seven, looked at his nephew, and without speaking a word, went into the bathroom. Ahmed could hear the running water from his uncle washing. After a few minutes, Caleb walked out and set the rug on the floor facing Mecca.

His uncle kneeled. "Ahmed," he called.

Ahmed stood next to his uncle. "Kneel with me, my son. It is time for you, a man of Allah, to enjoy Salah" (pronounced Salat).

Teru began weeping tears of joy.

Ahmed never felt such a pleasurable rush of energy. He kneeled and kissed the floor with Uncle Caleb.

After prayers, Teru set dinner for the men. Uncle smiled tightly across the table at Ahmed. "Honor is Allah's."

"Should we take him to the hospital for stitches after dinner?" Teru asked.

Uncle Caleb grinned and gently shook his head. "Keep the wound clean." He then looked at Ahmed. "Son, if anyone asks you how you hurt yourself, you fell on the way home from school. Being a teacher is not always easy." Uncle smiled. "I have some experience. We would not like to ruin a man's career for a transient moment of anger."

Ahmed was astonished. Uncle had not been in class with Ahmed, yet he saw more clearly than anyone who was.

"Yes, Uncle," he replied.

Abbaa Gudaa had begun, and now Uncle was continuing to make Ahmed a *nama goota*, a chivalrous man. Ahmed felt blessed to know, at such a young age, the meaning of chivalry.

After the event, life changed dramatically; Bones and his friends took Ahmed in as one of their own. They called him Amadeo, then just Deo. Ahmed looked up the meaning of the name Amadeo, "lover of God." This greatly satisfied him and for a while he became "Deo Selassie."

Bones quoted Jesus, who also disapproved of snitchers. He wanted us to take care of one another; "He who has not sinned, throw the first stone," and, "We are our brothers' keepers."

Jesus, or Isa, is the second most important prophet in Islam. Both prophets, Muhammad and Jesus, taught that we are all brothers. Ahmed, or to his Italian friends, Deo, liked being brothers with Bobby Bones and his gang.

Uncle woke Ahmed in the early morning and waited for him in the late evening for prayers.

Abby focused as much attention as she could on Ahmed from that day forward. They often walked each other home from school.

In the eighties, a fair-skinned girl walking with a darker-skinned boy drew attention. Convincing themselves that Ahmed was Italian, Spaniard, or Portuguese helped some sleep better. At that point in time, in the United States, Italians, Spaniards, and Portuguese weren't yet considered white, but were certainly preferred over any of the Arab populations.

One evening Ahmed read the front page of the *Times*:

December 21st 1983: Pan Am Flight 103 from London to New York exploded over the small town of Lockerbie, Scotland. All 259 people on board were killed, along with 11 on the ground.

"Uncle, what will come of our world?"

"My son, Gandhi said that there is enough for man's need but not enough for man's greed."

Uncle stared at Ahmed, realizing that he had not satisfied his nephew's thirst for resolve. "Son, the Middle East is the chessboard where great powers wage battles, for land, oil, glory and power. The people who live there are helpless pawns, and the soldiers who die there are mostly idealistic, unwitting hostages."

Ahmed contemplated his uncle's words. "But uncle, the flight was going from London to New York."

"While the suffering remains in the Middle East, the West will continue playing the game. Their populations do not complain, because they're unaffected and their companies are selling weapons, so they're actually rewarded for terrorism."

"Uncle, what does this occurrence mean for us?"

Uncle Caleb was satisfied with Ahmed's reflection and smiled at his young nephew before continuing, "It means that it will become more problematic to be a Muslim in our country."

"Our country, Uncle?"

"Yes, my son, this is also our country."

"What can we do for our country, Uncle?"

"As true Americans we can start by remembering that lying disparages honor."

Ahmed stared at his uncle.

"Ahmed, if a rose smelled like feces, would we still call it a flower?"

Ahmed smiled, fighting the urge to laugh out loud and not knowing if it would be correct to do so.

His uncle's expression answered. "Ahmed, many fellow Americans lie and call it protecting honor." His uncle paused and smiled tightly. "Now Ahmed, don't you have some studying to do?"

Ethiopia was often a dinner topic. According to Uncle, because of two decades of insurgency and civil war, Ethiopia fell into the grasp of a famine from 1983 to 1985. The government and their supporters claimed that it was caused by a drought. The situation worsened as the government used the disaster as an arm against the insurgents.

Uncle felt that the tragedy was political in nature, a tug-of-war between the resistance and the government. In the middle were the people. Ahmed witnessed his uncle cry while reading some of the horrific stories about Ethiopia in the *New York Times*.

Once, Uncle Caleb angered and described Mengistu Haile Mariam, the Ethiopian chairman, as "a fool who would take burning coals in his hand to gauge their heat, or use his head as a hammer to break a boulder."

For sixth grade, Ahmed switched to the Greenwich Middle School at 490 Hudson Street. Uncle examined Ahmed's books, nodding, smiling, grunting, and frowning as he traipsed through each one. Uncle added a selection of his own books for Ahmed to study. Most dealt in philosophy and history. Ahmed was soon a fan of Espinoza, Thoreau, and Voltaire.

One day after school, Ahmed and Abby were speaking in front of a grocery store close to Abby's home, when a very dark-skinned man appeared out of nowhere.

Abby scrutinized Ahmed as his eyes followed the fellow. She noticed a blatant transformation in Ahmed's facial expression. The man looked through Ahmed and continued to walk.

"What's wrong?" Abby asked.

"That was my uncle."

"You're lying. That was not your uncle."

Ahmed remained quiet.

"Why is he so dark?" Abby asked.

Ahmed studied Abby with his eyes.

"Does he frighten you?" Abby asked.

"No," Ahmed said plainly.

"Is he your real uncle?"

Ahmed remained silent.

"Ahmed, is he your real uncle?" she asked.

"Of course he's my real uncle. What kind of a question is that?" Ahmed replied.

"But he's so black," Abby responded.

Ahmed smiled. "Abby, the shade of one's skin is only critical when describing someone to a blind person. Culture defines a man."

Abby resented being lectured. She knew about race. Each questionnaire one fills out requires information about the color of one's skin. You can't turn on the television without hearing about race.

"He is my uncle." Ahmed paused. "In my country, we are a complexion rainbow, from very light to very dark."

Abby's smirk irritated Ahmed.

"But you don't even look like you're the same race," she ventured.

Ahmed took the time to weigh his communication. "What difference does it make?"

Abby was visibly irritated and glared at Ahmed.

"What difference does it make?" Ahmed asked more sternly.

Abby's eyes looked up, staring into a tree.

Ahmed shook his head. "Abby, why does the census ask people their color?"

Abby looked back at Ahmed and studied him quietly.

"I have never seen a white, black, yellow, or red man. Have you?" Ahmed probed.

Abby remained silent.

"Well, when you do, *point them out to me!*" Ahmed said severely.

Abby watched Ahmed and then giggled. "You weren't this angry the day Mr. Thomas slammed your head into the desk."

Ahmed's expression remained doubtful and wounded. "Yes, that's because Mr. Thomas is a moron. I expected much more from you."

Abby wasn't certain of the degree of Ahmed's seriousness.

"Well, you're right." Abby nodded. "I have never seen Crayola colored people. Anyway . . ." Abby paused. "I don't care."

Abby leaned into Ahmed to kiss him. Ahmed stepped back and headed home.

At dinner that evening, Uncle cleared his throat. "My son, bonds between men and women can be very complex. It is difficult to make a relationship work when both are from the same culture and the same religion. Imagine how it must be when they are from different cultures and different religions."

In October 1987, the world's stock markets crashed. Greenwich Village is not far from Wall Street, and the rumblings from the earthquake could be felt on every block. Uncle was particularly meditative and subdued.

Ahmed studied, and above all observed people and world events. He watched as:

In June 1989, college students took over Beijing's Tiananmen Square in a rally for democracy; thousands were killed as the government crushed the demonstration.

In the fall and winter, the Berlin Wall fell; communist rule ended in Bulgaria, Czechoslovakia, Hungary, Poland, and Romania; and nationalist movements in the Baltics were both literally and figuratively chipping away at the Soviet Union.

Iran, Greece, and South Africa all witnessed the election of reformist governments. A British scientist invented the World Wide Web, the first GPS satellite was launched, and an American company offered the public a dial-up internet connection for the first time.

Also in 1989, Ahmed was president of his graduation class. That wasn't reported in any of the major tabloids.

After eighth grade, Ahmed went to school at the Greenwich Village High School at 116 West 11th Street. He no longer saw much of Bones and the gang, but he still saw Abby, who also went to his school. In his mind, she had become the prettiest girl in New York City.

Ahmed endeavored to make Uncle Caleb proud. By the time he was a sophomore in high school, he and Uncle had kitchen table discussions as if they were colleagues. Ahmed gave profound comments on most any world event.

Saddam Hussein used Kuwait cross drilling into Iraqi oil fields as a motive for invasion, but Uncle Caleb stipulated that Kuwait had been a part of the Basra Province of Iraq until the end of World War I. It then became a vassal of the British Empire until 1961, when it won its independence.

Ahmed and most political leaders believed that Iraq had no valid reason for invading Kuwait, and on January 17th, 1991, the US-led coalition of thirty-four nations invaded Iraq.

The Kuwaiti Emir came out of an eight-week exile on March 15, 1991.

In December 1991, Teru died of breast cancer. The house was devoid of Teru's warmth. There was no one to prepare Ethiopian food. Ahmed felt as if he lost his mother for the second time and Caleb lost his best friend. Uncle was now sixty-six years old, and things had abruptly changed forever.

In the summer of 1993, Ahmed was soon to be a senior in high school. Uncle decided it was time for Ahmed to re-visit Ethiopia.

Ahmed got off the bus in Harar. His cousin Jafaar was impatiently waiting along with dozens of other cousins, aunts, uncles, and family friends.

Jafaar bumped his way to the front and hugged Ahmed. Ahmed's parents' house was now inhabited by his married cousin, Sa'eeda, her husband, Aakil, and their two daughters, Saa and Sabira.

Ahmed slept at Jafaar's home with Jafaar's parents, Ahmed's aunt and uncle. In the evening Jafaar and Ahmed romped in the center of Harar, conversing, kicking a soccer ball, watching women, and sipping coffees in one of the town's many cafes.

Ahmed loved Ethiopia's integrated society and valued the warmth that he believed was easier disseminated in a smaller space.

As a fan of singer Tom Jones, he especially remembered the verse "A man's place on earth is decided by birth." However, Ahmed believed that there was more possibility for upward mobilization in New York, so much so that he tried to convince Jafaar to return with him.

To Ahmed's surprise, Jafaar seemed to not even consider the option, responding that his family needed him on the farm.

After almost two months, Ahmed returned to Uncle in New York. After the loss of Teru, Uncle never recaptured the zest for life that he once had exhibited.

In 1994, Ahmed, almost nineteen years old, graduated valedictorian of his class and was ready for college. Thanks to Uncle's professor position, and Ahmed's grades and ranking in the SAT, he began taking classes at New York University.

Ahmed thirsted to combat injustice and majored in law. He was also a gifted linguist and took some of his classes in Arabic. He hoped to be attorney Ahmed Selassie someday.

Uncle knew of Ahmed's desire. One evening after prayer, while Ahmed was helping his uncle stand, his uncle looked in Ahmed's eyes. "Remember my son, a good Muslim is the defender of the weak. He fights for justice and compassion."

Ahmed smiled and hugged his uncle. "Of course I will, I will honor you, Uncle."

"Honor is Allah's son."

Ahmed nodded.

Ahmed worked in the college bookstore and excelled in every class. Uncle was delighted with his nephew, but rarely praised him. He didn't need to; Ahmed felt love and affection in his uncle's every word, every glance, and every breath.

In the middle of his third year of university, Ahmed showed Uncle his grades and ranking at the top of his class. Uncle Caleb smiled gently and two weeks later died of a massive heart attack.

After the smoke cleared, Ahmed learned why Uncle had been so absorbed during the stock market crash of '87. Caleb had lost all his savings and died with the few assets he was able to amass after that. Ahmed used his uncle's resources for burial in Harar and gave whatever remained to their family in Ethiopia.

The books, Uncle's most precious items and almost the only things of any value, were donated away.

Ahmed could no longer afford the apartment. He boxed up what he could and moved a few blocks west into a roach-infested studio. In dire financial straits and unwilling to put himself into a mountain of debt, he dropped out of school.

Alone and unsure of the road to take, he began looking for other occupations that would not require college. After not seeing each other for years, Abby and Ahmed met where he worked as a bartender in the White Horse Tavern. Abby was working on her bachelor's in marketing at NYU. They rekindled their relationship.

Abby was frustrated that Ahmed had dropped out of college. Also for this reason, she was fearful of telling him how much she loved him. After four months of revived romance, Abby arrived at the bar at 4 a.m. on a Saturday.

Ahmed was closing. He looked up and saw Abby. "What are you doing here at this hour? The streets are not safe for such a beautiful woman as yourself."

"I'm pregnant, Ahmed."

"Please tell me that you are kidding."

"I truly wish that I was."

Ahmed hugged her. Her arms remained at her sides.

"We'll marry," Ahmed whispered in her ear.

Abby remained unmoved. Ahmed sensed coldness. "Abby, this is a surprise, but all children are miraculous gifts from Allah, God."

"Jesus," Abby said, smiling thinly.

Ahmed smiled. "Children are gifts of Jesus and God."

"Is that all that you can say? What future could you offer a child?" Abby asked.

Abby wanted to see Ahmed be aggressive, to beg her to have the child, to explain to her that he would go back to college and become a lawyer. Instead, Ahmed just stared.

"Babies may be gifts, but this child will not be our gift."

"Abby, you're not considering aborting our child?" Ahmed asked, retreating.

"I'll figure it out. But, I'm not sure if I'd have the nerve to go through with it or the courage not to," Abby said.

"Abby, this is our child. We will get through this."

"Ahmed, I want more out of life than just being a mother."

"But there is nothing more beautiful."

"Then why don't you try it?"

Ahmed stared into Abby's ice-cold eyes. Ahmed reached for her arms.

Abby jerked away. "Let me be. I will sort things out . . . by myself. It's my life and you're certainly in no position to help me decide . . . or to do anything else, for that matter."

Abby coldly turned and walked away.

Ahmed was flabbergasted and had no one to talk to. He desperately hoped that Abby would reconsider, but was certain that she would not.

Abby waited for Ahmed to call, to arrive at her house, and ask to speak to her parents. He did none of this. He was not a man. It was convenient for him to just get her pregnant and then let her give the child up. He didn't care, and she wasn't going to beg him to reconsider.

The baby was snatched away at delivery and brought to Saint Anthony's Orphanage. Ahmed didn't ask to be there and wasn't invited. Neither of them ever saw the child. Abby did tell Ahmed that the baby was a girl.

Ahmed was bitterly frustrated and disheartened. Abby was a selfish, shallow woman who decided that a relationship with a poor, broken Ethiopian man was not what she wanted. He remembered the look in her eyes when he told her that Uncle Caleb was his blood uncle.

Periodically, Ahmed called her on the phone. Whenever she asked him what he was doing with his life, he responded, "Working and reading the Koran."

The two were physically only a few city blocks from each other but lived worlds apart.

Chapter 3

Iraq, We Must Change Our Situation

Ahmed struggled to deal with the loss of his family, Uncle Caleb, Abby, and his child. He wished with great certainty that Uncle Caleb or Abbaa Gudaa were around to advise him.

He told his situation to Jafaar by phone. Jafaar said, "Just because women don't know what they want does not stop them from getting it."

Ahmed took this as, "If it's meant to be, it will be."

In the book of Hadith, it is said that every morning, before the fajr, or morning prayer, and after completing the tahajjud, evening prayer, the Prophet Muhammad beseeched God, saying, "Oh Allah! I bear witness that all humans are brothers of each other."

Ahmed examined the world and the behavior of some "so-called Muslims." If the words of Muhammad were true, no one can kill or allow an innocent person to die, because as brothers and sisters, we must have love and concern for all. Ahmed understood this to be precisely what Islam, if correctly interpreted, requires of its followers.

After reading the Koran over and over, Ahmed began reading whatever he could get his hands on. By decoding the printed words in the different languages, he identified power-hungry leaders and war profiteers as the true enemies of peace.

Ahmed remembered Uncle's words: "If one is an extremist, he is ruled by emotion, instead of by reason; haste and impulsiveness, instead of patience and wisdom. Humanity is the only race. Extremism of any kind is a profound blindness to reality."

Ahmed began frequently corresponding with his cousin Jafaar and the rest of his family in Harar. They wanted him to return to Ethiopia, but New York had been his home for almost twenty years, and he had no idea of what he would do in Harar.

At twenty-four, Ahmed was confused and out of choices. He enlisted in the U.S. Army, selecting the Military Police Corps. He did not want to ever kill or injure anyone; MPC tasks were policing, detention, and intelligence.

Ahmed spoke Arabic, Amharic, English, and Oromo. He was a welcome addition to the MPs in the Middle East. Tension and complexity ran high between Iraqi civilians and the American troops. Ahmed's commander, Captain Gresham, along with many other military chiefs, was concerned about having Muslims in the US ranks.

Ahmed was called to the commander's office on his first day in Camp Buehring, Kuwait. Ahmed entered and saluted.

Captain Gresham nodded. "Please sit down, soldier," Captain Gresham said.

Ahmed sat.

"Soldier," the Captain said as he smiled, "I will not nurse the kitty, Kuwait and Iraq are Muslim nations. You are a Muslim. Your fellow soldiers are not."

Ahmed smiled, remembering the teaching in word and example of his wise uncle. "May I, Sir?"

Captain Gresham did not expect to be interrupted, but didn't want to block the recruit from speaking his mind. Gresham nodded.

"I understand your concern, Sir, and I appreciate your directness."

Captain Gresham smiled. Gresham's father was a Baptist preacher who preached of the brotherhood of man. Gresham also fervently believed that each person should be judged by his own actions and nothing else. "Continue, Soldier," Gresham said.

"Yes, Sir. Sir, the word 'Islam' is derived from the root s-l-m, which means 'peace.' In the Koran, the Prophet Muhammad is referred to as rahmat al-il alamin, or 'mercy unto the worlds.' He is thus a source of compassion for all of humankind, and not just Muslims."

Ahmed smiled. "May I continue, Sir?"

The Captain nodded.

"Sir, correctly interpreted, Islam is a religion of peace that condemns terrorism."

Gresham, somewhat impressed, stared into the eyes of Ahmed. Not wanting to be deceived by a heretic, he spoke. "My father was a man of God and I appreciate that, Soldier. But *you* were born Muslim in a foreign country. I'm sure that you can understand my concern."

"Of course, Sir, and I'd like to erase any doubt that you might have."

Ahmed pondered momentarily.

"And how would you do that, Soldier?"

"Sir, let me say that I was just as distraught as any American that I know of when the US embassy was bombed in Beirut or when the barracks were bombed six months and five days later."

Gresham noted the "six months and five days later." Even he did not remember the space of time between the events. Ahmed remained serious and attentive, not wanting to appear deceptively collaborative.

Gresham nodded. "It's rare that the MPC directly engages the enemy, however if this situation occurs you would have to defend yourself and your fellow US soldiers. Would you be willing to do so?"

"Sir, to the prophet Muhammed, Muslims, Christians, and Jews are all brothers. I would not let him or you down, Sir."

Ahmed grew into army life. After morning prayers, his days were filled with motivating and interesting assignments. Some days he worked as a translator, other days, a peacemaker, and still others a social worker or priest.

By the time that the Twin Towers came down, Ahmed was twenty-six years old and a sergeant. Some, noticing his talent, claimed that he should have had a few more stripes, but the brass was leery about Muslims, particularly about *devout* Muslims.

Their suspicions became louder still when it was reported that thousands of US Muslims were dancing in the streets as the towers plummeted. Though sixteen out of the nineteen hijackers were Saudi nationals, the United States invaded Iraq.

All Muslims became suspect in the United States, not only Muslims from Saudi Arabia.

In response to the downing of the Twin Towers, US President George W. Bush and UK Prime Minister Tony Blair claimed their coalition mission was "to disarm Iraq of weapons of mass destruction, to end Saddam Hussein's support for terrorism, and to free the Iraqi people."

Ahmed read with great interest that in a January 2003 CBS poll, 63 percent of Americans wanted Bush to find a diplomatic solution, and 62 percent believed the threat of terrorism directed against the United States would increase due to a war. Thirty-six million people across the globe took part in protests against the war in Iraq between January and April of 2003.

The invasion of Iraq was strongly opposed by long-standing US allies, including France, Germany, and New Zealand. Their leaders argued that there was no evidence of weapons of mass destruction in Iraq and that invading the sovereign nation was unjust.

Ahmed strongly agreed.

Some believed that Bush wanted to punish Saddam Hussein personally for the failed Kuwait assassination attempt of his father George H. W. Bush in April of 1993, and many Americans still believed that Saddam Hussein had a hand in the destruction of the Twin Towers.

Ahmed was strongly convinced that an invasion of Iraq was illegal, according to US morals and laws. He was troubled when his MPC squad was picked to be among the US troops to participate in the Iraq offensive.

The Iraq invasion was preceded by an airstrike on the Presidential Palace in Baghdad on March 20, 2003. During the initial invasion phase, 160,000 troops were sent in by the coalition. The US sent 130,000; the British 28,000; Australia 2,000; and Poland 194. Iraqi president Saddam Hussein and the central leadership went into hiding as the coalition forces completed the occupation of the country. On May 1, 2003, George W. Bush declared an end to major combat operations, but it was only the beginning of a long and bloody occupation.

Ahmed's life changed drastically in Iraq, as did the lives of all the invading troops. Ahmed became more solemn. To many, his silence was suspect. Ahmed was called into the base commander's office for counseling. The U.S. Army was trying to get a grip on a long occupation. Ahmed attended the mandatory classes given to all soldiers. Ahmed believed that many of the lessons were infantile and even factually incorrect. He remained silent through all of the lectures.

Many recruits avoided him. Still, Ahmed dedicated himself to making a positive difference for the Iraqi people. He considered leaving the army, but in 2008, he was promoted to staff sergeant and given charge of his own squad, made up of guys mostly from New York City. He reenlisted.

Initially the US-led force was viewed with curiosity and even joy by the political opponents of Saddam Hussein. But as the Iraqi civilian corpses mounted, their disgruntled family members began strapping on bombs and setting booby traps.

Peril was around every corner. The Military Police Corps was now in as much danger as the foot soldier. It was nearly impossible for Ahmed to believe that his beloved country could ever participate in such chaos. He faithfully believed that the people of the United States would eventually right the wrong and bring Cheney and Bush up on charges, hopefully resulting in imprisonment.

By the time Obama was elected on November 4, 2008, there were over four thousand dead US troops and over 200,000 confirmed dead Iraqi civilians. Still, Ahmed stayed positive. He was now Staff Sergeant Selassie and comfortably in charge of his squad, mostly other recruits from his own state, New York.

Ahmed fervently believed the United States to be a country of peace; that the United States did not torture, and that the United States certainly did not deceive their own citizens, resulting in the deaths of hundreds of thousands of innocent people.

Ahmed was confident that the United States would return to moral high ground, but by mid-January 2009, Obama made it clear that he would not investigate Bush or Cheney for war crimes. Ahmed cried tears of disappointment. Worse, in April 2009, Obama also refused to investigate the CIA for torture. Ahmed was flabbergasted. It was as if someone had repeatedly punched him in the gut.

Ahmed read articles from the sources he most respected.

Glenn Greenwald wrote, "President Obama is going to find it very hard to go around the world and say: 'We're now again a nation of laws,' if the first act he commits as President is to walk away from a confirmed war crime."

Rachel Maddow wrote, "How will people around the world not view us as an outlaw regime for not arresting war criminals on our own soil?"

Ahmed was confused. It appeared that many Americans were willing to overlook hypocrisy. How could Obama supporters not view as inconsistent Obama's attempt to tell the world that, "American values are restored and we're now a nation of laws again," after the US government's decision that confessed war crimes committed by its most powerful political leaders should go ignored, unpunished, and protected?

Ahmed lost faith in his nation's leaders and began losing faith in himself and his mission. The Iraqi people became angrier. Fewer and fewer of them viewed the United States as liberators.

For the benefit of the American public, camera crews staged Iraq support, holding up and paying for puppets like Nouri Kamil Mohammed Hasan al-Maliki, also known as Jawad al-Maliki or Abu Esraa.

Ahmed never mentioned a word about the sad transformation that he witnessed or his own feelings to his troops or anyone else. He kept his cool under incredible stress, as things went haywire everywhere, including in his own squad.

On a call to a small unnamed town outside Basra, Sergeant Ahmed Selassie and his troops were investigating trouble at a tiny, makeshift civilian hospital. They all knew that it could be a setup.

"Sergeant Selassie, are you out of your mind taking us to this rat trap? We'll be ambushed for sure," Kennedy said.

"That's possible," Ahmed responded, "and trust me, Kennedy, that's even more reason to keep quiet and stay alert."

"Hey Clark, have you ever noticed that *trust me* is often said by the people that you should trust the least?" Kennedy muttered.

"Yep, everyone's selling unicorn shit, Kennedy. Keep your eyes open," Clark responded.

After walking fifteen minutes, Kamar, an Arab soldier, and Holt, a lanky, dark-skinned soldier with a thin mustache, were twenty feet ahead. A grenade landed near them. Kamar froze; Holt didn't notice.

Selassie arrived, seemingly out of nowhere, and threw the grenade. "Down! Down!" he screamed as the hand bomb exploded in the air two hundred feet away.

Kamar referred to Ahmed as Isa after that event. Isa is the name for Jesus to Muslims.

Under incredible stress, and in chaotic situations, soldiers were expected to impeccably follow rules and regulations. This was a high bar for all involved with the invasion. Ahmed watched with not a small amount of bitterness as many soldiers were eventually imprisoned for (so-called) errors of judgment. Ahmed believed that many were sacrificial lambs for the growing malcontent at home.

Amnesty International reported that US forces engaged in rampant violations, including indiscriminate attacks that killed and injured civilians, secret detention, secret detainee transfers, enforced disappearance, torture, and other cruel, inhumane, or degrading treatment.

Ahmed believed it was easy for the politicians to criticize and make decisions on matters that wouldn't impact them or their own families.

According to the *New York Times*, only two House members had children who joined to serve in Iraq—and both joined as officers who would not likely see combat, according to a survey (*A NATION AT WAR: CHILDREN OF LAWMAKERS; Senators' Sons in War: An Army of One*).

Critics of the war say armed conflict might be less likely if the politicians who made the decisions to commit troops put their own sons and daughters at risk, according to an argument put forth by Representative Charles B. Rangel, Democrat of Manhattan, when he introduced legislation to revive the draft.

Some scholars say war itself might be waged differently if the children of the elite were involved.

With civilian cadavers mounting, US soldiers were more and more seen as enforcers of tyranny and not as liberators. Women and youths sought vengeance for dead relatives. Cans, sticks, toys, and even children could be booby trapped. Land mines were everywhere.

There was one family that the squad met in a village near Baghdad. A man and his twelve-year-old daughter were putting sheep in a pen. It was picturesque; some of the guys took photos.

Six weeks later, they went back and discovered that the daughter had died. She'd been dancing to music on her Discman and went to check on the sheep in the same place she'd been going repeatedly for months. There was an explosion.

Her father ran barefoot over to where it happened. His daughter's legs had been blown off and her body was burnt to toast.

It was nearly impossible to keep morale up, and in the spring of 2010, after hundreds of perilous missions, Ahmed's own squad was fatigued.

It was another sizzling day. The temperature was in the hundreds and Sergeant Selassie and his squad were sent to investigate rumors of an ammunition stockpile in Abu Zukhayr, a tiny town ten miles from Fallujah.

On March 31, 2004, Fallujah civilians killed four American troops, mutilated their bodies, burned them, and strung them up from a bridge. President Bush had answered in kind. The city of Fallujah had been the site of some of the bloodiest battles of the entire war.

The area had been quiet for some time but still, Ahmed was attentive and his troops were skittish.

Selassie's squad turned into a dusty street. When they all had entered the road, out of nowhere, the troops spotted two women carrying weapons. The *rat-a-tat-tat* sound of gunfire was heard.

The discharge of the troops' guns drowned out Ahmed's elongated yell. "Noooo!"

The two women lay dead. The weapons were pieces of ebony wood. The rat-a-tat-tat was a farmer hammering a piece of his tractor in a tin garage that bordered the dirt road.

Holt kneeled next to one of the women and cried.

Another squad of US soldiers arrived, guns blazing.

Selassie raised his arms. "We're good . . . we're good."

And now, after all the sacrifice and kindness dished out to the Iraqi people, he and his squad, according to the Army, were guilty of murder. Everyone except Selassie and Cowdar had discharged their weapons at the unarmed women.

Sergeant Selassie was now thirty-five years old and of average height and wiry build. With grave intent, he walked up to the drab and tan barracks. Corporal Hurt, a man in his twenties, was standing at attention at the entrance.

"Sergeant Selassie to see Colonel Drummond."

"I'll let him know that you are here, sir."

Sergeant Selassie knew Colonel Drummond to be a rigid yet fair man. Ahmed walked into the immaculately ordered headquarters. Drummond, in his early fifties, sat at his desk. His skin was coarse and brown, but his pulled-back sleeves revealed pale patches of skin. Drummond was sporting a marine-style crew-cut which he insisted originated in the Army. His chest was filled with medals of every color of the rainbow.

He looked up from the papers on his desk. Sergeant Selassie smiled and saluted. Drummond looked despairingly and returned the salute without standing.

"At ease, Sergeant," Drummond said.

They had never spoken on the subject, but Drummond's views of Iraq mirrored those of Sergeant Selassie. Drummond often marveled at how lying had become an accepted tool to "protect honor." What happened to patriots?

Drummond scanned his desk for some sort of solution. There was none to be found, and he reluctantly looked up. Standing in front of him was Selassie, a man that he liked and respected as he did no other.

Drummond cleared his throat and gazed up. In thirty years of his career, he did everything to keep his feelings under wraps. His mind was frantically racing to find the words that could change the predicament.

Selassie smiled tightly. Drummond cowered and looked to the side before speaking. *Funny how sometimes, seconds won't pass and years fly by,* he thought to himself.

"If you're here to ask for slack or a deal, you're in the wrong place." Drummond said. "You should be talking with your attorney, not me."

Ahmed stood perfectly still, as if meditating.

Finally, Drummond shattered the bitter, melancholy silence. "Do any of your soldiers have relatives that are senators or congressmen?" he asked.

"No, not that I know of sir."

"Of course they don't. If they did, they wouldn't be here. They'd be commissioned officers sitting behind some safe desk."

Drummond is the real Army and he feels personal guilt for what will likely happen to Selassie and his men.

"Politicians," Drummond said, as he looked up and thinly smiled at Selassie.

Selassie had reciprocal respect for Drummond and, strangely, felt certain that if he was in Drummond's room, and under Drummond's command, no harm would come to his men—men he loved as he loved Hessna, Fatima, and Muhammed, his own sisters and brother.

A tear formed in Drummond's eyes. He's disappointed in himself and raises his voice. "The taxpayer foots the bill for their vulgarity, and the poor fight the wars they start to promote capitalism."

Drummond tried again to smile. Sergeant Selassie remained motionless.

"Sergeant, I, like most of your squad, am from New York State."

"I know, Sir."

"Well then you must also know how difficult this is for me!"

"Yes, Sir. I realize that."

Drummond looked in Selassie's eyes, but it's as if he was watching the hunter trailing Bambi's mother in the Disney film of the same name. Drummond's whole body shrunk and he looked away.

"The Military Police Corp is here to protect civilians, not kill them," Drummond said deceitfully.

Drummond looked up. Bambi's mother was dead. There's nothing he could do to bring her back to life. "Are you sticking to your story, Sergeant, that you and your squad justifiably killed two civilians?"

"Yes, Sir. It's the truth."

"Do you like Kansas, Sergeant?"

"Kansas, Sir?"

"That's right, Kansas, as in Leavenworth Prison, Kansas."

Sergeant Selassie felt a lump form in his throat. "Never been there, Sir."

"Well, that's where you and your whole squad will be going for a long, long time if you don't change your story. . . . It's not going well for us here. To some, we're the war criminals, not Bush, not the Iraqis, not Cheney, and not Obama!"

Drummond recaptured his composure, hoping that maybe he could shake this decent man into thinking of something, anything to lighten the hammer-like blow coming down on Selassie and his men.

"Your squad killed two women!"

Sergeant Selassie still had the lump in his throat. He forced to push the wind out of his lungs around it to form the next words.

"We thought that we were being fired on, Sir."

"Save it for the judge. One of your men is testifying against all of you. He says that your men disobeyed your direct order not to shoot."

"Sir, it happened so fast." Selassie was getting used to speaking with a lump in his throat. The words exited a bit easier.

Selassie hesitated. "He was always an outsider, Sir. In a strange way he's getting revenge for never being accepted."

Drummond shakes his head. "Selassie, it doesn't matter to the court."

"And if we change our story?"

"If your men admit to not following regulations and killing the civilians and throw themselves at the mercy of the court, they may be more lenient. . . . But they'll still go away."

Drummond took a deep breath and looked at Ahmed as a mother might look at her dying child. "I can't help you. I'm sorry."

"Yes, Sir," Sergeant Selassie said, quietly raising his arm to salute and turn.

"They'll fry your men, Selassie."

Ahmed turned back out of respect for a man he knew was suffering as much as himself.

"They'll fry, and no one can help them," Drummond reiterated.

Ahmed stared.

Drummond softened his voice. "You see, the politicians that decided to make this war aren't held accountable for the carnal slaughter. But someone must be held accountable. . . . You and your squad are the scapegoats, and the 62 percent of the American public that wanted Bush to seek a diplomatic solution instead of an invasion will be waiting for you back home, screaming, 'Burn them! Burn them!'"

Ahmed could barely feel his legs. He's standing but not sure how or why. He looked at Drummond much as a little boy who witnessed his puppy squished under a car tire. He watched it, yet couldn't do anything to stop it.

"Every modern war is the same, Selassie. There is no chivalry," Drummond said, as he gawked at his own hand.

Sergeant Selassie was not sure if the colonel is done speaking. He thought of walking away but was not certain if he remembered how. He then heard Drummond's voice beckoning him back, and for an instant, Ahmed hoped that the good colonel may have thought of a miracle.

"You know, Selassie, brave men will always choose diplomacy and sacrifice over bloodshed, but the age of chivalry died when the king stopped riding out with his troops."

Drummond looked up and into Selassies's eyes. "I can't help you, I'm sorry."

"Yes, Sir."

Sergeant Selassie salutes. The colonel stands and holds his salute until Sergeant Selassie has turned and exited.

A few seconds later, Drummond heard Corporal Hurt knocking. Hurt continued knocking until Drummond responded. "What is it?"

Corporal Hurt entered. "Sir, Captain Ginsel is here."

"Show him in."

Captain Ginsel walked in and saluted the colonel. Colonel Drummond slapped his hand at the wind in response. Ginsel was an attorney representing a US officer who made a fortune selling US equipment to the other side.

"Captain, your client, that other captain asshole, sold our boys' supplies to Al Qaeda."

"Sir," Captain Ginsel said "let's get this straight. He was allocating products to civilians, and it was all okayed by Halliburton and KBR [a private defense and intelligence company]."

"Ginsel, do you know how many contractors were deployed in World War II?"

"No, Sir."

"Well, I'll tell you. One for every seven soldiers. Do you know how many contractors per soldier we have now?" Drummond yelled.

"No, Sir."

"Of course you don't, but I'll tell you! We have more contractors than soldiers, and they're shortchanging our boys' body armor protection and first-aid kits. Halliburton KBR is a fraud; billions have disappeared. But of course, you know what company Cheney was the CEO of."

Ginsel stared.

"Don't you?"

"Yes, Sir."

"Well, then say it, you gutless maggot!"

"Halliburton."

"And do you know how much they've billed the government?"

"Billions," Ginsel said timidly.

"Thirty-four billion!"

Ginsel nodded. "Yes, Sir. Sir, we'll take an undesirable discharge."

"Do you know how many soldiers we've lost here, captain?"

"Five thousand?"

"Close enough. Do you know what thirty-four billion divided by five thousand is?"

"No sir."

"Well, I do! It's six million, eight hundred thousand dollars per dead soldier."

Drummond stands and slams his hand on his desk. "Do you know what that means, Ginsel?"

Drummond is daring him to speak, and Ginsel gladly remains silent.

"They're selling our boys' lives!"

"Yes, Sir," Ginsel quips.

"Now let's get this straight you, human leech," Drummond said, staring at Ginsel's funny thin mustache. "You and your client are scum! It got so insane that many of our boys bought their own body armor. Those who could afford it. Their folks back home and their churches took up collections!"

A long pause was interrupted by the window air conditioner fan rubbing against the metal barrier.

"Sir, with all due respect, my job as an attorney is to defend. . . . You don't have proof that my client broke the rules. KBR was authorized by the president, and my client had KBR's blessing."

Drummond shook his head. "And he is the nephew of Senator Feinvine. Why don't you just have the balls to say so?"

"Sir, I don't like these political interferences any more than you. . . . We'll take an undesirable discharge without mention of the case or reason."

Drummond looked down at his desk. Without giving Ginsel the respect of looking at him, Drummond spoke. "The American soldiers in Iraq have been told that they are fighting to defend America." Drummond looked up at Ginsel. "But we both know that they are fighting and *dying*!"

Drummond slammed his fist on the desk. Ginsel jumped.

"For Halliburton, ExxonMobil, and Chevron. Halliburton's KBR subsidiary and their no-bid contracts are serving our troops toxic, bacteria-ridden food, putting untreated Euphrates River water into their canteens, and shortchanging their body armor." Drummond hesitated before speaking. "These American executives are treacherous cowards and traitors that should see the firing squad!"

Ginsel was perspiring, but he felt ice-cold.

"Members of Congress, the other ship's rats, ought to ask whether Halliburton's move to Dubai had anything to do with anticipated business. Had Cheney gotten his way the United States would have also attacked Iran."

Drummond was inflamed with anger. "There's no justice."

"Sir?" Ginsel said, waiting for a response to his proposal.

"I have no choice!"

Ginsel smiled tightly. "We all have choices, Sir."

Ginsel saluted and turned without waiting for Drummond to salute back. He stopped when he heard Drummond speak.

"Captain, that man who just left here, his whole squad is going away for a very long time. They got spooked and killed two Iraqi women. They arrived at that village to help, they had only sincere intent. . . . Instead, your client, Captain Kumball. . . ."

"Captain Kosel, Sir."

"Don't you toy with me, you cockroach shit of a person. Your client shortchanged our soldiers and sold their supplies to the enemy!"

"Sir, again, my client was authorized by Halliburton. You cannot prove his guilt."

"I don't need to! I know it! You know it! The White House knows it! The whole damned Army knows it! But it's not about guilt, is it Ginsel? It's about money, power, and political contacts. Today's presidents are vultures pretending to be eagles. They're hypocrites, like you and that client of yours! Now get out of here, Captain, before I come around this desk and kick your pansy ass!"

Captain Ginsel saluted. Drummond hesitated and began to head toward Ginsel, who turned and scurried away.

A tan barracks stood boldly against the parched blue sky. Inside were five uniformed men. Ahmed was not present.

Corporal Kennedy, a blond-haired soldier with a US flag tattooed on his right forearm, stood in the middle of the barracks and in the center of his comrades. "We're all going away! That pussy Cowdar is gonna rat us out!"

A short, thin black soldier with glasses, Corporal Harms, stood up. "But we're innocent. Those women made movements as if they were going to shoot. Then we heard gunfire. Who had time to think if it was really gunfire?"

Corporal Kennedy snidely eyed Harms. "Do you see what I mean, you geek? Which is it, gunfire or not?"

Corporal Holt stood. "Lay off the brother, man. It ain't going to do us any good to fight amongst ourselves."

Kennedy looked defiantly at Holt. "That's my point. It ain't gonna do us any good to fight anything. We got to run. The war's over for us, and the only thing waiting in the good old US of fucking 'A' is jail."

Kennedy looked over at Holt. "And when are you gonna shave that silly French mustache? You look like a goddamn faggot."

A short bald man with a hooked nose, Corporal Gallo, stood. "Hey man, I'm going back to Brooklyn."

A short, stubby guy with red hair, Corporal Clark, aimed his cigar and flicked it toward the sink, ten yards away. The cigar landed dead center. "Before any of us get back to New York, we'll spend a minimum of fifteen years in military prison."

"It ain't over till the fat lady sings," Kennedy said. "I say we get out of here before she gets her dress on."

"But we thought that they were shooting!" Harms yelled. "They could have been! It's not our fault! They butchered hundreds of us like that!" Harms ended his rant in a wishy-washy, weak-ended question. "The courts have to know that already, right?"

"Who's with me?" Kennedy asks.

Sergeant Selassie walked in. Hassan Kamar stood. "Isa, what did Drummond say? Will he help us?"

Kamar sees Isa's empty expression. "Isa."

"Damn you, Ay-rab!" Kennedy screams, "His name is Selassie, Sergeant Ahmed Selassie!"

"He saved my sand nigger ass twenty times. He's Isa to me, man."

"That's sacrilegious! 'Isa' is Jesus in Arabic. That's God, goddamn you! I told you a thousand times!"

Kamar was losing patience. "Hey man. Jesus is my guy too. I told you he's right after Muhammad."

"Well, he's number one to me!" Kennedy screamed.

"Leave it alone, Kennedy," Clark said.

Kennedy reluctantly listened.

Kamar grabbed Isa's arm. "Isa, will they cut us a deal? Will the army back us?"

Ahmed momentarily stared at Kamar and then looked down.

"Jesus!" Kennedy yelled. "I fuckin' told you! The army's gonna turn their back on us and watch the politicians hang us out to dry!"

"Isa?" Corporal Kamar asked feebly.

Ahmed looked at the ground and spoke, "If we admit to disobeying army regulations, killing those women, and throw ourselves at the mercy of the court, they might go easier on us."

"If we admit to killing those women, they might go easy on us." Kennedy said mockingly. "Fuck that."

"Easy, what's going easy on us mean?" Harms timidly asked.

Ahmed did not respond.

"Easy means having to fight every day," Corporal Clark said. "Except you won't be fighting the Iraqi sand niggers."

"Yeah," Kennedy said, "you'll be fighting to keep American dick out of your asshole in prison."

"Seems like we're already doing that right here in Iraq," Gallo added, "against our own, except for Harms, he likes giving up that *asspussy*." Gallo stared at Harms. "Don't you, Harms?"

Harms charged Gallo. A table was knocked over. An ashtray fell to the ground and cracked. Clark blocked Harms and pushed him back.

"Fuck you, Gallo! This is your motherfucking fault!" Harms yelled.

Gallo stood for confrontation.

Harms continued, "You fired the first shot! I saw you, you fucking wop prick!"

Gallo charged Harms. Harms came forward again, and Clark pushed him back, harder. Harms moved back. Kennedy grabbed Gallo and held him back.

"We were all there!" Holt said. "We all did it! It doesn't matter who fired first. They're not going to fucking care!"

Holts looked to the side. "Nobody cares," Holt muttered quietly. He sat down as if he was in a trance.

Kennedy and Clark were doing what they could to keep Gallo and Harms at bay.

"We didn't all do it," Kamar said. "Cowdar didn't fire a shot."

The room went silent other than for heavy breathing and the noise of thought.

The silence was interrupted by Ahmed, who looked collectively at his men. "We must change our situation."

It was 11:00 p.m. The roads of the army base were cloaked in silence. A few lights humbly attempted to display, but it was a quiet showing. Visibility was zero. The desert breeze reminded all hosts and guests that after the Sumerians, Akkadians, Babylonians, Persians, Greeks, Arabs, Mamelukes, Turks, and English have left, she will still reign supreme.

And tonight, the wind was particularly playful, picking up sand, rustling the palms, and singing a teasing song to remind the Americans that after they are gone and after their empire is destroyed she will still be here, giggling away as if nothing ever happened.

A shadow with a gun in hand stepped steadily and softly toward the Protective Custody Barracks. His appearance spooked the also-armed soldier guarding the entrance.

"Soldier, put the rifle down. I'm not here for you," the shadow said.

The sentinel laid his piece in front of him. The shadow cuffed his prisoner to the iron pole holding the flag. In this dark, it could be the flag of Iraq, ISIS, British Petroleum, Donald Duck, or the Chicago White Sox. This does give some solace to the natives; they're only American flags until the sun goes down.

The shadow took tape from his pocket and pressed it across the soldier's mouth. "Stay cool and stay alive," the shadow said to his prisoner.

The soldier nodded. The shadow quietly opened the door and tiptoed in. A glaring cigarette was the only bright light in the room. It rose with the shadow of the man who was smoking it.

"Corporal Cowdar," the shadow said firmly.

The smoking shadow flicked the cigarette away and moved onto the ground. The other shadow moved in his direction. Headlights from a passing vehicle revealed Isa holding Cowdar's face down by his hair. . . .

"You will die so that others can live. Make your peace and prepare to meet your Maker."

Two shots were fired. Isa laid Cowdar's head gently down on the floor. The lights of another passing vehicle showed blood painting the floor.

After the shooting, the army investigated the murder of the witness. Military brass figured that Ahmed went into the desert and was heading for Ethiopia. Ahmed had made many friends over the years and there was no one particularly enthusiastic about catching him, especially for the so-called crime of "silencing a canary." In fact, to most, including Drummond, Ahmed was a goddamned hero.

A week later, Corporals Kennedy, Clark, Harms, Holt, and Kamar stood in the half-lit Baghdad military airport hangar.

Holt was nervous. "If we get caught, we're history. This whole story will blow up in our faces. Aiding a murderer could carry hard times. They'll claim that we were all in on icing Cowdar. Then we're history."

Kamar began speaking, "If it wasn't for Isa . . ."

Kennedy interrupts him. "There you go again, it's Ahmed, you damn Ay-rab!"

"Isa," Kamar says. "Think about it, Kennedy . . . for once in your life, listen to someone besides yourself and Tucker Carlson."

For the first time that anyone can remember, Kennedy looked and remained silent.

"Jesus gave his life for the sins of others so that they may live," Kamar said.

"Then on the third day he was resurrected," Holt commented.

"Isa did it for us. I'd die for him," Harms said.

Clark flicked his cigar butt about fifty feet into a box. "You may have to."

"Isa," Kennedy mumbled.

"That's who he is from now on," Clark said. "We'll get him home."

"He should be here any minute," Harms said.

The hangar floor was filled with black body bags.

Clark pointed randomly, "Empty that bag, we'll ditch the body. That's Isa's seat home."

"Where will we ditch it?" Holt asked.

"Holt, we're in the middle of a frickin' desert larger than the state of New York," Kennedy said without looking at him.

"How do we know they'll put him on the plane and not in with the cargo to freeze to death?" Harms asked.

"The decomposed go in the hold. These are the fresh arrivals," Kennedy said.

Harms and Gallo unloaded a mangled body from the bag. They all watched as they shoved it into a large plastic bag.

Isa arrived. Kamar, Clark, Harms, and Holt walked toward him. After greetings, Holt and Gallo broke off and wiped down the inside of Isa's new travel compartment.

Holt looked at Isa. "Stay cool, brother."

One by one, they all hugged Isa.

"Isa, remember Gallo's cousin at JFK," Clark said. "Don't budge until you hear 'and on the third day he arose according to the scriptures.'"

Isa got into the body bag.

"And Isa," Clark said, "when it's our turn, we'll not let you down."

Isa smiled at each one of them. "I know, but remember," Isa said, looking sharply at Clark and then one by one, at the rest. "If there is ever any danger of me being exposed, take me out. One should not be the risk of all."

Harms openly cried. He handed Isa a water bottle and a K-ration. "Goodbye, brother."

Isa winked.

"Don't forget to drink, man," Harms said.

Isa nodded and smiled warmly. "Goodbye." He laid down, and Clark zipped him up in the body bag.

With no witness, the army tossed the case around until it was dropped. For months, Drummond's beam could light the Atlantic Ocean. The rest of Isa's squad served out their time and returned to New York.

PART II

Chapter 4

It Could Be a Bestseller

It's a Friday evening, ten years later, 2020, at an office party in the Gent America Media offices in Manhattan. GAM is one of the largest book publishers in the world. The "GAM" sign is huge and in multicolored metal, upright inside the reception area. People are standing with drinks in their hands, talking and laughing. Waiters with white vests and gloves are holding appetizer trays.

A blond man in his thirties, Bob Herman, is quietly sitting alone watching Mark Koss, a seventy-year-old man with dark dyed hair, a bushy mustache, and bifocals.

Koss lowers a pipe from his mouth. "I own this place and I say when it's time . . ."

All eyes are on Koss, the owner of GAM. From behind Koss a sixtyish burly, gray-haired man, Ted Basle, arrives and whispers in Koss's ear. Koss listens intently, then appears surprised. Koss mutters something into Ted's ear. Ted nods and moves away.

Koss regains his composure. "Yes . . . and when I say it's time to eat."

Koss glares at his paycheck-collecting, captivated guests. One by one they look at each other. Finally, the consensus is to laugh. They compete to gain favor in a laughing contest.

When Koss sees that all are hooting enthusiastically, he smiles into the cerebral void created by fifty vassals and yells, "It's time to eat!"

Everyone laughs harder than before and each one files into two glass doors. Then, one by one, they stand in line to fill their plates with the restaurant-made processed garbage.

They all sat at a conference table and scattered smaller ones. Waiters served beverages. An attractive forty-one-year-old redheaded woman, Gael, and a pretty, younger blond woman, Jennifer, are conversing. Bob Herman is to the left of the redhead.

Jennifer laughs. "Gael, you're crazy."

"He almost faints with all that blood rushing to fill that thing! It's a pleasure that I'll never get the privilege to experience . . . that's what's crazy," Gael says.

Jennifer notices Bob next to Gael, eavesdropping. "Hi Bob," Jennifer says.

Gael turns her head into Bob Herman's gaze. She leans in closer to him and whispers, "Gay men. They're hung, you know? *Penis enlargers*."

"Yes . . . No! I mean I don't know. Not personally. I've never . . . I don't . . ." Bob stutters nervously.

"Oh?" Gael hesitates and looks at Jennifer. "Well, if you decide to broaden your horizons, let me know. I like to watch."

Gael winks at Bob. He looks away, embarrassed.

Gael then looks at unamused Jennifer and laughs. The laugh trails off to a truly disappointed expression on Gael's face. "Men, they've become such stumbling wusses. Most are still disappointed that you can be prosecuted for unwanted sexual advances on a crowded subway."

Mark Koss has heard pieces of their conversation from across the table. He stands. "Gael, leave that young rooster be. He's turned corporate sales around. A toast to Bob!"

Everyone looks at Bob and raises their glasses.

"No . . . no Sir. That's Bob Phillips . . . I'm Bob Herman. I'm a Special Projects Manager."

"Yes, of course you are," Koss says.

Guests raise beverages up to a momentarily uncomfortable silence.

"Well, eat and drink up, this party's costing me a fortune."

Everyone laughs on cue. Bob tightly grins and sips his drink. The party billows out around Bob until he is no longer in sight. He just disappears. No one noticed that he was gone, except maybe Jennifer.

Bob climbs onto an empty bus heading home. He swipes his transit card and heads back. Street people pepper the spaces. A brown bag wrapped with rubber bands sits in an empty seat. It's torn open at the top from wear. Papers can be seen inside.

Bob sits and watches the world outside the window.

A homeless man approaches him. "Do you want to help a brother?"

Bob's on another planet. "What?"

"Do you want to help a brother?"

Bob snaps to attention. "Uh, I don't know . . . I mean . . . what do you mean?"

"What do you mean, what do I mean, man? Do you want to help a brother or not?"

"I'm not sure what . . . do you mean money?"

"Oh man . . . you got a dollar?"

"Yes, but I . . ."

The two look at each other in silence. Bob averts his eyes first.

"You mean yes, you got a dollar but no you don't want to help a brother? . . . Man, you wishy-washy."

Bob looks at his feet as the bus stops. When he looks up, the man is getting off. Bob glances over at the brown package. He loosens his tie and faces it. He looks away, looks back, and then glances at the driver who is oblivious of him. He looks out the window again, pauses and looks again at the bag.

Shortly after, Bob is in his tiny, cluttered, one-bedroom apartment. His jacket, tie, and shirt create a trail from the front door to the bedroom. The unmade bed takes up almost all the available space.

Bob lays on the bed. A cat jumps onto his bare chest. The brown bag is open on the bedside table revealing pages of a manuscript. Bob's reading. The cat licks his face. Bob's eyes turn from wonderment to frustration. He tosses the pages on the floor and pushes the rest of the manuscript off the bed, frightening the cat away.

He shuts off the light and turns on his side. "Goddamn good writers. I hate them."

The next day, Bob's in his tiny, neat office nibbling on a carrot and staring sideways at a desk folder on his computer entitled "Bob's Stories."

People are filing out of the office. A graying forty-five-year-old man, Lou Mell, pops his head into Bob's office. "Lunch, Bobby . . . ? Bob, Herman, earth to Bob . . . Herman!"

Bob is startled. "Sorry . . . What?"

"Come on Bob, why don't you come to lunch anymore?"

"No thanks, I'm good."

"Bob, I want to ask you a question, buddy."

"Shoot."

"You're not jealous because I got picked for editing, are you?"

Bob hesitates before answering, knowing that the answer is a gigantic *yes*. "No, no, of course not, Lou. You deserve it more than me."

Bob forces a smile.

"Good to hear, good to hear. . . . And for once, you're right. Well, enjoy your carrot." Lou turns to leave then stops. "I know that you have author ambition. How's your own writing going? Got anything for the new editor yet?"

"I'm working on it."

"Good to hear, good to hear. What's it about?"

Lou perches himself on Bob's desk, towering over him.

"Oh, well . . . you know, the usual . . . stuff."

"Maybe it's good. Can I see some of it?"

"No, it's not ready and I may never show it to anyone. . . . The best manuscripts never get read. . . ."

"Listen Bobby, you win some, and you lose some. I'm sure Koss will give you another chance at being published. Dickens tried a hundred times before someone published him. I mean, you've been working on stuff for years. You must have something worth reading."

Bob looks up, faking the face of an adoring little brother, knowing that Lou got picked because he's been kissing Koss's ass for years. Some say that he didn't stop there. "Thanks so much for the encouragement, Lou. It really means a lot to me."

"All right, buddy, have a good lunch. And don't worry . . . I watched Koss gloss over your last story. He clicked off after less than a minute. Can't go anywhere but up from there, right?"

Bob stares, resisting everything in him that wants to get up and strangle the guy. Instead, he reinforces his melancholy face.

"Right, and thanks. Have a good lunch."

Lou turns. Bob gives the finger to Lou's back. The phone rings, Bob answers it. "Bob Herman, Special Projects Manager."

Out of the corner of his eye, he notices Ted Basle slipping into a colleague's office.

A few days later, Bob is standing on a crowded bus reading the manuscript.

"This should be published," a voice says.

Bob turns and sees Lucia, a petite, mixed-race beauty staring at him. "A writer, huh?"

Bob's not sure if he's nervous because the manuscript is not his or because he's never, ever spoken to such an enchanting vixen. He jerks. The manuscript falls to the ground. Together they gather the pages.

Lucia reads a line from the manuscript. "We can never be truly exultant until we've been truly desolate."

They look up at each other.

Lucia smiles. "Sounds like a gold mine."

"Yeah, no kidding?" Bob quips.

"Oh, modest, huh?"

Bob's body starts to feel wet with mini droplets of perspiration. "I didn't mean, it's not really . . ." he stutters.

"I like confidence in a man. Hungry?"

Bob doesn't get it. Is this vixen asking him to dinner? "Um, yes. Yes," (Bob firms his voice) "*I'm hungry.*"

Bob and Lucia are eating in Grand Sichuan on 7th Ave.

Lucia cuts to the chase. "I'm tired of men. They never want to commit, no matter what you do for them."

"It's hard to believe that men have a hard time committing to you."

"You look at the exterior and say that."

"No one can be that beautiful outside without having beauty inside," Bob returns.

"Thanks." Lucia purposely blushes.

They stand and leave the semi-crowded restaurant.

Once outside, Bob turns to his new associate. "Can I walk you home?"

"Sure." Lucia pauses. "I don't usually pick men up on the bus like this."

"Is that what you did? Pick me up?"

"Sort of, I guess," Lucia says coyly.

"How is it that someone like you is not . . ."

Lucia interrupts him. "Not occupied? Well, my mother is Italian. My parents adore each other and I want to be just like them. With the media pushing perversion and calling it liberation, there just aren't a lot of 'death do us part' guys around anymore."

"I see," Bob says, holding on to her every word.

"My only guy was Italian too . . . but it ended sadly," she adds softly. "Tony. He said he'd take care of me. What a laugh."

"Oh. I'm sorry," Bob says meekly.

"Don't be. He's the boxer, Tony Russo? Have you heard of him? He was number nine in *Ring Magazine*."

Bob shakes his head.

Lucia says, "I hate boxing. You're not a boxer, are you?"

Bob fights to gain confidence. "No. No. Too pretty for that." He smiles.

Lucia stares in his eyes. "Yes, you are."

"Thanks for dinner," Bob says, not knowing what else to say.

"It was the least I could do after that mess I made on the bus."

"It's okay. I enjoyed the mess. Anyway, next time dinner's on me. You choose the place."

"You said you worked for Gent, Gent America Media. That's a pretty powerful corporation."

"You know your stuff," Bob says, wishing that this evening would never end.

"I hear things here and there. I'd love to read your book."

"Uh, really, why?"

Lucia moves closer. "I don't know, I guess something about you makes me think it would be good."

Bob looks at her, hesitates and babbles. "You can't . . . it's not done . . . it's not good."

"Oh, come on. A big publishing company like GAM wouldn't hire a bad writer."

"Actually . . ."

"Be positive, stop being unpretentious. Drive, Bobby, drive."

Bobby nods. At this point he'd do or say anything to gain favor.

"Is this your only copy?"

Bob nods.

"Well . . . why don't you give me your number? I'll call you and maybe I can read it at your place."

"My place?"

Lucia takes her phone out.

"Uh, you want my number?" Bob asks.

"Unless you don't want me to have it."

"No, of course not. I mean, of course I want you to have it."

Lucia taps Bob's number into her phone. "Thanks. That will suffice for now."

They walk past a bookstore. Bob stops and stares at a sign:

Bob is with Lucia on a billboard:

Famous author Bob Herman, accompanied by his beautiful wife, will autograph his bestseller today.

He slows, staring at the bookstore window. Lucia walks ahead of him.

"Bobby," Lucia beckons, with the tone of the owner of a German Shepherd at a dog show.

Bob is not sure who's calling him and doesn't want to leave the book signing. He then realizes that he's imagining and recognizes Lucia's voice. "Coming?"

Bob smirks, shakes his head and looks back at the poster that is an advertisement for a series of self-help books. His eyes glue to the bold phrase, *Tired of going nowhere?*

That night, Lucia and Bob make dinner plans by text.

Chapter 5

Just Technicalities

Bob is on an almost empty bus later that night. He moves next to a sleeping drunk and clears his throat. "Excuse me . . . excuse me," Bob says.

The drunk doesn't respond and Bob touches his shoulder. The drunk slightly opens his eyes but Bob doesn't notice and looks away. When he turns back the drunk is wide eyed and staring at him. Bob is startled.

"What do you want?" the drunk asks in an extremely unfriendly tone.

"I found a brown paper bag with a manuscript in it, the other night on the bus. Is it yours?" Bob asks.

The drunk looks Bob over and purses his lips. "What are you selling?"

Bob answers nervously, "Selling? Well, actually, I'm talking about a story."

Suddenly, the drunk doesn't appear to be intoxicated at all. His eyes are crisp and his gaze is sure.

Bob smiles politely and retries. "I found a brown bag with a manuscript in it the other night on this bus route and I'm looking for the owner. It's a great piece and I'm in the writing business. Is it yours by any chance?"

The man sits upright.

"Sir, is it yours?" Bob repeats.

"Mine? Son, I'm glad that you found it. Yes, son, it's mine."

"Oh, wonderful, sir. It's a powerful piece. I was wondering . . . if you would like to uh, my name's Bob, I work at a publishing company. I think that with just a few changes, the manuscript could go places. We could publish it together. You could be a coauthor."

"Coauthor?" the man asks firmly.

"Author . . . well that's not important now. The important thing is that I've found you. Are you interested in being partners, a writing team?"

The man nods his head gently. "A writing team? Sure. I think that would be enjoyable."

"Great. Uh, do you need a place to stay?"

"Truthfully," the man smiles gently. "I'm a bit down on my luck. Might you have fifty for a room at the Sun Bright Hotel in Chinatown?"

Bob instinctively reaches his hand into his pocket. "Fifty, let me see. . . ."

Bob removes his hand with his business card and three twenties. The man fixes his eyes on the twenties and then on Bob's face.

Bob smiles broadly and looks out the window, "Ahh damn, my stop's coming. Take this. Call me first thing in the morning."

The man takes Bob's business card and the three twenties. "Sir, I'm sorry, I don't have change," the man says.

Bob looks momentarily confused. "Change, oh you mean for the sixty. That's fine, don't worry about that. Please, as soon as you get up, call my cell phone."

Bob shakes the man's hand and pulls the bell cord. The man smiles broadly. Bob turns and walks toward the front of the bus and looks back from the door. "Sir!" he yells, "what's your name?"

"My name?"

"Yes!" Bob cups his hands around his face and yells, "What-is-your-name?"

The man smiles sincerely. "Why, it's Ernest."

The bus stops and the door opens.

"Sir, please exit, I have a schedule," the bus driver says.

Bob steps down and looks back at the man. "Ernest what!" he yells.

The man looks at the window and then at Bob. "Hemingway!" the man yells back.

Bob steps onto the street and watches the bus pull away. He wanted Lucia, and to have her, he knew that he needed to produce. To do that he needed to make some sort of deal with the book's author.

Later that night, Bob is back on the same Broadway route. The bus is stopped at a light. Bob is sitting in front, almost next to the driver. He's the only passenger.

"Hey," the driver says, "I like the company, but you're better off going home. There's not many passengers at this hour. Tell you what, give 'lost and found' a ring tomorrow. If someone's looking for a lost manuscript, they'll tell you."

Bob is happy to hear any kind of advice.

The driver continues. "If no one claims it after sixty days, it's rightfully yours anyway. Of course, you'll have to first turn it into MTA lost and found."

Bob watches the traffic light turn green. "I don't . . . can't hand it in. It's in delicate condition. But thanks, that's a great idea. I'll call them. If someone is looking for it, lost and found can send them to me."

The next day in the offices of Gent America Media, Lou Mell is sitting on Bob's desk, laughing. His umbrella is dripping on the floor. Bob is watching Lou, but doesn't seem real amused.

"Boy oh boy," Lou says, "I just had to tell someone about her. Who'd have thought that a little ole editor could score something like that on a whim?"

Lou looks down at Bob. "I'd have gotten into her pants even if I hadn't told her that I would do what I could with her novel. She was fantastic and so into it. I was on top of her for thirteen minutes plowing."

"Seriously, Lou," Bob says, "I need to make the right choice."

"I have the clock radio on the right side of the bed. I looked when I saddled her up. It was 11:13. I started riding, you know softly, then I started taking longer strides and finally after three minutes, I looked at the clock, it was 11:16, I started galloping. . . ."

"Lou," Bob interrupts.

"Wait, Bobby. It's like she knew. All of the sudden her fingers dug into my arms. She knew Bobby, she knew that the ole cowboy was going to clear the hurdle and move out into the prairie."

Lou places his hands in front of him as if he was holding onto the rein. He moves his chest and hands front and backward. "I bolted, I mean, I rode her at a sprint."

Bob watches, doubting the story, but Lou has mesmerized himself with his own tale.

"She started sweating. Her nails dug further into my arms. She was overflowing, and almost frothing at the mouth." Lou winks. "I pushed it like Mario Gutierrez on the final turn of the Kentucky Derby."

"Lou," Bob says impatiently.

"Oh, calm down, calm down Bobby." Lou stares seriously. "When I finally hopped off, the clock read 11:26. Shit, Bobby, the Kentucky derby only lasts two minutes."

Lou stares at Bob, who disappointedly seems unmoved.

"She thinks that I'm going to get her published for one carnival ride? Hmphh. You know Bobby, those toothless monsters can destroy your life and I'm not even sure that I could get her book published. Of course she doesn't know that."

Bob wasn't paying a lot of attention. "Toothless monsters?"

"That's what I call them," Lou responded. "What do you call them, sausage wraps?"

Bob impatiently blows air out.

Lou claps and rubs his hands together. "Okay, give them to me again, I'll focus."

"Candidate number one has fifteen years in CBS corporate headquarters."

"Mmm hmm. Okay. Then . . ."

"Candidate number 2 has a master's in communication and has published lots."

Lou nods his head approvingly.

"Candidate number three has great references, she'll work for 20 percent less than the other two."

"Who'd you say this was for?" Lou asks.

"Marketing, Dan and Scott."

Lou momentarily concentrates. "Well, that's easy then."

Bob smiles and looks at Lou, "Okay, tell me then, who should I pick?"

"The one with the biggest tits," Lou says.

Just as Lou moves away to the door, Jennifer walks in. "Bob, got the bus company on line four."

"The bus company? Oh. Thanks Lou," Bob says.

Lou winks at Bob and smiles at Jennifer. "Anytime. Bus company? You know Bob, the bus doesn't give frequent rider miles."

Jennifer lingers.

"I got it, Jennifer. Thanks . . . thanks," Bob says.

Lou watches Jennifer as she leaves and turns to Bob. "Have you ever taken her out of the barn? You know she wants you. Everyone notices how she watches you," Lou says.

Bob smiles tightly, "Let me get this."

"The bus company can wait. Have you done her or not?"

Bob sighs impatiently. "No."

"Why the hell not? I'd do her," Lou says, "I'd love to have her and the filly I rode last night in the same race, or Jennifer and Gael. I know Gael comes and goes. I'd do 'em in a heartbeat," Lou winks. "Both of them."

"I'm sure you would," Bob reaches for the phone. "That's the difference between us." Bob studies Lou as he hits the fourth green light. "For you, they just have to breathe. I must be attracted."

Lou shakes his head. "When the fruit is ripe, you eat all you can, Bobby. The season doesn't last forever."

Lou walks away.

Bob blows out, "Bob Herman." Bob looks around, making sure that he's alone. He speaks quietly into the mouthpiece. "Yes, it was a brown paper bag with papers of some kind in it . . . no one asked for it?"

Jennifer walks back into Bob's room. He puts his hand up as if he were a cop in London stopping traffic. Jennifer freezes.

"Okay, thanks then, I really appreciate the information. Bye," he says, hangs up and looks at Jennifer.

"Bob . . . some of us are going for a drink this evening after work. Would you like to join me . . . us?"

"Tonight? No, got plans tonight."

Bob looks down at his desk and then at his phone. It's late. At 5:30 he rushes out and forgets the manuscript on his desk.

Bob walks into Il Mulino, an Italian restaurant on Third. The maître d' seats him. The place is packed. Bob felt out of place in the fancy restaurant. After an hour Bob is still seated by himself. He rolls a spoon in his hand and glances to the left and right. He gets up and walks to the host who is looking at his reservation pad.

The host glances at Bob, looks down and then calmly looks up. "Yes sir, may I help you?"

"Yes. Are you sure . . . I mean my date was supposed to be here an hour ago." Bob fidgets.

"Sir. I assure you that there is no way to get by me. Your name is Herman, isn't it?"

"Yes, yes, it is," Bob says, smiling gingerly as if the maître d' is about to give him good news.

"Well, Mr. Herman, just relax. As soon as she arrives, I'll seat her."

Bob turns to leave, and as he does, he spots Lucia nonchalantly entering. The host looks approvingly.

Bob smiles quietly and then moves toward Lucia. "You're late. You look beautiful, but you're very late."

"I know. I'm sorry. I got tied up. I was shooting some pictures for my portfolio."

"Your portfolio?"

"Yes, months ago, I met a guy who says that I'm a natural to be a model."

Bob touches her arm gently. "Oh, good, let's sit down."

They walk to their table. They sit and he looks at Lucia. "So you've been here before?"

"Here? No. It just looks so beautiful. I've always wanted to come. I guess I just had to wait for the right person to bring me. That's why I asked you to bring me here. I'm glad you waited."

"So . . ." Bob pauses. "Modeling? I thought you were a secretary. Two jobs?"

"Bobby," Lucia says, as she looks in his eyes and prepares to unload the dirt. "I have to look out for myself. I mean, who else will? Who else ever has?"

"Well . . ." Bob hesitates, not sure if he should say what he's thinking.

Lucia continues to shine. She also notices that Bob's getting ready to dive into the cool bay.

Bob smiles. "Well." He pauses. "Well, there's me, now."

Lucia smiles huge and beautiful. She wants Bobby to feel that he's in control. *Go on boy, jump*, Lucia thinks to herself.

To hell with it, Bobby thinks. He perches out and dives.

"Although I think that you'd make a beautiful model, you'd make a beautiful anything. . . . It's not an easy profession. Most women end up being hamburger meat for the photographers, agents, financiers, or magazine editors sooner or later."

Lucia pretends not to hear, but she has recorded each word, and each pitch of each syllable. They both open their menus. Bob nervously looks at the prices. He dove in, but now he's got to get out of the water. It's freezing.

Lucia stares at him fondly. Bob can feel her eyes beginning to sear a tattoo on his forehead. He's not sure that he wants a tattoo on his forehead. He looks at her.

Lucia smiles. "Bobby, would it be all right if I call you Bobby from now on?"

Bobby swoons, like the mate of a Chinese mantis.

"Jesus, I'm starved," Lucia says.

After a hundred minutes, and what Bob feels like, has been as many courses, they are finally finished. *Bobby* literally begins to sweat when he notices the waiter heading toward him with the bill. He'd rather be facing a firing squad or enlisting in the Israeli Defense Force, and he's not even Jewish.

Bob stares down at the bill.

"This was beautiful Bobby, really. Thank you so much," Lucia says.

Bobby smiles tightly. He's afraid to get up because the bill has had the effect of a gigantic enema. He scribbles his name, adds a tip, and smiles.

The waiter takes the check and nods. Bob nods mockingly back. What the hell was the waiter nodding at? Was he nodding at the fact that he had just ripped Bobby's eyeballs out through his anus?

As they're leaving the restaurant. Lucia overhears the waiter and the host commenting. "Next time, don't do me any favors. He had the table the whole night and left me three dollars. What made you think that he was a big tipper?"

"Last of the big spenders," the host says. "Sorry, I owe you one."

Lucia and Bob walk out onto the street. Lucia takes his hand. "Got any wine at home? I think now would be a good time to take a look at your book."

"Uh, no. But . . ." Bob's face is chalky and pained.

"What is it, Bobby? Don't you want to have me over?"

"Yes, yes of course," Bobby says. He hesitates and looks up the street. "It's just that . . . I don't know."

"I know what this is Bobby, I'm on to you," Lucia says.

Bobby breathes out, heavily through his nose, with his mouth closed. "Hmph, do you?"

"Yes I do. You're going through a confidence crisis."

Bob studies Lucia. She's ravishing. He'd buy arsenic, for personal use, from her, if she offered.

She continued, "You're a writer, I read it in your eyes the first time that I saw you."

Lucia takes Bobby's hands strongly into her own. She jerks them and he stares at her.

"You see, Bobby," she says, "men never catch women that don't want to be caught. I want to be caught."

Lucia looks hard, and yet softly into him. Bobby feels like he's being bound by a beautiful goddess.

"I want to be caught," she continues, "by a writer, a blond, handsome writer. Are you him, Bobby?" She moves in closer.

"Yes I am . . . I mean, *yes, I'm him.*"

Bobby would have said yes to her if she asked him if he'd like to jump off the Empire State building with her, or maybe without her.

"Yes, you are . . . now, let's go back to your place." She pecks Bobby's cheek.

Moments later they're standing in silence waiting for the bus.

"I'd figure a guy on the brink of being published by such a big company would have a car, or at least an Uber account."

"I'm planning on getting a car soon. Uber's not for me. They used 'Greyball,' ripped off the cities and their drivers. Didn't you read about it? All or nothing, that's me. I wait till I can have the best. No compromising."

Lucia stares at him, knowing that he's trying to make roses out of weeds. "My kind of man," she says.

The bus pulls up and they get in.

A half hour later they arrive at the building that Bob lives in. Lucia looks at the entrance and is uninspired. They get on the elevator and take it up to the eighth floor. Bob leads the way to 8H. He lets Lucia in.

As soon as they enter, he nervously attempts to straighten the clothes and clutter. Lucia, not minimally impressed, sits on the couch. Some things just can't be concealed. She knows that it's his sorry-ass apartment.

"So, is this just your writing studio or . . . ?"

"This? No, I mean, yes, I like to live modestly."

"I guess," Lucia says to herself, while looking at the drab furniture.

Bob opens his midget refrigerator. "So." He looks at her but she's paying no attention. "I don't have any wine," he continues, "but I've got some apple juice."

Bob doesn't get a response from Lucia. Bob's cat rubs her leg. She grimaces and pushes him away. Her cell phone rings.

"Hello?" she responds softly. "Hey . . . um, no, false alarm," she says.

Lucia watches Bob fill two jars with apple juice. *Oh my God*, she thinks, *no one drinks out of jars anymore.*

"Yes, yes, I will. I promise," she whispers into her phone.

When she hangs up, Bob hands her an apple juice and awkwardly leans to kiss her. "Bob. Don't."

"I'm sorry. Is there something wrong?" He takes her hand.

"Don't do that. Bob, don't do that." She pulls her hand back.

"Lucia," he says.

She takes a deep breath, "Bob, that was Tony."

"Tony? Your ex Tony?"

"Yeah, Tony my ex. If he ever found out . . ."

Bob interrupts, "I thought . . . I mean, what did you tell him?"

"You heard. I didn't really tell him anything."

"I thought that it was a closed department?" Bob stares at her.

Lucia lays the jar on the floor. The cat sniffs at it, waits until she looks away and then sticks his tongue in the juice.

"No, not closed, dead," she says.

Lucia forces herself to remember when she spilled a Coke and Rum on her fur. Her eyes begin to tear and the waterworks flow rapidly. She sniffles, "I gave him everything. He was my first, my only . . . in the end he beat me and cheated and . . . I just, I don't want to be a fool again. What if you're not what you seem? It's possible, you know. I thought he was a good man and he was . . ."

She's grateful that Bob interrupts her. She didn't know what else to say.

"*I am what you think.* I am!" Bob says forcefully.

"I'm just, I know this doesn't make any sense to you . . . it doesn't make any sense to me . . . maybe I'm feeling a little emotional and confused right now."

She gazes into Bob's shallow puddles. "I think I should just go home," she says softly.

Lucia stands and walks to the door.

Bob would do anything to keep her there. "Wait," he says.

"I'm sorry, I should just go."

"Why? What's wrong? Why should you go?"

Lucia cracks the door slightly open. She turns and looks at Bobby. The tears have made the skin under her eyes moist and sensual. She's the most erotic woman Bobby's ever seen. He must have her, at any price. He must have her.

His thoughts are interrupted by an angel. "I'll call you," Lucia says as she turns.

"Let me walk you to the elevator," he says softly.

As the elevator doors close, he quietly says, "I love you."

The following morning, Bob sludges through the hallway to his office, his head hung low. A small crowd is at his desk. Koss has pages in his hand. As Bob enters, Koss quietly passes a page to Gael.

No one has noticed Bob's presence.

"Humph," Koss says, "I knew that this Phillips had something."

"This is Herman," Gael says, "Phillips is the head of corporate sales."

"Technicalities," Koss says.

Bob clears his throat. The group acknowledges his presence. "What's going on?" he asks.

"Herman," Koss says, at the same time, looking at Gael for confirmation that this is in fact Herman.

Gael nods and Koss continues. "This is good, Herman," he says.

Bob gently grips the papers in Koss's hand. "It's nothing really, sir."

Koss holds them tight. He looks at Bob with the determination of a honey badger. "I like it. I like how it flows. Lou said you were piddling with the writing again, but I had no idea how far you've come."

Bob releases the sheets, mechanically looks away, and places his hands at his side.

Koss shakes the pages in front of Bob's face. "Still needs a little work, though. The voice isn't quite you. A bit forced. It needs more . . . rectitude. Take it home and work on it. Have a revised copy on my desk by next Monday."

Everyone stares at Bob, who stands quiet as a Trappist monk.

"You've got one week, Herman," Koss says firmly, again looking for assurance from Gael.

Gael again nods. Koss continues, "Don't let me down, Herman."

Koss smiles at Gael; he got his name down now. Everyone leaves, except Gael.

"Hmm," she says, "you of all people. Who would have thought?"

Gael takes Bob's face in her fingers. "Don't let us down, Bobby." She brings Bob's head close to hers and then tweaks it, gently down toward her breast. He stiffens, she drops her talons and leaves.

Bob feels that he's been staring for hours when Jennifer walks in.

"I'm sorry Bob, I didn't mean to snoop. I saw the manuscript and was curious, then Gael came in and one thing led to another."

Bob continues to stare.

"It's really good Bob, really. I'm happy for you." Jennifer kisses him on the cheek.

Bob couldn't tell you exactly how he lived or what he did in the next collection of hours. Confusion attacked his mind, leaving a disorganized idea of ecstasy. He pondered, *had fate finally closed in on him?* He slowly recovered. He needed to find the author, the real author.

Making changes to the manuscript would be like revising the smile on the Mona Lisa. Other than some grammar, he couldn't imagine making alterations that would improve it.

In one transitory moment, he realized that he was going to be a published author. The next instant, he called Lucia. She didn't answer. He dialed and dialed to no avail.

Bob returned to his apartment. Bob placed the manuscript on one side of the room and purposely sat on the other side. After a few minutes, he walked, stood over it and blankly stared down.

Bob looked at the cat. "What should I do?" he asked.

Cat, the cat, blinked and stared at him, thinking, *do anything you want, but keep that bitch out of here.*

Bob stared. "I know, I need to find her," he said.

Cat watched impatiently. It was pathetic. Even he knew that Bob needed Lucia like one needs Ebola.

Bob flips through the printed morsels and begins looking up synonyms for various passages. As he grinds down the pile, his face changes appearance dozens of times. Hours sneak into morning, and exhaustion wakes him and carries him to bed.

On Monday morning, Bob knocks on Koss's office door. Koss himself greets Bob, and they walk inside. On Koss's desk is the jacket artwork for *Standard Deviations*.

Bob's eyes move down the cover. He reads *by Robert Herman*.

Koss puts his arm around Bob. "Well, son, I gave you a week to do your part. I'm sure you won't let us down. To be truthful, I'd publish it the way it was, without a change, but I wanted to give you some time alone with your work. I'm sure you invested it wisely."

Bob stares blankly. He doesn't know how to respond. His look of null unsettles Koss.

"How do you like what the designers did for your cover?"

Bobby remains statuesque.

Koss winks at him. "Bobby, it's gold."

Koss kisses Bobby's cheek. "You've always been like a son to me. I knew from the moment that I hired you."

"Gael hired me, sir," Bobby says gently.

Koss smiles largely. "Technicalities, Bobby, technicalities."

Chapter 6

Find of the Century

Koss is beaming brightly. Bob Herman is standing in front of his desk. "Sit down," Koss says as he winks and motions Herman down. "I'll get Arnie Schuman. He's the best agent in the country, he'll take care of you."

Bob sits. Koss takes the phone and winks. "Mark Koss here. I got one. I'll sponsor . . . how many did Selton sell this year? . . . . This kid will double that . . . Herman. Robert Herman."

"Bobby . . . I'd like to go by "Bobby," Herman says firmly, in a low tone.

Koss nods and winks again. "Bobby Herman. He's one of mine."

Koss sets the phone down and again winks at Bob. "You've arrived, my boy. You'll become a pillar around here. A piece of this place will belong to you someday . . . I can feel it."

Bob watches.

"Don't you have anything to say, Bobby? Anything to ask? GAM is part of you, Bobby, and you are part of it."

Koss winks yet again, and Bob is starting to wonder if it's a tic. Bob notices Ted Basle pass the doorway.

"I do have a question."

Koss winks and nods.

"Who is Ted?" Bob asks blandly, kind of like potatoes without salt.

Mark winks, smiles, stands, and puts his hand on Bob's shoulder. "Do you like baseball, Bobby?"

"Baseball?" Bob pauses, "Well, kind of, if I'm really bored I guess." Bob pauses. "It beats football."

Koss rubs Bob's shoulders. Bob would rather have two Brazilian Wandering Spiders on him, and a low concentration of Brazilian Wandering Spider venom causes impotence.

"Well, in the old days, teams didn't have billions to buy forty players for a roster. Each team had a guy that could do it all, who got the job done. . . . When the center fielder was having a bad day or the catcher or the shortstop, they called in the utility man. Somehow, someway, smoothly, not so smoothly, ethically, not so ethically, he got the job done. Ted Basle is Gent America Media's utility man. He gets the job done. We all need utility men, Bob."

Koss removes his hands from Bob and steps in front of him. Bob shrugs his shoulders, hoping to shake off any shed snakeskin.

For the first time, Bob's role is unambiguous. Koss needs him and not vice versa. He eyes Koss how a newborn might gaze at the world. Koss's nose resembles that of a pig.

"Even the president of the United States has utility men, a whole department of them," Koss insists.

"Never heard of them."

"Sure you have . . . FBI, CIA. Wake up Bobby, no one writes like you who doesn't know the score. Three percent of the US population own seventy percent of the wealth. One man owns more than the bottom thirty percent. It's *far worse* than the old feudal system, at least for anyone who isn't rich and part of the scheme."

Bob uncomfortably digests the words. He certainly can find no fault in them but knows that it's not politically correct to speak about these things freely. He wouldn't want anyone to think that he was a socialist.

Koss loves enlightening; it was his calling. In the military, he spelled it out for the other brass who couldn't figure out the game plan. He knew that war was all about dollars; billions of dollars.

"How do you think the powerful manage the peons, Bobby? The masses? *We* keep them running the gerbil wheel, making the elite richer." Koss winks and raises the tone of his voice, "And when they get out of line *we* start a war and send them to the wolves, making big bucks on the weapons *we* sell to both sides, Bobby!"

It would be interesting to see Koss foam, so Bob watches and waits.

"Bobby, come on, we're a part of it!"

Koss stares and winks before continuing. "The media, Bobby. When we rob the public of health care or distract them by telling them to look at Greece or Islamic terrorism; it's all a scam Bobby. You know it." Koss winks. *Maybe it's not a tic,* Bobby thinks.

Koss continues, "I know it and we benefit from the system. We couldn't, Bobby, without the Ted Basles of the world."

Koss winks again. For sure it's a tic.

"*Standard Deviations* tells me that you understand that. You're not like the rest of the boys, Bobby. You're a man, and don't worry, Bobby; we take care of our own here. If you ever need a utility man, it's carte blanche."

Koss reaches into his drawer and gives Bob Ted's business card.

Bobby nods and mumbles, "Utility man," to himself.

"That's right, Bobby."

Koss makes his hand into a fist and hits Bobby gently on the arm. "Now get back to work and start your next baby. You're not a famous writer . . . yet."

Bobby beats Koss and exaggerates winking again and again.

Koss squints and scrutinizes his new find, "You better get that checked, Bobby," he says seriously.

Later that day, Bob is chipper and whistling, collecting his things to go home.

Jennifer enters his office. "Bob, how did it go with Koss?" she asks.

"He's going to publish it."

"I'm so happy for you! Do you need someone to celebrate with?"

"No. . . . Thanks, Jen. I have plans."

"You're a busy guy," Jennifer says quietly.

Bob smiles and walks out.

On the bus, he stares at the manuscript with a far-gone grin. As people walk on the bus, he covers his name, especially from anyone looking homeless. He passes his usual stop and continues on, toward Chinatown.

Bob looks up at the building. He scans the names and spots "Lucia." He excitedly presses the button next to her name. No one answers. He rings and rings and rings.

"Bob?"

Bob turns to see Lucia approaching with groceries.

"Lucia! Why haven't you returned my calls?"

She seems harder than before. "What are you doing here?"

"I've missed you so much, you look beautiful. Where have you been?"

Lucia glances around and pulls him into the door with her. They make it up four flights of stairs, and she unlocks a shoddy door.

Lucia's apartment is a tiny, gypsy-like space full of trinkets. Beads hanging from the ceiling separate the living space. The bed is a mattress on the floor surrounded by white hanging droplets.

Bob takes one of them in his hands. "These aren't plastic . . . they're stones," he says more to himself than Lucia.

She hears him. "Of course, they're not plastic. Won't find anything plastic here, except maybe the garbage liner."

"They're some kind of mineral stone."

"They're Brazilian," she says.

"Wow, classy, I like them, the texture, the color."

Lucia's hearing is selective. At the moment, she's paying *zero* attention, not purposely being impolite; it's who she is.

Bob walks to a shelf on the right side of the bed containing jade pieces of a buddha and elephants. He picks up a piece of paper. "Christie's Auction Certificate of Authenticity."

Lucia continues to put her rations away at a leisurely pace. Bob looks to the right and notices cocaine dust and a razor on a small mirror. He's not overly concerned. There are seven times more cocaine users than lawyers in the United States; we should be relieved. Of course, some cross over into both categories.

Finally, when the bags are empty, Lucia begins reciting. To most anyone it sounds like she's said the same speech a thousand times. But as is apparent, Bobby is hooked past his gills. "You don't know me," she says. "You don't know who I am, what I've done."

Bob's virgin. "Stop it, Lucia. Damn . . . I don't care. I know you. I don't care. We can start fresh."

"Another fresh start for a coke fiend? Are you a preacher Bobby? You uncuff slaves?"

Bob hesitates. "Yes, *yes*."

"A fresh start from murder? From murdering a baby?"

"What? What baby? What are you talking about?"

This horse is docile. Lucia's got free rein. "Tony's . . . and mine," she says as an apparent matter of fact.

"What! Are you trying to press buttons? There are a million legal abortions in the United States every year. Should we condemn every woman who believes that her happiness is more important than an unknown fetus?"

Lucia enjoys the game and, as always, is willing to go to the next level. She walks to Herman. "It was not a fetus. I was seven months pregnant . . . too late for an abortion, a hospital one, anyway. Unless you have big money. If you have a lot of money you can have the doctor do it to save the mother's life."

Bobby's in unchartered territory. *What the hell is she talking about? She obviously didn't pay attention to Dr. Derek Shepherd of* Grey's Anatomy.

Lucia stared at him. *The idiot was probably thinking of* Grey's Anatomy's *Dr. Derek Shepherd.*

She raised the pitch of her voice to get him back to New York. "Tony took me to the gym locker room. His doctor was waiting. They sedated me, forced the birth, and left the baby to die. I woke, and there the angel laid; red and tiny and blue and beautiful."

Lucia sobs on cue. "The baby was still faintly breathing. There was no one there to help me. I picked the baby up to run to a hospital. Tony's doctor blocked me. The baby fell. Its little body moved on the floor."

Bob is staring, imagining the scene.

Lucia sobs again and takes a breath. "The doctor injected a syringe into the baby's chest. The baby jerked."

Bob interrupts the void left by Lucia's completion of the story. "And what did they do with it?"

"Him! Him! He was a beautiful boy! Don't call him an 'it'!"

Bob ran his hand over his hair and stared at the crash. *How could he have called it an 'it'?*

"They took him, Bobby, *him* into the bathroom." She wept uncontrollably. "I heard the toilet flush, once and twice and again and . . ." Lucia begins to sob, "leave me alone, Bobby. I ruin everything I touch."

She takes his face in her hands and walks him toward the door. "Oh Bobby, I want to be with you, I just wish he were dead! I know that's awful, but sometimes I think it's the only way."

Herman was never in the marines or any military, but he felt the calling of the marines deep down within him, "from the halls of Montezuma to the shores of Tripoli, and all that . . ."

"*We'll have babies*, our own babies! I will take care of you," he says softly.

Lucia pushes him. "Leave me alone. Don't call me. Don't think about me. It's for your own good . . . do you understand?! He won't let us, and I don't want to ruin you . . . do you want to be ruined?!" Lucia blubbers.

She opens the door and shoves him out, leaving him standing in the hallway. Her voice is almost inaudible, "Maybe call me sometime down the road, Bobby."

He knocks on the door. "Lucia?"

A scrappy looking, middle-aged woman opens her door. "Hey lover boy, take the soap opera back in there or get out of the hall. Some of us like peace and quiet."

Lucia takes a jade elephant lovingly in her hands. She rubs it against her face and then sits it besides several other jade pieces. She hears Bob on the other side of the world.

His voice is muffled and distant. "Lucia," she hears him whisper.

Bob gently bumps his forehead against the door and between his flattened hands. He hesitates, turns, and slowly walks away. Bob walks down the street back to the bus stop. A dark-skinned, middle-aged man watches him.

A squad car is parked up the street. The driver, a stubby middle-aged male with red hair, Detective Clark, is smoking a cigar. The passenger is also a middle-aged male, Detective Kennedy. Kennedy has a tattoo of the US flag on his arm. They're both watching the dark-skinned stranger and Bob.

"You think there's anything to worry about?" asks Detective Kennedy.

"I hope not. If Isa's ever discovered, we're all as good as gone. The whole cover-up will be on our laps," Clark says.

"We'll do a check on this guy. If there's a problem, remember Isa's command. Cowdar died so we all could live. If they get to Isa, there's closure," Kennedy says.

"You mean Isa expires." Clark looks at Kennedy and begins pulling the car into traffic. He flicks his cigar out the window at a street sign. It hits the sign dead center. "I still got it," he says smiling to himself.

The squad heads in Bob's direction. Bob gets on a bus. The squad follows him, unnoticed until he enters his building.

Bob Herman's in his apartment that evening, pacing and disheveled. He looks at the phone lying on the bed and then sits down next to it. He has Ted Basle's card in his hand.

Phones represent a lot of things. At the moment, Bob's phone represents some sort of reprieve, some sort of second chance at bliss. He gently moves his hand along the bed, kind of sneaking up on the phone and the hazard it represents.

Ted is in his den wearing a silk robe. He looks at the caller ID and places the electronic lifeline to his ear. "Hey ya, Bobby!" he says.

"Uhuh," Bobby didn't expect Basle to have his cell number. He gets nervous. "I'm sorry, wrong number."

Bobby hangs up. The phone immediately rings from an unidentified number. It happened too quickly for it to be Basle. Maybe it's Lucia.

"Hello?"

"Robert. It's Dad."

"Oh, hi Dad."

"How are you, Robert?"

"Good, Dad, and you?"

"Good. You haven't called in a few months. I hope that you're okay."

"Me? Are you kidding? I've never been better. I was actually going to call you."

"That's good to hear, son. One should call . . ."

Bob interrupts his father. He knows the script by heart anyway. "I'm going to be published, Dad."

The lack of enthusiasm loaded into the silence almost busts Bob's eardrum. Fighting pain, Bob blows softly and away from the mouthpiece. "Dad, I know that I owe you lots."

"No flag running up the staff yet," Bob continues, "as soon as the royalty check comes, I'll get it to you."

"Robert, me and your mother are in a bad situation. We took a second mortgage out on the house to help you and . . ."

"Yes, Dad, I'll get it to you. Maybe you weren't listening, *too worried about money to hear what I said.* I'm getting published."

"Son, you know, I'm happy for you. How much money will you be getting?"

"A lot, I don't know exactly how much, but a lot."

"They don't tell you?"

"Well, they told my agent. He takes care of the economic things."

"Son, make sure your checking account doesn't get eaten up by your online gambling account."

"I won't gamble it away, Dad. Those days are over. I would have called you sooner, but I didn't want to jinx it. . . . I haven't gambled for a while now."

"How big is the book?"

"It's a few hundred pages, I guess. It depends on the marketing department, the font, margins, all of that. I could give you a summary"

"That's fine son. I'll wait until I read my published, autographed copy."

Bob knows that his father doesn't believe him and frankly, why should he, except that fathers, good fathers, anyway, should always believe their sons.

Bob rummages around for words. Finally, he offers a lackluster, "How's Mom?" Bob waits for a response but only hears quiet. His father has already hung up.

"Love you," Bob whispers.

Months flew by like moths around the light bulb on the back porch.

Standard Deviations became everything that Koss promised. The book is everywhere, in everyone's hands. The reviews rocket Bob Herman into the skies with Miley Cyrus, Kim Kardashian, Justin Bieber; talk about basking in class. . . .

Further on, Bob's seated and surrounded by stacks of books at the King Cole Bar and Salon in the St. Regis. His facial expression is not one of a man who has a long, *long* line of people who spent fifty on his book, waiting for an autograph: his autograph!

Bob scribbles in a book and waits for the next sucker customer. His face on the back of his book glares at him.

Arnie Schuman, a sixtyish man with white kinky hair, walks from behind and rests his hand on Bob's shoulder. "The *Times* says that you're the find of the century."

Bob grooms his hair back, smiles, turns, and opens a book, sword in hand.

Mark Koss smacks him on the back. "Hi Bobby, my boy. I'm waiting for your second jewel. Is it coming?"

Bob smiles. "Yes sir, just polishing it up."

Mark Koss makes a gun out of his hand, winks, and shoots it at Arnie. He wishes it was a real gun.

"See what I mean?" Mark Koss says, looking at Arnie, "Jewel . . . polishing . . . polishing his jewel. . . . He's got it."

Koss slaps Bob on the back again. "Looking forward to it, kid."

Koss glances at Arnie. They hate each other. "I told you Arnie. He's a rare one."

"Yeah," Arnie says, "like thunder in a snowstorm."

Koss analyzes the words for a land mine. "Schuman, he doesn't know how to speak any other way, him and his overestimation of self-worth."

Later, Bob is at home on his computer. "And that takes care of that," he says.

Cat hops on the desk and reads a few lines. *Looks like shit to me*, he thinks to himself.

Bob takes Cat's head into his hands. He looks in Cat's eyes knowing that he can always count on his support. Bobby thinks, *No more credit collector calls. Nothing but blue skies ahead. All I must do is write another amazing book . . .*

Bob looks to the side and at Cat. The smirk on Cat's face reminds him that to write "another" amazing book, implies that he needs to write the first one . . . and he hasn't done that. He must write the first amazing book that he hasn't been able to do for years of trying.

Cat understood the entire situation and didn't think that Herman had it in him. Cat read a few more lines and thought, *Still looks like shit to me*. He wouldn't tell Bob if he did talk. Bob changed the kitty litter, and no one was going to make him live in an apartment that didn't have someone to change the kitty litter.

Bob scoots Cat off the desk and stares at the screen. He hesitates and writes a few lines. He then erases the letters one by one. He takes a deep breath and looks for Cat and speaks. "It's okay. I have plenty of time. Anyway, I think I deserve a little celebration."

Online betting is great but not like the excitement of being there. Bob's standing with two guys, Chuck and Van, at the Aqueduct Race Track.

In the background the announcer is calling the race. "And it's Blue Bonnet from behind . . . Blue Bonnet by a nose . . . hold your tickets for the final."

Bob looks down at his tickets.

"You may have published a bestseller, but your luck hasn't changed here," Chuck says.

"You must have lost twenty grand," Van throws.

"I wish," Bob grunts.

Koss called Bob several times a day for an update. Bob had to hit the iron while the coal was still hot. Koss wanted to read the first chapter, the first three chapters, sample chapters, and get a summary; he knew he wouldn't get a book proposal, so he wasn't asking for one. He wanted something, anything, but time quickly passed.

A few months after Bob shot to the *New York Times* bestseller list was the perfect time to announce the second book. If he waited too long, readers wouldn't know Bobby Herman from Herman Munster.

Koss was more than impatient. GAM had invested heavily in Herman. PR was far from cheap, and getting him on the *New York Times* bestseller list cost an arm and two legs.

Arnie Schuman was also getting antsy, and Koss knew it. Most big shots in the industry thought that their shit didn't stink. Arnie was above the tribe. He thought that his shit was a commodity.

Koss sat at his desk playing Pac-Man 256. The phone rang. He knew it was Arnie. "Hello Arnie, my *Yakiri*" (*my treasure* in Hebrew), Koss said.

"Mark, I'm sorry if I insist, but you know the business well."

Koss felt the jab. Arnie would never have said that Koss knew the business as well as he. "Yes Arnie. I do know the business well. Hell, I've got lots at stake here. It was my dime! I paid his advance!"

"Yes, Mark, I realize that. I'm not only thinking of myself, I'm thinking of you, *ach*" (*brother* in Hebrew). "Talk to him."

Koss rolls his eyes. He wished he had an Uzi (Israeli open-bolt, blowback-operated submachine gun) and that Arnie was here, so he could personally silence that Israeli *zavua* (hypocrite).

"Yeah, Arnie, I'll talk to him," Koss affirmed.

Koss firmly hits the intercom. "Jennifer, did you tell Bob Herman that I wanted him?"

"Yes sir."

"Well, go and get him. Now!"

Jennifer walks into Bob's office. She doesn't say a word nor does she need to. Bob looks up from his screen and nods.

Bob walks into Koss's office and sits on his desk.

"Where are we at, son?"

"Writing books is not like writing magazine articles. I've started like five books. I'm just having some difficulty deciding which road to take."

"Well, bring what you have to me. I'll give you my opinion." Koss hesitates and beams, "I was spot on with *Standard Deviations*. Give me a shot, let me help you again."

"I'm not showing them to anyone. They're just not ready." Bobby squeezes out a smile.

"Son," Koss said in a fatherly tone, "you hit the iron when it's hot. Tomorrow the schleps that bought your first book will forget your name. Do you know what it cost me to get you on the *New York Times* bestseller list?"

Bob was naive. He believed that the *New York Times* bestseller list was a reputable club.

"It's business, Bobby, bring me what you have, and we'll get a ghost."

Bobby stares at Koss. "But . . ."

Koss doesn't give him space. "Bob, this firm stuck its neck out for you. Every GAM shareholder is counting on you to deliver. We made projections based on the success of your first book. It means a lot to the bottom line. . . . Do you like being a writer, Bobby?"

"Yes, yes I do."

"Bring me what you got."

Bob nods.

"Good boy, Bobby."

Bob stands and leaves.

Later that evening on the bus, Bob walks up the aisle. He notices a stack of newspapers on one of the seats. He shuffles through them. There's no book.

He gets off the bus and treads to his apartment, sits at the computer, and runs his fingers through his hair. He punches the tab key with his finger. He punches it harder and harder, stops and shuts the computer off.

Suddenly he stands. It seems that he's made a critical decision. He rises and pulls one of his old manuscripts from the file cabinet. He begins scanning the pages into his computer.

Jennifer walks by Gael at the office's Marzocco espresso machine. "I think Herman bought *Standard Deviations*," Gael says.

"What?" Jennifer hesitates before continuing. "Bob wouldn't buy a manuscript. It's not possible."

"Not possible? Where have you been? They all buy scripts. It's the author's name that sells, not the content. Besides, I've seen other things that he's written." Gael's nose rises, she purses her lips and shakes her head. "He doesn't have it."

"That's loathsome . . . even for you," Jennifer shoots.

Bob heads toward the women. Gael slowly walks away backward, still looking at Jennifer and purposely speaks loud enough for Bob to hear. "Anyway, he'd better buy or find or write something decent soon, *if he wants to stay in this office*. Koss didn't like him from the beginning."

Gael impudently glares at Bob and then turns away.

Bob looks at Jennifer, back at Gael, and then at Jennifer again. "Can you make me a coffee? I'm no good at it."

Chapter 7

Gambling Guarantees

Bob walks back to his office with an espresso in his hand. He sits behind his desk. Jennifer enters and softly closes the door behind her. "Bob, did you write *Standard Deviations*?"

"What kind of a question is that?" Bob squirms. "I never figured you to be one that followed office gossip."

Jennifer holds her ground. "I'm not. Are you the author?"

"Jennifer. I've written another one that will convince them all. Koss is reading it right now."

Jennifer smiles. "Good, Bob, I'm counting on you."

She leaves. Bob pours down the scalding black liquid. He stands with his mouth half open, sucking in cool air.

Koss, meanwhile, is at his desk resting his jaw on the palm of his right hand. His head sinks until his palm is holding up his skull. He looks sideways at his computer. Nothing happened. The words were the same.

Koss snaps the phone before it rings a second time. "Arnie. I can't figure it out. It's all garbage, just trash, I mean it's infantile. . . . This wouldn't sell to your average Fox News viewer."

"Are you sure it came from Herman?" Arnie asks.

"Yes, it came from Herman! He gave it to me. He scanned it off one of his older manuscripts but there's not even a sliver of gold. Hell, there's not even a sliver of tin in it."

Koss hung the phone up and stared at the *Standard Deviations* book on his award shelf. He suddenly stands and heads out the door.

Employees have seen Koss plod this way before. His stride resembles an angry hippo sloshing through the African swamps. No one dares to greet him or even look his way.

Koss charges into Bobby's room. "Bobby, what are you trying to pull?!"

Bob does not respond.

"First you give me a piece of gold and then you give me a piece of shit. Look, I understand that for some, the second novel is harder than the first, but *you've got to rise to your potential, man.* Do you understand me?!"

Bob nods.

"We want you to do well. You want you to do well. Do it!" Koss screams.

Koss leaves Bob, who uncomfortably swallows the rest of his hot brew.

That evening Bob is walking on the dark street in the drizzly rain. A bus passes. Bob notices Lucia on the bus. "Lucia! Lucia!" he yells while waving his arms.

Lucia ignores or doesn't see him. Bob runs after the bus. For a few blocks, he stays close but then stops. A heavily bearded man walks out of the shadow behind him and is looking at the bus that Lucia is on. Lucia looks back. The man looks at Bob, who wipes his mouth and crouches down to catch his breath.

Bob looks up at the man. "Do you want something?" Bob asks panting.

The man smiles. "We all want something."

Bob looks around, the street is empty. "Where did you come from?"

"Come from?"

"Yes. Where did you come from?"

"Well, my people were from Ethiopia. I grew up here."

"Oh," Bob says, still trying to catch his breath.

"My family is related to Haile Selassie."

"I never heard of him. Was he some sort of black hero?"

"Black? No. I'm not much darker than you. Ethiopians are African, Arab, and Asian. People who categorize others as Crayola colors are infantile. Don't you think so?"

"Oh? Think?" Bob asks. "You're here now, I mean in this country. That pretty much makes you black."

"Thanks for letting me know," the man snipes back.

Bob is out of breath. Bob has never seen this bum before, but he doesn't seem to be a threat. Bob looks at him again, in desperate need of entertainment.

"Such a foolish notion, separating people into five Crayola colors. It's almost as imbecilic as the politicians who believe that changing flags on building tops will ease the pain of the past. They should leave them there to remind us of the truth."

Bob hasn't the foggiest notion of what this guy is smoking or snorting but if he were to indulge, he'd want to get the same stuff.

"Only when we reside with truth can we understand when we are living a lie."

Bob digests the last sentence and recalls the ones prior. Suddenly, something about the man and his dialogue intrigues and even seems familiar to Bob, but he has other things to be concerned with. "Okay, have a good night," Bob says as he begins to walk away.

"What do you want with the girl on the bus?"

Bob stops and turns. He analyzes the man's eyes.

"She is certainly a beautiful woman," the man says.

"Yes, she is. I have to go now," Bob says.

"In a hurry?"

"Look . . . I don't know you nor do I . . ."

The man interrupts. "Yes. Even so, someday I'll ask you to do something very important for me." The man turns and walks away, crossing the street.

Bob notices a bound brown bag in the man's arm. A car passes, blocking Bob's view of the street. "Wait! Wait!"

Bob walks quickly in the direction that the bum headed, but the man has vanished. Bob runs down the street and into a dead-end alley just as his hope tank runs dry. He saw the needle on empty this afternoon when Koss screamed at him. He just didn't see any Hope Stations on his way home. He kneels. "No! Where did you go? Please!" he sobs.

Bob catches his breath. Newspapers move and two homeless people rise from the rubble.

"Hey, I'm right here. How's about helping me out with some change?" the first homeless man says.

"I'm right here, help me out too," the second man says.

Bob backs out of the alleyway and quickly turns the corner, nervously looking back. He notices two other men behind, following him. Bob ducks into Bino's, a small, dimly lit saloon.

The walls are crowded with hanging autographed photos of fighters. Bob begins reading their names. He gets to the middle of the bar and reads "Tony Russo." Bob examines the photo. Tony looks to be in his thirties but has boyish features and a head of choppy hair. Bob finishes analyzing the snapshot and then looks around.

The two guys that he feared were stalking him never entered and the homeless guys from the alley probably wouldn't enter. A few guys are sitting at the end of the bar. Bob steps up and orders.

"Shot of Chivas," he says.

The bartender silently serves him.

Bob shoots the elixir down. "Another please."

"What race are you in?" the bartender queries.

Bob tightly smiles. "Please just pour me another."

Another three shots and twenty minutes later, Bob is unsteadily heading back from the bathroom.

A patron enters. The bartender yells, "Hey Tony, what's up, my guy?!"

Bob stops in his tracks. He looks at the wall and focuses on the picture of Tony Russo. He then moves back to his spot.

The bartender approaches. "Refill?"

Bob looks at Tony. Tony's actually shorter than Bob, 5'9, 5'10, maybe. Tony's wearing a black leather jacket and you can see that he's fit.

"Refill?" the bartender repeats.

"Yeah. Yeah man, refill," Bob says trying to regain composure.

The bartender pours. Bob guns it down. The bartender begins to walk away.

"Wait. Is that Tony Russo?" Bob asks.

The bartender stares back at Bob. "Why? He go with your girl or something? If he did, I don't want no trouble here. I'll lose my license."

"Another please," Bob says.

"Hey, it's your stomach." The bartender pours another drink.

Bob downs it. The bartender suspiciously watches as Bob nervously pushes his hand into his pocket and walks toward Tony.

"Hey Tony!" the bartender yells, "this guy . . . Tony!"

Tony looks at the bartender then at Bob. Bob's hand is in his pocket shaking and pointed toward Tony.

"Madonna!" Tony yells.

Bob continues to move toward him.

Tony focuses on the bulge in Bob's jacket that's pointing at him. He raises his hands. "Whatever you got I don't want none of it. I ain't bothering nobody."

Bob is momentarily confused. *Did this idiot just use a double negative?*

Now Bob is irritated. It just irks him to no end when people use double negatives.

Bob feels alcohol confidence. Tony seems skittish. Bob has no idea why.

Bob looks from side to side, unconsciously pushing his hand further into his pocket. The jacket is now pointed directly at Tony's chest.

"Please, please," Tony begs. "If Mikey O sent you, I can fix everything. I swear."

Bob jerks his head to gain poise. He musters up a mean face. In fact, if someone saw him that didn't know him, they might say that his name should be "Meanface."

"I'm a friend of Lucia," Bob says in the best Pacino he can foster.

"Oh, yeah," Tony says faintly, "Lucia."

"Leave her alone," Bob says.

Tony is frozen.

"Leave her in peace. You got it?" Bob repeats.

"In peace, sure, I'll leave her in peace. I got it."

"If you don't," Herman says, "I'll be back to straighten things out."

"Sure, sure," Tony says. "I'll leave her in peace, don't worry."

Bob's eyes have Tony's eyes by the collar. Bob pushes his hand further into his pocket and moves closer until he's within inches. "You better get it . . . or you'll really get it."

Bob lowers his arm and walks out of the bar.

Tony is obviously relieved.

"Who was that guy, Tony?" the bartender asks.

"I don't know, but he had me spooked," Tony spews.

Outside Bino's, Bob trots down the street, turns the corner, stops, and gasps for breath. He glances back around the corner. No one is outside of Bino's. He defiantly moves back onto the sidewalk, easily visible for anyone who wants to find him. He waits almost twenty seconds and then turns back around the corner.

Bob pulls the cell phone out of his pocket and walks steadily to the bus stop. He's just in time. Seated, he relaxes, smiles, and finally chuckles out loud.

Minutes later, Tony runs out of Bino's and jumps in his car. He speeds to Lucia's. He soars the four flights of stairs to Lucia's apartment. As he arrives at her door, an elderly, well-groomed man heads out. Tony stares at him. The man looks away.

Tony enters and is face-to-face with Lucia. "I thought you said you dropped that dirtbag."

"Which one?"

"I'm not the one you play with, Lucia. That young blond, professional faggot-looking guy."

"Oh, I'm sorry baby. You mean the wannabe writer. I did drop him."

"You didn't drop him hard enough. He just came into Bino's and threatened me with a gun."

Lucia laughs, obviously amused. "What? Are you trying to be funny?"

"Oh, is that funny Lucia? A guy pointing a gun at me two inches from my face, is that funny to you?"

"He wouldn't hurt a fly, couldn't hurt a fly," she says almost disappointedly.

"Why's he still sniffing around if he ain't paying no bills here?"

"Probably the same reason you are." Lucia playfully smiles.

Tony presses her up against the wall. He reaches his hand down to her crotch. "This is why I'm here. And I'm the only one who gets it for free. You know the rules. If you can't get nothing from them, you dump 'em. And don't get me angry or . . ."

Tony moves his hand to his belt buckle and chokes Lucia with the other hand.

Lucia begins gagging. She's terrified and speaks in monosyllables. "To-ny, he-don't-come-a-round a-ny-more."

Tony loosens his grip. Lucia continues. "He wrote some bigshot book. He's going to make some serious scratch when the royalties start coming in. He's like a little puppy dog. I think he wants to have a relationship. Still, I don't think he understands that I'm only interested in his money . . . if he has any."

"Do you want me to explain it to him?"

Lucia regains self-control. "No, Tony. It's not worth it. He's harmless, really." Lucia begins smiling. "He thinks that I'm a nice girl."

"You are a nice girl, baby. You're my nice girl. You ain't goin' sweet on him, are you?"

Lucia looks away.

"You ain't soft on him, are you?" Tony asks.

Lucia remains still. She knows the script. Tony opens his fly, looking to toss Lucia on the bed. As he's carrying her forward, he notices Bob's photo on the back of a book. He freezes.

"Hey I thought you said you were just interested in his money? *You falling for this fag?*"

"I was trying to tell you. That book is a bestseller."

"I don't believe it. That guy?"

"I know," Lucia smiles. She touches Tony's chin with her inch-and-a-half-long fingernail. "Did you bring my candy?"

Tony kisses her hard then tosses her on the bed, at the same time wrapping her legs around him. "We're a team baby, don't ever forget it," he says.

"I know, baby. I'll never forget it." Lucia focuses her gaze on a picture of the Blessed Virgin hanging over her entrance. She begins crying as noise and grunts turn into panting and moaning.

Late that night, Bob's asleep face up, holding *Standard Deviations*. He's hoping he can absorb something of it if he sleeps with it. He'd eat it if he thought that there was a snowball's chance in hell that it might help. He hears a knock and jerks into consciousness. He instinctively looks at the digital clock, *4:03 a.m.*

Bob fumbles up and walks to the door. He's still half-drunk. Before he arrives, there's another loud knock. He looks through the peephole. Whoever's outside has the peephole covered. There's another loud knock.

"Who is it?" Bob asks.

There's no response.

"Who is it?" he asks louder.

Bob sobers up in a hurry and grabs a knife off the counter and slowly opens the door leaving the chain latched. "Gael?"

As always, she's dressed to kill. "I want to talk."

"At 4 a.m.?"

"I do some of my best talking in the morning."

"Are you on something?"

"If so, all the better for you."

"Gael, I'm not interested."

He tries to close the door. She stops it with her hand.

"Is this the way you treat your partner?"

"Partner?"

"I knew all along you didn't write *Standard Deviations*. . . . You don't even know what 'standard deviations' means."

He again tries to close the door. She again stops it.

"You've produced only crap since you plagiarized that book. I take it that you're having trouble." Gael's smile is so wide that her ears move. "I can help," she says.

"Oh. How are you so sure?"

"For poetry's sake we'll call it women's intuition. The point is, I can help you," she says in monosyllables.

A door down the hall opens. "Hey, some of us work. If you don't take it inside, I'm calling the cops," the male voice says.

Gael gestures to the chain. Bob unlatches it and opens the door. She walks in and closes the door behind her.

Bob cleans his eyes with a tissue. "Make it fast, Gael."

Gael doesn't seem to have much intention of doing that. She lights a cigarette.

"Don't smoke . . . please don't smoke. My landlord will fine me. It's a nonsmoking lease," Bob says.

Gael blows a cloud of smoke in his face. "Are there also restrictions on fornication?"

Bob shakes his head. "Gael, say what you have to say and leave."

"It's all too much for you, Bobby. Your life needs a woman's touch. Without it, you'll spiral down and crash. I'm here to catch you. I don't care that you didn't write the book. I'll help you anyway . . . and you'll help me."

"How will you help me?"

"I'll be your manager."

"Koss got me a manager, Schuman."

"Schuman's a literary agent. You need a situation manager, someone to hold you on top. You'll pay support, and it will be the best move you ever made."

Bob is feeling the effect of the alcohol but is suddenly sobered by desperation. He's emotionally drained and willing to consider any proposal or any kind of arrangement from anyone, that gets him to where he needs to be, even Gael.

Cat rubs against Gael. She calmly looks down and kicks him against the wall.

Another bitch, Cat thinks. He runs back and tries to scratch, hoping to leave runs in her nylons. He gets it right but the nylons don't run like they used to—tougher fabric. He tries to dig into her leg, but her other foot catches him and he flies against the refrigerator. *Women*, he thinks, *we don't have a chance.*

Bob gets a can and places it on the chair for Gael to use as an ashtray.

"That's it, Bobby. . . . And Koss will approve. I know the ropes and *he* knows that he can always count on me to bring home victory."

Cat's safely watching from under the table. Gael's smiling so wide that Cat's hoping her lip will split; unfortunately, she closes her smile, just in time.

"After all," she says, "everyone wants the same thing, your success."

Bob's drunkenness enters and exits, giving him the vision of a driver in a pouring rainstorm. Tragic reality bangs him occasionally, giving him momentary glimpses of the road.

"Get real, Gael," he says.

"Oh, I'm for real, Bobby." Gael gently grabs his shoulder and reaches her right hand down into her purse and pulls out a small pistol.

"Jesus! Is that *a gun*?"

"Did you see me light my cigarette with it?" Gael hesitates and smiles.

Cat shakes his head and pushes around in his litter box. He has no idea where he'll go if she kills Herman but boy, does he have it coming. That bitch could have killed Cat and Bob didn't even say a word, let alone raise his voice. That's the last time he'll lick Bob. It doesn't matter how much cream he dips himself in.

Cat continues to shake his head and muses, *Where does the idiot find these pups, anyway?* (Calling felines "chicks" never worked in the cat world).

"Did you see mamma light her cigarette with it?" Gael asks again.

Having a gun waving in your face does wonders for stopping a monsoon. Bob sees the road clearly.

"Now, get into the bedroom Bobby. If we're going to be partners, you've got to get used to taking orders."

Bob looks at the gun, already knowing the answer to his dumb question. "Are you insane?"

"Criminally," she says.

He should have expected that. How else would a woman get to be an executive at a top publishing house? Well, there are a few other possibilities, and Gael looks like a natural "apple-bobber."

"Bobby, let's just say that I'm very, very resourceful. You'll come to appreciate that part of me. . . . Move."

Bob turns into the bedroom. Gael keeps the gun pointed at him as she follows him in.

"Undress," she says.

"This is rape," Bobby says.

"And who'd believe you?" Gael makes a gesture toward his pants. She smiles. "Can't shoot with them on."

"Really Gael. *This is rape.*"

"Bobby, it's politically correct, social engineering. It's our turn to be victims, even when we humili-rape you. I mean look at me, Bobby," she quips, "any judge would be jealous and try to lower his hammer on you for even reporting such a wet dream."

"You're going too far," Herman implores.

"Shut up, you cupcake of a man. Most men and half the women I know fantasize about being forced to have sex at gunpoint." Gael smiles keenly and points her gun at his crotch. Bobby removes his pants.

"Half of all rape charges could be avoided if you *dutzes* would just have the courtesy to call us in the morning," Gael says seriously. "Anyway, it would be my version against yours. And Bobby," Gael pauses and smiles. "The underwear as well, stud."

Bobby reluctantly pulls his elastic band down.

"And Bobby, the media would write it my way," Gael laughs again out loud. "Mike Tyson got convicted and she showed up at his hotel room in her pajamas. Welcome to the twenty-first century. Nice, isn't it?"

Bobby has his underwear down to his knees.

"Compliments, I see you're happy to see mamma," she winks at him.

He almost deflates as her winking reminds him of Koss.

"I'm very inspired," she pauses.

Gael undresses and pushes him on the bed.

Gael gets on top and begins singing, "Woman, hear me roar in numbers too big to ignore . . ."

Cat watches the duo as he pisses in Gael's shoe.

The digital clock ticks to 5:30 a.m. and the song, "Living Without You" by Patrick Girondi and the Orphan's Dream blares.

Gael rolls off Bob. "To be honest, I'm very impressed."

Bob smirks. "Thanks."

"Why do you get up at 5:30?"

"I write best at daybreak," Bob answers.

Gael ignores his response. "So, what is it? You paid some guy for his book?"

They're both almost dressed.

Gael looks in Bob's face. "Pay him for another."

Bob's face wants to engage in a conversation but his mouth won't collaborate.

"Spill it," Gayle says.

Bob smiles tightly. What choice did he have? "It goes like this, Gael . . ."

They speak until almost eight o'clock, when Gael gathers her things, and pecks Bob on the cheek. As she closes the door behind her, she turns and finds herself face-to-face with a noticeably shocked Lucia.

Gael doesn't miss a beat. "Don't expect a lot, honey. He's probably a little tired."

Gael forgot her lighter. She turns and knocks lightly. Bobby opens the door smiling with Gael's silver lighter in his hand. His eyes land on Lucia, who's heading back down the hall.

"Lucia!" he screams.

Gael grabs her lighter, shakes her head, and tilts it to the side. "It really wasn't that important. I only smoke before I fornicate."

Bobby gawks down the hall where Lucia was seconds ago.

"She's cute, partner," Gael says, "real cute . . . maybe we could share her."

Bob shoves Gael out of the way and runs down the stairs.

"Don't make Mamma jealous," Gael calls after him.

Bob makes it out onto the street. He arrives just as Lucia drives off in a cab.

"Shit!" he says.

Bob doesn't notice Gael exiting the building. His eyes are still fixed on Lucia's cab. In his eyes, the cab quickly becomes tiny and distant.

Lucia's cabdriver is a middle-aged, dark-skinned man.

"You look distressed, young lady," he says to her. "Can I do anything for you?"

"Yes, keep your eyes on the road."

The cabdriver's appetite is obviously aroused by Lucia's beauty. "That guy who came out after you in his underwear . . . is that your man?"

Lucia stares out the window. After ten seconds, she speaks. "I don't know who he is. . . . I don't know who I am. I don't know who I want . . . I don't know why I went there."

"Seems to me you want him," he pauses. "No?"

The cab pulls in front of her place. Lucia rummages through her purse. It's loaded with money. "I forgot my wallet. How much is it?"

"It's $19.50," he says.

Lucia smiles. "I'll run up to my apartment, or would you like to have me in your debt?"

The cabdriver smiles. "The day is young and mmm, mmm. I'd love to have you in my debt."

The cabdriver hands Lucia a card. "This is my number. I'll be your personal chauffeur anytime."

Lucia takes the card and smiles, "I'll be in touch."

Lucia walks to her building. The cab pulls away.

Chapter 8

Author, Meet the Author

It's Monday morning. Bob is in his office, listening to Lucia's answering machine. *Beep.*

"Lucia, how many times do I need to tell your answering machine that she means nothing to me? I only think of you. Please, I must talk to you. I'm a published author now . . . I'm good. I can take care of us. You'll see . . . please, call me . . . I'll do anything. I love you."

Bob hangs up. He rises and walks into the hall and past Lou's desk.

"Asshole," Lou murmurs.

Bob ignores him but thinks he understands. *GAM management are also shareholders of the same. The company invested considerable in the marketing of him and* Standard Deviations. *Lou, like everyone else, is regretting the investment while waiting for the second book.*

Koss passes and pats Bob on the back. "That's my boy, Bobby."

Bob's confused. He glances back at Koss and then turns into the coffee room where Gael is stirring an espresso.

Bob looks at Gael. "What's going on here? Koss just said that I was his boy."

"He knows that you're my project now," Gael says. "He's confident that the situation will be resolved."

"Yeah, well, Lou just called me an asshole."

Gael smiles. "He knows that you're my project too."

"So?" Bob asks.

"Bobby. I'm a liberated woman. Some call us perverts, but they're just jealous, or flabby, or just plain ugly."

Bob nods knowledgeably.

Gael continues, "Bob, I get my bell rung three or four times between my periods." She purses her lips, squints, and looks up at empty space. "Sometimes,

I actually play through them. Now that you're my project, Lou's afraid that he won't be ringing anymore."

Bob is trying to do the math and connect the dots in his head.

Gael doesn't want to see him strain himself. "Bobby," she pauses. "You know when Lou and I leave for our workouts?"

"Yeah," Bob says innocently.

"We work out."

Bob leaves, Jennifer walks in, and Gael winks at her. "He's been allocated to me, honey. I honestly don't know what you see in him. He's about as manly as a pink dress," she pauses. "But when pushed, he can perform and has nice equipment. I'll give him that."

Jennifer leaves without saying a word.

Ted Basle is in a parked car watching Ahmed walk on the street toward him. Ahmed gets closer and Ted takes pictures of him. After Ahmed passes, Ted turns the car around and follows him until Ahmed enters the New York City Rescue Mission.

Detectives Kennedy and Clark are parked. They have been watching Ted while he was watching Isa.

"Shit. Now who do you think this asshole is?" Kennedy asks as he scratches his bare arm below his US flag tattoo.

"We've got a problem," Clark says without answering Kennedy's question.

Gael is in her office, doing her nails and working at the computer. She goes to Google and hits search. Ted enters and dumps pictures of Isa on Gael's Desk.

Without looking at them she speaks. "Got him?"

"Yeah, I got him but I still need his name."

"How hard can it be to identify a street person?" Gael asks. She takes a picture of Isa into her hands and begins studying it.

Ted scrutinizes her expression. "Hundreds of thousands of them die every year without ever being identified. He may be joining them. Ugly, huh?" Ted asks.

"You're not paid for your opinions, but personally, I don't like beards." She continues to look at one of the photos. "He looks like a wolf man."

Ted squints. "I have the feeling that you're hiding something from me."

"You know what I think?" Gael pauses and glares at him. "I think you're too smart for your own good." She reaches into her purse and takes out a stack of hundred-dollar bills. She counts fifty of them. "You won't get another dime without his name."

Ted takes the cash and smirks. "Why are you so tough with me?"

Gael returns to looking at the photos. "There can only be one king of the forest."

"Men," Ted says, "we don't stand a chance."

Bob is standing on the bus and staring blankly out the window. He hears a voice behind him. "Don't turn around. Get off at the next stop." Bob instinctively begins turning.

"Don't," the voice says. "Get off and go into the Euro Café at the next stop."

Bob straightens his collar. Isa follows him and they sit in a corner booth.

"You're the writer of *Standard Deviations*, aren't you?" Herman asks.

"I arranged the words, but we are all the writers of *Standard Deviations*," Isa replies.

Isa studies Bob. Bob is still pondering Isa's words. "There are things you don't understand," Isa says.

"Boy, don't I know it." Bob smiles. "It's great to finally know you, sir. I can't tell you how important it is for me to speak to you," Bob says.

Bob extends his hand; Isa doesn't accept. Bob clears his throat. "I wanted to find you, really, I looked everywhere."

Bob wants Isa to believe him in the worst way. "Then people read your book and one thing led to another . . . it all happened so fast. . . . I meant no disrespect," Bob pleads.

Isa remains silent.

"I saw that you carried another manuscript the other night. I'd like to buy it," Bob says.

"My arrangements of words are precious to me. I will not sell them."

"But you can get off the streets. You can live in a nice house. You can have your own barber." Bob smiles, trying to be charming. "And he can shave that beard."

Isa shakes his head gently. "Ownership is slavery. No, I won't have it."

"What's your name?" Bob asks.

"My name is not your concern."

Bob stares at the condiments on the table, thinking about how lucky the saltshaker is to have no problems. "But, this means everything to me."

"Curious things often occupy a lot of space in trifling minds," Isa replies.

Bob smooths his hair back, "I'm begging you."

They stare at each other like *High Noon.*

"You just don't understand," Bob says, with the seriousness of a personal injury attorney.

"Don't I?" Isa smiles knowingly. "I've been observing you," he says.

"Me?" Bob points to himself. "What do you mean?"

"You and the people you've hired must stop looking for me."

Bob clears his throat and loosens his tie. "*So,* you've watched me struggle, all along knowing that all you had to do, to help me, was show your face. . . . And I didn't hire people to follow anyone."

Isa impatiently shakes his head. "You've made a big mistake."

Bob's been jammed too long. He jumps out of his playpen. "Coauthor the book with me. You can be rich!"

Isa is unaffected but people at surrounding tables glance their way.

Isa steely stares Herman. "You must stop looking for me." Isa rises.

"Give me another book and I will," Herman lobs.

Isa thinks long and hard and then looks down at Bob. The steel has melted. It is now honey. "There's something you must do for me."

Bob's face shows relief. The world is being lifted off his shoulders. "Anything, anything," he pleads.

"You must start being a man of honor."

Bob stares. *What the hell is this bearded lunatic talking about now?* Isa turns to leave. The planet falls down, smashing Bob's back.

Bob feebly speaks, from under Antarctica, "But . . ."

"Do not follow me." Isa leaves.

"Honor? What the . . ." Bob doesn't finish the sentence. Instead, he takes out his cell phone and dials. "Gael, Bob."

"I know it's you, you moron, your number's memorized."

"Okay, okay," he says anxiously, "I found him."

"How did you find him?"

"Don't worry about that. I'm no slouch." Bob pauses, almost believing it himself. "But forget about that. I don't think that he'll play ball."

Herman has no idea but Gael's outside the Euro Café in the passenger seat of Ted Basle's car watching Isa leave.

Gael speaks into the phone. "Don't sweat it, sweetheart."

She nods at Ted, then ends the phone conversation.

Bob is still inside the booth and desperate. "Gael? Gael?" Frustrated, he lays his phone on the table, staring first at the salt and then at the pepper shaker.

Gael gets out of the car and walks into the Euro Café. Ted drives off to follow Isa.

Gael sits down next to Bob. "So, that was our laureate?"

"Where the hell did you come from?"

Gael smiles. "We'll get him. He's got a tail."

"A tail? Jesus, maybe you should just let me handle this, Gael."

"Like you've handled it until now? Time's money. . . . You don't get it, do you?"

"If I can't convince him, how will you?"

Gael smiles.

Bob concentrates, putting seriousness into his next words. "He's not that easy."

Gael looks back at Bob with the same intention. "Neither am I. . . . Besides, Africans are way overrated. The Latins are where it's at. Give me a young Italian, Brazilian, or Greek any day."

Bob stares at perversion. *Is it possible that everything in her world has a carnal side to it?*

Gael gets up to leave. "You've turned over our savior. Take the day off, Bobby. You've earned your thirty pieces of silver."

Gael leaves. Bob waits a few minutes, rises, and walks to the door.

"Hey," the owner calls, "who's going to pay for those coffees and water?"

"Who else?"

Bob pays, walks out, and spends the rest of the day walking around, looking for Isa.

In the evening, Bob goes home and dedicates himself to his favorite hobby, speaking with Lucia's answering machine.

Cat watched Bob in disbelief for almost an hour and sincerely wished that the hot bitch (*did you catch that, pup, bitch?*) from the other night had left her gun. He'd have figured out a way to put this moron out of his misery. It was the only truly feline thing to do.

"Lucia, I have to stop calling you but I can't. Why won't you just contact me? We have something, damn it! I'm sorry, I didn't mean to swear . . . just, I need to find you. I need you." His voice trails off and he closes.

He looks at Ted's card, dials the phone, then hangs up. After a moment, he dials again.

An hour later, Bob and Ted are sitting in Toad Hall Bar with coffee in front of them.

"You read my mind, Bobby," Ted says expressively.

"What do you mean, I read your mind?"

"Well, Bobby . . . let me put it this way. Mark Koss is on top of the wall, if you know what I mean."

"What, like Humpty Dumpty?"

"Precisely. And I'm the guy that makes sure that Humpty Dumpty doesn't take a fall, 'cause all the king's horses and all the king's men couldn't put Humpty together again. . . ."

Bob watches Ted, thinking that his next book ought to be about Gent America Media. Ted notices that Bob's distracted. "Bobby."

Herman almost jumps.

Satisfied that he has his attention, Ted continues. "And because I occupy this position, you could say that I'm the most important man in GAM. I was going to call you because you've become an important resource. Our stock is counting on you. I'm a large shareholder, so I'm counting on you. . . . Now how can I be of service?"

Bob clears his throat before speaking. "Ted, a writer's emotional stability is everything. If I lack confidence or tranquility, I can't work. I've fallen for this girl, but something's not right. She's got wild stories and expensive clothes, and I just don't want to be taken for a ride."

Ted knows that Bob is a fraud, but nods gently as any understanding parent would.

Bob's consoled, or feigns comfort.

"You know what I mean," Bob says.

"Bobby, this is Ted you're talking to. Now, you're no writer, everyone knows that now. But you're an important part of the team. You're our man, and I want to keep our man happy. What is it with this girl? What's her name?"

"Lucia, 234 East 2nd. I'm not really sure of anything else, but she does live there and 'Lucia' is the name on her door," Bob says.

"Sure, Bobby. That's more than enough. Now, what kind of information? Medical? Criminal? Scholastic?"

"Yes, yes, all of it."

Bobby places Saint Bernard's eyes on Ted.

"You got it Bobby. I'll get you info on her family, her lawyer, doctor, arrests, lawsuits, credit cards, and exes. You'll have it all."

"Thanks Ted." Bob reaches, Ted smiles sinisterly (Bob thinks it's a friendly smile, kind of like a python's victim thinks it's a friendly hug) and squeezes Bob's hand tightly.

"I'm your friend, Bob. At GAM, we're all one big happy family. Of course, like any company, the most important part about GAM is the bottom line. You see Bob, I guard the bottom line. If someone messes with you, they're messing with the bottom line."

Now Ted beams the Wicked Witch of the West smile. "And they're messing with me."

Bobby tries to remove his hand from Ted's grip. Ted holds tight and speaks softly. "Anyone who messes with the bottom line is messing with me. . . . Anyone. Got that?"

Bob pays more attention to the utility man than he would an oncologist.

"Yes. Thanks, Ted. I got it and I really appreciate it. Listen, don't tell anyone about this, okay? Just our secret."

"You just go home, Bobby, and leave it up to me."

Ted releases Bob's hand. Bob feels the blood circulating again but doesn't want Ted to notice. Ted stands, smiles, and leaves Bob uncomfortably alone.

In Bob's apartment, later that evening, he's at his laptop with a pencil in his ear looking industrious. He hears a knock. He jots something down, makes a frustrated face and walks toward the door. "Who is it?"

"Police."

Bob clears the page on his laptop and opens the door. Two plainclothesmen are in the hall. "What can I do for you?"

They flash their badges. "Are you Robert Herman?"

"Yes."

"Can you please come to the station with us, Mr. Herman?"

"Why?"

"Sir, please get your jacket. I'll explain on the way."

Bob is muddled. "Can I see your badges again?"

The officers remove their IDs again. Bob examines them. "All seems in order."

"We're happy you're pleased," one of the officers says, flashing a Hollywood smile.

In the station, Detectives Harms and Clark are talking near the filing cabinets. In the background Bob Herman is sitting at a desk.

"We've got to hold this guy," Detective Harms says. "He's on to Isa."

"I told you to avoid using his name," Clark whispers.

"If this thing blows up, it will be front-page news. We'll all go away for a very long time," Harms says.

Clark seems unimpressed.

Harms continues. "Isa eliminated Cowdar for us all, and we were all a part of it." Harms stares at Clark.

Clark drags long on his cigar. "Stop talking."

A female police officer passes. "Hey, Clark, no smoking in the building."

Clark takes another long drag and blows out smoke as if he's completely unrelated.

"You men all think that you're above the law," the officer says as she turns the corner.

"Yeah and two women officers got shot with their own guns this year . . . cum recipient," Clark mumbles.

Harms comes up next to Clark. "You've got to book Herman."

Clark looks disappointedly at Harms. "If I booked everyone that had reason to kill Russo, we'd be filling out paperwork for a year."

Harms looks toward Bob, who is oblivious to what's going on.

"We need to get him to confess to assaulting Russo, or to lie about knowing him, then we can book him," Clark says.

A while later, Bob's sitting in front of Detective Clark. Detective Kennedy is in the corner of the room.

"*Standard Deviations*, isn't it, Mr. Herman?" Clark asks.

Bob nods slightly.

"I loved it," Clark says, smiling with an unlit cigar in his jaw.

"Thank you. Now, will you please tell me why I'm here."

"You don't know?"

"I'm not one to be dallied with, Officer."

"Of course, Mr. Herman. I'm sure you're not and I would never dally."

"I need to know why I'm here. . . . Now what is this about?"

Clark stares at Bob. "Do you own a gun, Mr. Herman?"

"I want my attorney."

"Sure, Herman, you can have ten of them. Now answer me. Do you own a gun?"

"A gun? No, of course not."

"Well, if you don't own a gun, you will voluntarily give us permission to search your apartment then, won't you?"

"My apartment? Why? I want to call my attorney."

"If you'd like. But I think we could settle this quickly. If you'd just cooperate."

"No, no. . . . I want my phone call."

Clark puts Bob in a holding cell.

"I want to call my attorney," Bob says.

Clark ignores him.

An hour later Clark walks Bob into the interrogation room and removes his cuffs.

"Sit down, Herman," Clark says.

Bob sits down.

"Do you know why anyone would want to kill Tony Russo?" Clark asks.

Bob seems sincerely shocked by the news. "Tony Russo? I don't even know him."

"Book him!" Clark yells.

Detective Clark stands up. Kennedy approaches Bob.

"I want to call my attorney," Bob says.

Chapter 9

From Stars to Cut

Twenty minutes later, Arnie Schuman and Ted Basle arrive at the police station. They're allowed into the interrogation room. Arnie and Basle nod at Herman. Bob nods back at them.

Arnie and Basle patiently wait for the police to cut to the chase, but they're playing the usual cat-and-mouse, good-cop-bad-cop game.

And we trust these morons to protect us? Arnie thinks to himself. *Terrorists or whoever is trying to harm us must not try too hard, or they are real morons.*

"We're not getting anywhere. Stand up, Herman," Clark says.

"Officer, we still don't know why you arrested my client," Arnie says.

"Wait a minute," Bob interrupts. "I met Russo once."

Clark doesn't lose an instant. "Did you point a gun at Russo in Bino's bar?"

"No. I was telling you the truth about that. I don't own a gun," Bob says.

"Yeah," Harms adds. "Writers have a selective process regarding the truth. What other lies did you tell us?"

"None. Russo was messing with a girl I know. I went into the bar. I've never been there before. By coincidence, Russo was there. I asked him to leave her alone."

"You've never been there before?" Clark asked.

"Tell the truth, Bob. You have nothing to hide," Arnie hesitated, "do you?"

"I pointed at him with my cell phone in my pocket. He may have thought it was a gun."

"Did you tell him it was a gun?" Harms asked.

"No."

"Did you tell him it wasn't a gun?"

"I was surrounded by five of his friends. Would you have told him it wasn't a gun?" Bob pauses. "Is he really dead?"

Kennedy now engages front and center. "Should I book him?" he asks.

"Not yet. Would you like some water, coffee, Mr. Herman?"

"What kind of game are we playing here, Detective?" Arnie asks.

Ted Basle is observing every move that Harms, Clark, and Kennedy make.

Clark stares at Ted. "May I ask who you are, Sir?"

"He is my assistant," Arnie says impatiently.

Clark continues to look inhospitably at Ted. "Are you an attorney?"

"No," Arnie answers.

"A paralegal?" Clark asks menacingly.

"No," Arnie replies.

"A relative?" Clark asks mockingly.

The hairs on Arnie's back stand up. "Detective, who are you interrogating here?"

Kennedy smiles and nods his head at Arnie.

"It is late," Arnie continues. "If you're going to book my client I wish that you would do so without wasting any more time. . . . Otherwise I insist that you release him."

Ten minutes later Bob walks out of the station with Arnie and Ted. Clark and Kennedy are in the background watching them sally down the police station steps.

The next day, curiosity dragged Bob to the gate of St. John's Cemetery in Middle Village. He was wearing a hat and sunglasses. The procession carrying Russo to his final resting place enters. Bob slouches down until the parade passes and then follows, two hundred feet behind.

Bob waits until the last have exited their cars. He then walks closer, to another grave site, feigning to be paying his respects.

They carry the casket to the front of the group next to a dug-out hole in the ground. The priest stands at the crown of the plot. Old Italian women clad in black begin to howl and cry on cue.

Bob scans the crowd and spots Lucia. She's standing erect and lifeless. He can't make out the expression on her face.

After about twenty minutes the priest finishes his gibberish.

The crowd makes the sign of the cross, and Russo slowly begins his final trip down.

As Bob, again, tries to scrutinize the expression on Lucia's face, a hooded man walks up to him. Bob's startled.

"I thought you'd show up here," Isa says. "I have what you want."

Isa shoves the book into his stomach.

Bob moves away to absorb the blow.

"If you're an honorable man," Isa says, "you will make sure that you, and your people, leave me alone."

Bob is ecstatic to be holding the book. He smiles quaintly, fighting the urge to scream for joy. Bob nods his head to Isa's request. Of course, at this juncture Bob would have agreed to anything.

Isa scans Bob's face. "If you do not leave me alone, you risk the world finding out who the real author is, and more." Isa hesitates. "Much more than you or your people could understand."

Bob's smile respectfully expands. "Yes sir, I will, I will. Thank you."

Isa steps back.

"Wait," Herman says, "please, let me give you something." Bob reaches into his pocket.

Isa smiles sarcastically. His voice raises. "These are the clothes of a freeman! You will not enchain me!"

Bob's terrified. Isa's yelling could disrupt the funeral ritual and make him look pretty foolish to everyone at Russo's funeral, including Lucia. He keeps one eye on Isa and the other on the Russo party. Fortunately, it seems that no one else heard.

Bob watches Isa walk through the entrance gate. Bob walks toward his Zipcar and takes his phone out, "Gael. I have the second book."

"How?" she asks unbelievably.

"He was at the funeral."

"Whose funeral?"

"The funeral of a friend."

"What friend of yours, Bobby, died without you telling me?"

"It doesn't really matter, does it? What matters is that I have the second book."

"He found you at the funeral of a friend? Does he know your friend?"

"I told you, I don't know who he is. I don't think he knows my friend, but he some-how knew that I'd be there. I've spent months looking for him," Bob reports.

"How would he know to find you there?"

"Gael, I don't know. He seems to know lots of things, he's spooky."

There's three seconds of silence before Bob continues. He measures his words articulately. "Gael," Bob breaks in, "he said that if we don't stop following him . . ." another pause, "he'd let the world know who the real author was."

Bob didn't wait for Gael to respond. He put the phone in his pocket and cheerfully walked through the cemetery toward Russo's end and his beginning, Lucia.

When he gets about a hundred feet away, he's confronted by Bino's bartender. "Hey. I wouldn't go up there," the bartender says.

"Oh?" Bob says confidently. The last time he saw Russo and this guy he had them running for the hills. And *now*, he even has a second book.

"You weren't his friend. Were you?" the bartender asks melancholically.

"No," Bob offers, without a trace of arrogance.

"A little consideration then," the teary-eyed bartender says, looking away.

Bob remains still. The bartender turns back to him. "He might have been a jagoff, but he was *our* jagoff."

Bob gently nods and moves to the parked cars on the road. The bartender walks away. Ted Basle is also parked in the cemetery, and *he's caught the whole matinee.*

Bob stands by his car and indiscriminately opens the package. He reads page 26, "*The general replied, 'because the Gulf War was about liberating as much as the invasion of Iraq was about halting terrorism, as much as Vietnam was about fighting for justice.*

'After tens of thousands of brave American women and men have gone to their graves, let us look each other in the eye and admit that these theaters were open to promote the legalization of slavery, of all men under the sponsorship of the global elite.'

Bob turns to the last page. *I devote this book to all the hopeless romantics who fought battle in conflicts created by civil division through invention.*

Bob wanders through the manuscript, reading random paragraphs. He vividly pictures the Iraq War. When he raises his head, the Russo funeral has disappeared. In fact, he's the only living being (soul?) in the cemetery.

Bob sneaks back into the east end of Manhattan and parks his Zipcar.

The world has changed. He decides to walk it up the eight flights of stairs. On the way, he bounces, wondering what he might have said to Lucia at the cemetery and what he might say to her when they next meet. He arrived at his floor, the eighth floor, and was not even out of breath.

The next morning, Bob's sleeping on his bed with pages of the second book under his hand. The phone rings. He fumbles to answer.

"Hello," he says.

"Bob, it's Jennifer."

"Jennifer, what time is it?"

"It's 10:30," she says.

"In the morning? Yes, in the morning," he answers himself, as he looks out the window.

"I want to come over and talk to you," Jennifer says.

"Why? Is something wrong? I was going to come to the office anyway, today," he says.

"Please, Bob," she says.

"Do you know where I live?"

"Yes, I do," she answers gently.

"All right then, if it's really important, I'll wait here for you," he responds.

Bob stands, walks into the bathroom, and turns the water on.

Jennifer hangs up her phone. Gael walks in. Jennifer tries to compose herself. She fears that Gael knows who she was talking to. There are just too many coincidences lately at BAM, "Bent America Media" (that's what Jennifer calls it). Jennifer looks to the side, contritely.

"Should I know who that was?" Gael asks mockingly.

While Jennifer gawks at the sharp-cut wrinkle in Gael's cheek, she garners twenty-eight grams of courage. "Koss may allow you to run everything in this company. But you don't run my personal life."

"Not yet," Gael playfully smiles. "Lover boy's done with book two."

"Oh, so soon?"

"Genius . . . is that what you most adore about him?"

"Truthfully, Gael, the thing that attracts me to him the most is that he's nothing like you."

Gael has never seen this side of Jennifer and she truly, truly likes it. She feels aroused and makes the most seductive smile she can muster.

"You said that the second book is on the way. Stop riding him, Gael. You got what you want, now leave him alone," Jennifer says curtly.

"Oh Jennifer, I'm going to keep riding him until he can no longer stand. You might try it yourself." Gael turns to leave and then turns back. "Oh, that's right, you offered, but he doesn't want you on his horse."

"I'm not interested in his horse. Of course, you're a modern woman, and couldn't possibly understand what I'm referring to." Jennifer rebelliously stands and is now face-to-face with Gael. "He'd have nothing to do with you if he wasn't forced to."

Gael is a teensy, weensy bit intimidated and intellectually frightened. Maybe the arousal she felt had nothing to do with physical urges. Maybe she was attracted to courage. Nah, too late in the game for decency.

Through the obvious time gap Gael explodes through and exits with an obnoxious gaping smile. "Don't bet on it. Trapped manhood can be very cooperative." Gael pauses. "And if challenged properly, virile."

"Well leave him alone, he's not part of your typical diet anyhow. *Canis simensis* eat rats."

Gael is not used to being defied. "*Canis* what? What is that?"

Jennifer smiles, in complete control. She knows much more than is necessary. "The red fox of Ethiopia. It lives by eating rats."

Gael is thrown off balance momentarily. She regains her stride. "Oh, how quaint. A wolf biologist, are we, dear?"

Jennifer steps back and grabs her purse.

"And if I don't leave him alone?" Gael impishly asks.

Jennifer approaches Gael again. "Gael, look in my eyes."

Gael remains immobile.

"What do you see Gael?"

"I see a little, half-witted, lovestruck maiden."

"Little, half-witted, lovestruck maidens can knock Humpty Dumpty off the wall." Jennifer walks defiantly past.

Gael stands, staring like Michelangelo's *David*. There was something strange going on.

Jennifer walks the eight flights of stairs and knocks. Bob answers, thinking that there's no one else from GAM that he'd rather see.

"Come on in. Let me make some coffee."

Jennifer looks around the dingy apartment, thinking that she'd like to be there more often.

The two sit and sip their coffee as if they were in Montmartre. They are chasing the same dream, just with different people.

After the usual pleasantries, Jennifer cuts to the chase. "But Bob, why would you sleep with someone that you don't love?"

Bob doesn't have the vaguest idea what he'll do with that.

A furious emotion mounts in Jennifer's deep waters. "These homos, transvestites, metro sex, bi sex, lesbians, transgenders are all screaming that it's all right to be different, all the while pressuring us to be the same as them."

Bob's face becomes a human question mark. "The same?"

"Yes, the same!" Jennifer shakes her head in disgust, "Sick perverts. It's not natural for women to be promiscuous. They want to have a loyal partner and then when they can't find one, Harvey Weinstein goes to jail."

"Jennifer," Bob pauses. "I'm a man. . . . Sometimes a frightened man, but all the same a man. You may not have noticed, but men aren't always particular."

"Well, neither are contemporary women. I hoped that you were different, that your moral compass was still true north."

"Being moral, sleeping only with people we love. . . . Jennifer, those things died along with the virgin bride."

Bob's face betrays bottomless, unadulterated sorrow with his ill-fated life. Disappointing Jennifer only adds to the shit in his cesspool.

"In the end, you're just putty in Koss and Gael's hands," Jennifer continues. "Bob, you need to find someone else to publish your work."

"I can't."

"Of course, you can. *Standard Deviations* made it to the top. You're one of the best new talents in the country."

"It's not that simple," Bob says as he looks away.

"It is that simple! Why would you want to stay with these people? You're not like them. You could find a nice woman, raise children. I just don't understand you."

Bob looks back at Jennifer. He'd like to raise children with Lucia. He'd love to get out of GAM, but he's trapped.

Jennifer's glassy tone shatters the gray ice. "Did you write that book?"

Jennifer stares in his eyes. Bob looks away. He turns back. "Jennifer, have you ever been in love?"

"In love? Yes."

"I'm in love," he pauses, "and love makes people do stupid things."

Jennifer stands.

"Where are you going?" Bob asks.

Jennifer has the information she came for. She's heading for the door but turns back to Bob. "I wanted to alert you about Gael and Koss. I'm going back to work. We're all not authors."

Bob doesn't want her to leave. She's the only real person that he knows that will still have anything to do with him.

She turns around at the door. Bob stares at her, hoping that she will smile and say, "See you at the office."

They stare at each other, each one wishing that they could have what they wanted.

Jennifer interrupts their dreamland, "And as far as love's concerned . . ."

Bob stares harder. He wanted to know if Jennifer possibly had the secret.

"If love finds you worthy, it will guide its own course." Jennifer opens and shuts the door so quickly that she doesn't leave, she disappears.

The following evening, Bob is in his office at GAM, enthusiastically working in the dark with a bureau lamp on. He could work from home, but the office's serious atmosphere is stimulating.

The second manuscript, *Square Pegs in Circles*, is on his screen. He's combing through it, correcting grammar and misspelled words, and is beginning to feel that he's a part of the piece. He gets to the end of chapter 7, rises, and exits. The offices are empty. He heads to the elevator.

Bob walks past the lobby reception. The guard smiles, "Good night, Mr. Herman."

"Good night, Donny," Bob says.

Bob always liked Donny. In fact, tonight he likes everyone and everything, especially his new outlook on life. After all, he now has the author's permission. He's worked on the books firsthand. Tomorrow, if there's a scandal, it will turn into a ten-year court case. No one would be able to prove that Bob was not an author of the books. He may have not written them word for word, but he edited them, and that's an integral part of writing them. And by the time a court case would be finished, Bob would have learned how to write like his mentor.

Bob goes through the revolving door. Donny dials and puts his cell phone to his ear. "He just left . . . no, ma'am. He's by himself."

The next day Gael is sitting at a table in the Smith restaurant on Second Avenue.

Ted Basle approaches, "Hey, Gael."

"Sit down and lower your voice. I pay you for discretion," Gael slithers.

Ted sits down and taps an unlit cigar on the table.

"Well?" she asks.

Ted takes out another picture of their bearded novelist. "He's called 'Isa.'"

The face of the man in the picture is far more detailed. Gael stares. "Is he? Isa what?"

"That's all I got. There's nothing on him anywhere. He sleeps at that New York Rescue Mission. The place is run by a nun named Sister Brenda. No one there has any idea who he is. He just showed up one day."

Detective Clark is in the background sipping coffee at another table. He grabs his cell phone and makes a call. "Meeting, thirty. I've got Isa's tail."

Shortly after, Detectives Harms, Holt, Kennedy, Gallo, and Clark are together in Kennedy's home basement.

"The tail is professional, sort of professional. We'll get back to him." Clark says.

"What happened to the Hollywood author?" Holt asked.

"He's nothing to worry about. Isa would never tell him anything." Clark grins. "Anyone remember a guy in Baghdad supply named Basle?"

"Yeah, I remember Ted Basle. He got a lot of the brothers strung out on drugs, but never went away, had some sort of corporate or political connection," Holt says.

"Yeah," Clark quips, "modern-day fascism; industry and government are one." Clark looks to the side and then back at Gallo. "Thanks, Mussolini."

Gallo looks slightly offended. "He made the trains run on time." Gallo shrugs before continuing. "and then they hung him on a fence," he returns defensively.

"Yeah," Kennedy says, "and that's exactly how the politicians and the CEOs should end up here—pieces of maggot feces. True patriots should be taking them out, one by one."

Each man looks at Kennedy knowing that he's on target.

Kennedy feels elevated, for once he's the guy. He continues, "I mean, those hypocritical, puritan cowards are what's left at the water station after you filter shit and piss."

"It used to be," Clark says, "that the corporations and the rich had the Republican party and the workingman had the Democratic party. Reagan started killing the unions. In twenty-five years, they went from powerful to powerless. Then the Democrats turned to Wall Street for their graft; now the rich have both parties."

"So what about Ted Basle?" Holt asks.

Clark smiles. "Old Basle's a private investigator now and he's Isa's tail," Clark fires.

"For who?" Harms asks.

"Hard to tell . . . a woman named Gael Veenstra, from Gent America Media . . . he does some work for her." Clark rolls his eyes. "She's got her own story," Clark quips.

The men listen on the edge of their seats. Clark chuckles. "It seems that Isa and Gael may have a shared past . . . and maybe something that links them to the future."

Some weeks later in the packed Four Seasons lobby, a billboard reads, *Bobby Herman Square Pegs in Circles book signing.*

Bob's seated, unenthusiastically signing books. Koss, Arnie, and Gael are standing behind him.

Arnie whispers to Koss. "*Square Pegs in Circles* will sell twice as many copies as *Standard Deviations*."

Koss smiles snidely. "How nice," Koss says, really, wishing that the lump that they found in Arnie's chest would have been malignant.

Bob looks up. His eyes focus on Lucia, who's in line with a book in her hand.

Bob stands and ignores those ahead of her. "Lucia."

"Hello, Bobby."

"I-I . . . I miss you so much," he says.

Lucia embraces him melodramatically. "I miss you too, Bobby. I miss you too."

Koss and Arnie stare at the lovely vixen. Bob sits back down and fervently continues signing books. Koss mentally counts the people and estimates the number of books left in the boxes. He smiles broadly.

Finally, there are no more books available. It's a first for GAM to ever sell out of books at a signing.

Later, arm in arm, Bobby and Lucia walk out of the Four Seasons and duck into Le Bilboquet on Sixtieth Street.

The owner has read both of Bob's books and notices him. He claps his hands, and a table is brought from the back and placed in front of the restaurant. Everyone stares at the exhibition; most are disgruntled. But when Pierre announces that this is the famous author Bob Herman, the tables fill with smiles and admiration. Each of the patrons will have bragging rights. *They ate near the ingenious, famous author.*

Bobby and Lucia are holding hands and doing what lovers do when they refind each other. Everything was now perfect and the absence would only make their union stronger . . . right.

"Tony was killed, and I had no one to turn to," Lucia says.

"How could you have ever been drawn to him?"

"I was desperate for security. I still desperately need security, Bobby."

"Lucia, I love you, I have since the day we met, but I don't want to just be a replacement for Tony."

"Bobby," Lucia whispers, "who's Tony?"

Bobby beams and nods his head. "Lucia, my life's been filled with disappointment, my own disappointment. But not anymore. We'll both start over," he winks (strangely enough, he thinks of Koss). "We'll be unstoppable," he closes.

They kiss.

The following Monday at GAM, Koss is in his office staring out the window. Gael is in front of him.

"That ungrateful punk." Koss slams his fist on the desk and stares at Gael. "You know, I never did like him. That leech! He ran off to the Bahamas with his book advance! I'll never get the three books I need from him to break even. If I could get what I've invested, I'd flip him to someone in a heartbeat." Koss again slams his fist on the desk. "If he doesn't produce, this firm is in jeopardy. I'm fucked. Doesn't he get it?"

Gael responds, "I'm not sure what he gets. There are other books. There must be. What if we get ahold of them and cut out the middleman?"

"Cut out Bobby?"

"All he is to us at this point is a name," Gael says. "We silence him, and go straight to the source for the books. We'll just use Bobby's name . . . and we give him what we want."

Koss puts his hand to his chin. It's as if Gael has finally opened his eyes. "Cut out Bobby, huh? You don't think it's too soon?"

"No, I don't think so. Not at all."

"And he'd let us?" Koss boyishly asks.

Gael smiles. "Definitely. He'd have no choice."

"Really?" Koss beams, "Oh God, I love you. How long would this take to orchestrate?"

"Not sure, but it's important that he doesn't suspect a thing."

PART III

Chapter 10

Locker 117

A month later at the Gramercy Room in the Peninsula, Lucia and Bob are kissing at their wedding reception. Lucia feeds him cake.

Mark Koss stands up with a champagne glass in his hand. "I took this boy under my wing. He is now a man. He does things a bit differently, like going on his honeymoon before he got married."

The vassals laugh, at least the ones that are within eyeshot of Koss.

Koss continues. "I wish him and his bride a long and happy life. And many, many more bestsellers!"

Lucia laughs. "Hear! Hear!"

Mark raises the glass. The banquet of eighty people toast. "Hear! Hear!"

Shortly after, Lucia is reentering the hall.

Gael walks to her. "All my best, Lucia."

Lucia stares coldly. "The name is Mrs. Herman."

"Come now, honey. I only stole him from you for a little while. A real lady doesn't hold a grudge."

Lucia steps on Gael's foot as she walks away.

"Ah!" Gael says in pain. "Bitch."

Weeks later, Bob's sloppily dressed, sitting at his desk. Lou Mell passes.

"Must be nice to do nothing and get paid for it," Lou says.

Bob runs his hand over his head. He looks toward the computer. He turns it on, stands up, and walks out. He turns into Jennifer's office.

"Jennifer, get me a copy of *Standard Deviations*."

"*Standard Deviations?*" she asks.

"Yes, you heard me, a copy of *Stan-dard De-vi-a-tio*ns. You've heard of the book before?" Bob hesitates, "Maybe if I study, really study it, something will come to me."

103

"Like what?"

"Get me *Standard Deviations!*"

Jennifer stands. "They're in the back." *Oh, God, how did she ever fall for this moron?* Jennifer thought to herself.

Koss enters. "How's the third one coming, Bobby?"

Bob and Lucia have rented a new condo at 100 Barrow Street in the West Village. Bob walks in. Lucia is reading a magazine. The television is on a random channel, dispersing the same reused vomit.

Lucia smiles. "Hi Bobby, I need some Jimmy Choo shoes. Did you take care of my CCB?"

"Let's not talk about money," Bob volleys.

"I know you hate talking about money. I'm not talking about money. That's why I call it a CCB, Bobby. But unless you pay my *credit card bill* I can't buy my Jimmy Choos."

Bob is ready to collapse. "What's for dinner?"

"Honey, I didn't marry you to cook. We're eating out."

Bob goes into the den and reenters the room holding a stack of receipts. "These are yours, all yours! You're spending money faster than the mint can make it! We're broke!"

"Cool it. Get an advance on your third book."

"I already got my advance. I got an advance on my advance all the way to my fifth book!"

Lucia is unaffected. "Go to your parents."

"I was supposed to pay them out of the advance—the advance that paid for our wedding and our trips and your clothes and they don't have a dime left to give me." Bob pauses, "Even if they were crazy enough to want to give it."

"Well, you better think of something."

Bob stares. Lunacy, pure, untainted lunacy. "I'm tired of thinking! My mind hurts from thinking. Why don't you just go to your parents? They didn't come to the wedding, the least they could do is send us a gift!"

"I can't ask them for money," Lucia says.

"Why?" Bob fires back.

Lucia is now physically charged. She points at Bobby. "Because, you promised to take care of me! I should have known better!"

Lucia leaps to her feet as if she's going to trounce her husband. Her face gets within two inches of his own. "Well believe me, I will take care of myself, if you don't!"

Lucia turns and walks away.

"What does that mean? What does that mean?" he yells to her back.

Bob's intimidated. He knows exactly what she means.

Lucia slowly turns and sinisterly smirks. "Bobby, do you know what Santa Claus and free sex have in common?"

Bobby scowls at low volume, "Goddamn soul assassin." He runs his hand through his hair and walks out, slamming the door.

"They're both make-believe," Lucia says to the door.

Across town, Isa is holding a bag and walking out of the New York City Rescue Mission. He makes his way to the Star Bright Hotel in Chinatown. The hotel entrance is full of homeless folks and people who work at the heart of New York's food industry. On lucky days, they become clients.

Isa walks up the shoddy stairs and turns into a long dark hall. He pulls a key out of his pocket and puts coins into the slot on locker 117. He places his bag in the container, locks it, and exits the hotel.

At the same time outside, Ted and Gael are panicking. They can't find anywhere to park. Gael jumps out of the car and walks toward the hotel. She's fifty feet away, and Isa comes out of the entrance. Gael feigns that she has dropped something to avoid being seen.

Isa stops. "Ma'am, may I help you?"

"No," Gael says coldly. "No, I don't need assistance."

Isa hesitates. There's something familiar about the woman's voice. He doesn't need added attention. He moves on.

Gael remains kneeling for another thirty seconds. She stands and looks down the block. Isa has disappeared. Ted arrives.

Gael looks at him. "Uggh," she gnashes, "old man Koss has no idea what he'd be without me."

"You?" Ted asks, "I just paid a guy a hundred to park the car in a restaurant loading zone." Ted pauses. "For fifteen minutes!"

Gael shakes her head. "This is getting complex, and I fear that it will continue going in that direction."

"Maybe you should start working for yourself," Ted says.

"Maybe I should," Gael replies.

The following day, Ted and Gael meet at 6 a.m. They drive to the New York City Rescue Mission and park. After a few minutes, Isa comes within sight.

"There he is. Go and get him," Gael points.

Ted opens the door and takes his gun from his holster. He rushes behind Isa. "Just a moment, fellow, NYPD."

Isa ignores Ted and continues to walk. Holt and Harms are in an unmarked squad, watching the event unfold.

"Shit. What do we do?" Harms asks.

"Just hold on, brother. We won't do anything yet. Call Clark," Holt banters.

Gael opens the car door and quietly follows Ted and Isa.

"Turn around or I'll shoot," Ted says.

Isa continues to walk. He then stops and purposely lets the manuscript fall out of his hands. He stops to pick it up. Without looking at Ted he says, "Go ahead, shoot."

Isa picks the manuscript up, stands, and glances at Gael before he walks away.

Later at Gregory's Coffee on Park, Bob is sloppily groomed and sitting with Ted Basle. Bob is unaware of the run-in between Ted and the author of Bob's books this morning.

"Look," Bob runs his hands through his hair. "Ted. I'll give you anything if you find this guy, anything, I swear."

Ted looks to the side and smirks. "All you've told me is that he's a light-skinned, Arab-looking street person with a beard that gave you some manuscripts and that hangs around Chinatown."

Bob's eyes are inflamed. "I told you, he's some kind of philosopher. He doesn't care about fortune or fame. He's in great physical shape," Bob grabs Ted by the collar. "I'll give you anything. . . . Anything."

Ted smiles and removes Bob's hands. "Sure you will, until I ask for it."

"Try me," Bob says grimly.

"All right," Ted says. He takes a pen from Bob's pocket, grins, and writes on a napkin. "He lives at the New York City Rescue Mission. They call him Isa. Sounds like a girl's name to me."

"You knew?" Bob looks at Ted in disbelief. "You bastard, you knew all along."

"Look, Herman, it's my business to know things that others don't. Why else would people pay me?" Ted musters the seriousness of cancer and waits until Bob is focused. "And Herman, I collect when the time comes."

Back at GAM, Gael is standing in front of Koss's desk. Koss is disheveled. He looks up at Gael, trying to give the appearance of being the man in control. "I don't get you."

Gael knows the difference between being strong and being ruthless. *Weak people need to be merciless to counterbalance others' strength.*

She stares back at her soul twin. He never fooled her, because she never fooled herself. Both would just as soon eliminate each other as they would swat a mosquito. The world would miss the mosquito more.

Gael chuckles. "You don't need to get me. I'm here to take Herman off your hands."

Gael has Koss's complete attention. Years ago, he wanted her, but that was before Ted turned him onto the world of heroin and crack whores, where you get laid by hungry, crazed twenty-year-old stars for $20–50. And the pharma companies crank hundreds more out every day.

Heroin is a great substitute for painkillers and antidepressants and a lot cheaper, Koss thinks. *The only thing left for the drug company execs to do is to cut their price and start selling the product directly to the dealers, cutting out the middlemen.*

Gael knows all about the filth that's crawling around in Koss's garbage truck. He's probably thinking of where he's going to meet his heroin-addict girlfriend today. Gael's tired of waiting. She rests her hand on his desk.

He looks down at it.

"You said that all you wanted was your investment back," Gael says.

Koss looks up from her hand. "It would take the profit on his next three books to do that."

"That's exactly how I calculated. I'll match what GAM has invested and you'll release Herman to me?"

Koss wishes that he had more time to think. It's like a rat that discovers a dead cat on the street but must figure out how he's going to drag it into his hole. Koss smiles. "You got to let a guy make a little profit, Gael. I mean, my time is worth something."

"I will. Do we have a deal?"

"Gael, you come to me with this proposal. I have no idea how you will follow through. It's a lot of dough."

"Mark, let's not toy. You know me to be a serious woman."

"Very, you're a very serious businesswoman, which is why you'll ask me about this again next week. Give a man time to think."

When Brenda was a girl she always knew that she would be a nun. She was the oldest of five siblings. Her family lived in Elizabeth, New Jersey, down the road from the St. Walburga Monastery on Broad.

The Monastery nuns were respected by the townspeople. Their every desire was fleetingly answered. Men offered to drive them, women cooked for them and brought them gifts.

Brenda was a plain-looking girl and her life was uneventful. Different from her brother, Tommy, she never gave a smidgen of trouble to her family. They were all ecstatic when she was ordained a Benedictine nun in 1990.

Brenda tried to help Tommy when he was released from prison. She noticed the great void for ex-convicts and homeless people. In fact, many homeless people are habitually incarcerated throughout their lives.

Sister Brenda received permission to move from where she worked at Saint Anthony's Orphanage to open a soup kitchen and homeless shelter on the Lower West Side in 2011.

Sister Brenda was a practical woman and believed in finite boundaries. She was willing to assist but not willing to be taken advantage of. Each homeless person who decided to take up residence had his or her chores. She permitted no amorous relationships, and if she even suspected misbehavior of any kind, she did not hesitate to show a person the door.

The community relied on her, and local merchants donated heavily. She maintained a full-time staff of five. Their compensation would not ever make them rich, but there were perks. They got dibs on all the leftover food, meaning that they did not have grocery bills.

The workers were also permitted to have first dibs on the clothes, furniture, and all other nonmonetary donations that arrived. If one was smart, he could make a living just off hustling through the treasures. Often, antique furniture, precious art pieces, and even expensive jewelry ended up in their hands.

The existence of the fringe benefits kept her costs low. Sister Brenda was cognizant of the situation, and things worked smoothly. One would do whatever he or she could not to be fired.

Isa showed up some years ago and became a permanent fixture. He had his own five-by-ten-foot room in the basement. He was incredibly efficient at building maintenance issues and saved the good sister tens of thousands yearly.

Sister Brenda was not sure what Isa's story was, but certain that his past, like the past of every other guest, was soiled. Initially, she prodded, but it was more curiosity than necessity for her to know where he came from and or who he was.

After all, if Isa had a criminal past it was better that the good sister knew nothing about it. This way if the police ever made an arrest, she could honestly plead ignorance. What was essential was that he kept the roof from leaking, the boiler working, windows repaired, the building tuck-pointed, etc.

She noted that he spent most of his free time at his computer. She knew that he was a writer, but aren't we all? She herself had contemplated writing her life's story and eventually would certainly do so.

From time to time, the good sister noticed Isa walking around with bags of paper. She assumed that they were his prose. She also enjoyed reading what she wrote on regular paper. To her thinking, there was no comparison between the computer screen and pages.

She curiously noticed him scurrying around with his literary pieces. She didn't understand why or what he was doing and was, quite frankly, too "open-minded" to believe that a homeless person could ever have anything worth writing about.

Isa kept his room immaculate, and this offset any urge for her to pry. There were few things that Sister Brenda abhorred more than a messy room.

Sister Brenda knew that Isa also had some sort of relationship with the Star Bright Hotel in Chinatown. He was spotted toting his manuscripts there. Several guests, hoping to garnish favor, informed Sister Brenda of Isa's movings.

The New York City Rescue Mission was much larger than the Star Bright, where Isa changed light bulbs and fixed leaky pipes from time to time.

The New York City Rescue Mission basement was two underground floors of weaving crypts and tunnels.

Fire from the water heater and furnace gave little light to the room that housed them. The center, always on a Spartan budget, had little concern that there was not proper lighting in the mammoth underground dungeons.

This morning, in the second-floor underground, a light went onto a stack of bound papers. A person picks up three of the stacks and leaves.

At GAM, Koss wanted to see Herman about as much as he wanted to see "cold sore Nadine."

Nadine was the drop-dead gorgeous Irish heroin addict that he had been in a relationship with for almost two years. Unfortunately, the last time he saw her, about a month ago, she had a humongous cold sore on her lip.

Koss was steamed; he had already taken his tadalafil pill, a generic version of Cialis from India. They worked just as well, but he got them for less than a buck each.

He probably didn't need them and convinced himself that he took a five milligram pill a day for an enlarged prostate.

The cold sore scared him and he made up an excuse not to make a deposit in Nadine's oral orifice.

Thanks to Ted, Koss had a rainbow of young girls salivating to get together with him. They came from India, Poland, Italy, Africa, and Sweden. What were these girls' parents thinking when they sent them to the United States?

Koss was a publisher and up on world events. A place like Italy with 60,000,000 people has 500 murders a year in the whole country. There's that many in the city of New York alone.

US marketing; no one does it better. Propaganda versus news, reality versus perception. Trump had it right. Most news is fake, especially when it's disseminated by people that benefit from lying about it.

Koss was sure that a couple of the girls had real feelings for him, and why not? He was only seventy-one, in good physical shape (he thought) and showered regularly. He'd much rather be with an attractive, clean seventy-year-old than an ugly, fat unbathed twenty-year-old, himself.

The media tried to create these finite boundaries. The poor seventeen-year-old girl was having relations with men three times her age. So, what? She was probably doing threesomes since she was thirteen, and at least most older guys didn't beat her.

Nadine now stalked him. She called, cried, and begged. Sure, Koss thought, her pushers were tired of taking blowjobs and sex in exchange for the product. She needed men with cash, and with the way the corporations decimated the middle class's piece of the pie, there were fewer and fewer men out there with thirty dollars to spare.

When Koss first met Nadine, he contemplated marrying her. Of course, that was fantasy. His wife would destroy him in court. Affirmative action and politically corrected judges in the judicial system have made many men paupers.

He treated Nadine like gold until he realized that thanks to the utility man he could have a hundred Nadines. If the milk costs fifty bucks a day, why would anyone in their right mind ever buy a cow who could cost you half of everything you worked for all your life?

He'd get with Angela later that evening. She was a beautiful Italian girl who came to New York a few years back looking to be a singer. Her voice wasn't bad, even beautiful, but the world's full of beautiful voices.

She was entertaining to listen to. She sang in English with an Italian accent.

Koss couldn't understand why an Italian singer would ever want to sing in English when they sang in the most beautiful language in the world, at least to him. Of course, the answer again lies in propaganda.

Angela had thick black hair and lips of a goddess and Koss loved grabbing her black locks and pulling and pushing while she bobbed for his apple.

Unfortunately, in the middle of all of Koss's philosophical thoughts, Herman arrived, and now was standing in front of him.

"Bobby, I really love you and that wife of yours, and would hate to lose you, but if you don't produce in a hurry, Gael and the people that she's dealing with will take you over."

"Don't do it . . . I'll get things right, I promise. Just give me a little more time," Bob pleaded.

"I'm sorry, we don't have any more of that," Koss shook his head. "Get back to me with a solution boy, in a hurry, or Gael will foreclose." Koss paused. "You went through the banking debacle; you know, sometimes the best solution is to punt."

Bob walks into the New York City Rescue Mission. The place is huge. As he saunters around, no one seems to notice him. He walks into the double doors of the cafeteria. It's empty, except for the workers in the kitchen and Isa, who is sitting at a table, reading. Bob walks over and sits in front of him.

Isa barely moves. He's got another one of those bestsellers in his hands.

"How did you find me?"

"I have my ways. Why do you reread your stuff on paper and not on the computer?"

"Words seem to have a different flavor when you just can't backspace and abolish them. They're a step closer to life."

Isa looks up from his work and looks in Bob's eyes. "I'll burn the rest of the books before I give them to you."

Bob's attention peaked. "Rest? How many are there?"

Isa stands.

"Wait, wait, please. I'll be ruined . . . my wife . . . " Bob implores.

"Money or a lack of it cannot destroy what's not already ruined. If you crash, you'll be a better man for it . . . for you and your girlfriend."

"Isa, please, she's my wife."

Isa stares. "Your wife?" Isa hesitates, his facial expression changes. "Well then, face the truth and make your bread another way."

"Writing is all I know how to do."

Isa takes Bob's hand. "Until now, all you've done is plagiarize. I'm sure that you're capable of something else, something honorable."

"What, are you some kind of prophet? Honorable! You're no different than the rest of us. You're here hiding from something or someone. If that wasn't the case, you'd be a celebrated author, living on Park Avenue in the summer and Collins Avenue in the winter."

Bob hesitates to exact sincerity. "Ruin me, Isa, and I'll ruin you!"

They begin to draw attention from people working in the kitchen, one of whom has already beckoned the good Sister Brenda, who is spying from a distance.

"Get out," Isa says.

"I'm sorry," Bob beseeches, "please, just one more book, and I'll leave you alone forever."

"Get out!"

Bob storms away. Sister Brenda heads out the back exit and meets Bob at the mission's entrance. "Come with me to my office, sir."

"I'm sorry, Sister. I was just leaving."

"But I'd like to help you, my son."

Bob follows the nun to her office. They sit. "We're all fond of Isa. He does maintenance here. He's been a huge help; he doesn't seem to know the word no."

"Yes, Sister. I'm sure that he's wonderful."

"One has to be quite resourceful to keep a structure like this open," she says.

Bob's mind races to catch the school bus he took to Catholic school when he was a kid.

"I heard your talk and I know who you are," she says with the kindness of an old-fashioned mother.

Bob remains silent.

"And I know what you've done, Mr. Herman."

"What are you talking about?"

"The Bible isn't the only book I've read, Mr. Herman."

Sister Brenda pulls a stack of manuscripts from the floor behind her and dumps them on her desk. Bob reaches for them but Sister slaps a ruler hard on the stack.

"This mission needs money. The building is too valuable. The city, developers, and the owner want us to lose our lease."

"How much do you want for them?" Bob asks.

Sister Brenda nods. "Whatever the price, I want you to know that the funds will go for the Lord's work."

Harms, Clark, and Kennedy are sitting at a foldable card table in Detective Kennedy's basement. Laundry is stacked on the floor next to them.

"Why would GAM Publishing care about Isa?" Harms asks.

Clark puffs on his cigar. The words come out with the smoke. "Herman and Gael Veenstra both work for GAM. *It has something to do with the company.*"

"In this crazy world, anything's possible," Kennedy says.

"Yeah," Harms says, "that loony bird tweeter got into the White House, anything is possible."

"You people just didn't give him enough time," Clark says.

Harms ignores Clark. "Who owns GAM?" Harms asks.

"Mark Koss," Kennedy says.

"How old is he?" Harms asks.

Kennedy shrugs his shoulders, "Sixty-five? Seventy?"

"What do we know about him?" Harms asks.

"He was an officer in Iraq," Kennedy responds.

"Is that verified?" Clark asks. "Are you sure?"

"Yeah, it's verified. He's even a member of some VFW in Brooklyn," Kennedy says. "He couldn't get in otherwise."

"Have you talked to them yet?" Clark asks.

"I wanted to meet with you guys first," Kennedy says.

"Maybe that's the connection," Harms queries.

Clark looks at Harms and Kennedy. "I don't like it. . . . It's too risky. If they discover that Isa was resurrected out of a body bag, we're all done. The investigation of those two women shot will explode again. The politicians in Iraq will demand justice, and the politicians here will give them our heads on silver platters."

Kennedy mockingly smiles. "We'll soon be selling lots of Coca-Cola, Microsoft software, Levi's jeans, and McDonald's in Iraq." Kennedy pauses. "The only god-damned thing that can save this country from the rich is a revolution."

"We can do that later, brother. For now, there are more pressing things," Harms says. "Let's get into this. We need to understand the situation."

They stand and walk out.

Sister Brenda is sitting at her desk below a large wooden crucifix.

A large, young, dark-skinned guy, Larry, comes to the door. "Sister, Mr. Herman is here to see you."

Sister nods and smiles. "Thank you, Larry, please show him in."

Bob enters and waits for Larry to exit.

"I have a check for you, Sister," Bob says.

He hands it to her, and she examines it.

"I had expected more," she says.

"More? I can't afford this."

"Mr. Herman, do I have to remind you that we are the rightful heirs of Isa's property? He is a nonpaying tenant. You see, Mr. Herman, those manuscripts are part of his estate. We have legal ownership and the right to protect the integrity of the art."

"Don't even think about it, Sister, it wouldn't be in your best interest."

"I'll decide what's in the best interest of this center."

"Sister. I'll double the check, but I need the next two books."

"It may not be the best strategy to piecemeal these books. I was thinking about selling them in a block. I have another interested bidder."

"These books are worthless without my name on them. They're just manuscripts. Don't outsmart yourself, Sister Brenda."

She pushes the check back at him. "Regardless, you'll have to do better than this."

In Midtown, Ted and Gael are seated in Ted's car. She's smoking a cigarette. "If we get the books, Bob works for us. We'll be in the chips."

"Gael, I've always liked the way you think, maneuver, act. I've always liked everything about you."

Gael smirks. "Yeah, Ted, I'll bet. You're not starting to tire of opioid addicts, are you?"

The car jerks as Ted speeds away.

"Where are we going?" Gael asks, glad that she stung him.

"To see another lady who thinks she knows all the answers," Ted says coolly.

Chapter 11

Abby Gael

Ted and Gael walk out of the New York City Rescue Mission to Ted's car. Ted turns to Gael. "Can't argue with the nun's logic. The manuscripts aren't books without Herman's name on them."

Gael spies Ted scornfully. "I control him." Gael reaches for the door as Ted enters the car. Isa walks from the mission with a package. Gael stares at Isa and Ted looks in the direction of Gael's stare.

"There's our author again," Ted says.

Gael moves, intending to head Isa off at the corner of the building.

"Where are you going?" Ted asks.

"To deal with him."

"To deal with a shit bum?"

Gael runs but Ted passes her.

Isa walks to the end of the building. As he turns, he is greeted by Ted, Ted's pistol, and Gael.

"Stop, or I'll really shoot this time," Ted says.

Gael stares at Isa and then at Ted.

"Put your gun down, Ted. Sir, we'd like to buy your manuscripts." Gael squints as she looks at Isa.

"They're not for sale," Isa says.

"Everything has a price," Gael throws back.

Isa stares at Gael.

"Ted, leave us alone. I'll handle this," Gael says.

Ted looks in disbelief. "Are you nuts? Leave you alone with this bearded street scum?"

"Leave. . . . Damn it, just leave!"

Ted turns to leave then looks again at Gael. "Do you want my gun?"

"How many do you think I need?" Gael asks calmly.

Ted leaves, and Gael removes a pistol from her purse. Isa stares.

"Where are you going with these books?" Gael asks.

"To a place where they can be safe."

Gael smiles. "They'll be safe with me."

Isa shakes his head, "You people just don't understand."

Gael smiles, "Locker 117 should be almost full. I could just shoot you now. Fewer than 20 percent of US homicides end with a conviction."

"Oh," Isa says, "the way the government security forces play with numbers, I'd bet you're on the high side.

Gael breaks a long silence. "I always wondered if I'd ever see you again, Ahmed, Amadeo, Deo, Isa." Gael smiles. "How do you know what name to answer to?"

"Abby, I wanted to be with you, but you made the decision to abandon our daughter."

"You didn't care. You lived two blocks away. You could have come by anytime. But you buried yourself in your religion. You didn't give a damn."

"Abby, it's a long story."

"My parents named me Abigael. I was Abby to you and my old friends. But, now, I'm Gael."

Gael hesitates and then with as much spite as she can muster, "Just Gael. Get it?"

"Abby, I'm sorry, but it is a long story, and I had few choices. You'd never understand. The situation is complex."

"If you call me Abby again, I'll shoot you right in your control tower." Abby points the gun at his penis. "I knew that if I ever saw you again you'd give me that shit. I'd have recognized you sooner without the beard. Are you incognito?"

"You should know something."

"Nothing that you could tell me could change anything," Gael says rebelliously.

"I'm not so sure."

"Oh Ahmed, you always liked to dramatize."

Isa nods his head and smiles thinly. "We'll see. . . . Lucia is our daughter."

Gael holds her head for a moment. She looks aside. When she looks back tears are running down her face. "The Saint Anthony orphanage said she was adopted by people out west. Are you sure?"

Isa gently nods. "I want you to know that I could not contact you. It was a question of honor. If I was found many would have suffered."

Isa tries to read Abby's face.

Isa breaks the silence, "I, myself, have only recently found out about Lucia. I have been coping."

"And that is honorable? You're a coward!"

116

"Abby!"

She moves the safety and points at his crotch.

"Gael, my squad was in trouble. To rectify the situation, I murdered a man."

Gael does not give him time to speak. "And what about me? Did you care that you killed me, my soul? Had you shown more concern, had you insisted and demonstrated how we would have lived. But no, instead, you ran away and buried your head in your holy book."

Gael points the gun at Isa's face. "Man of honor." Gael nods. "So, let me understand this. You murdered someone in Iraq and have been hiding ever since? Why hide? That's what soldiers are supposed to do."

"I murdered an American." Isa says slowly.

"I'm not stupid. I figured that out. Why else would you live like a dog in the shadows? How chivalrous."

Isa looks at Gael with the eyes of a child. "Without chivalry, life is not worth living."

"I don't need to hear about it." Gael begins to openly cry.

"If you speak about this, I will be dead before I make it to trial."

"What do I care?!"

Gael lowers the gun, rubs her forehead, then raises it, pointing it in Isa's face.

"Life is filled with tough choices. If you shoot, I only ask that you take care of our daughter," Isa says.

Gael falls to the ground crying.

Isa walks into the building. Gael collects herself and joins Ted in the car.

Isa decides to not sleep at the mission. Wind ruffles the newspapers that partially cover him as he sleeps on the grass in Central Park. A shadowed figure moves over him with a large knife. The knife raises.

A voice is heard in the distance, "Isa! Isa!"

The shadow stabs Isa in the chest. Isa grunts but blocks the second thrust. The shadow turns and sees Clark running toward him. Clark shoots but misses. The shadow turns and runs away.

Clark arrives. "Isa. Shit. Are you all right?"

"Yes, but I have a cut on my chest."

Clark helps him up, puts him in the car, and brings him to Kennedy's house. They lay Isa on a mattress in the dimly lit basement utility room. Harms, Clark, and Kennedy stand over Isa.

"This is getting crazy, crazy," Harms says.

"I couldn't make him out. I shot hoping he'd stop so I could identify him. If I had wounded or killed him, there'd be an investigation and . . ."

"Why were you even in Central Park?" Kennedy asked.

"I followed Isa from the center this afternoon. I knew that he was in Central Park. It's not the first time that he's slept there. I went to check on him," Clark said.

Isa looks up at his friends. "It's time for closure."

"No fuckin' way," Harms says.

Isa repeats, "It's time for closure."

"I said, 'Fuck you,' Isa," Harms says.

Kennedy looks at Harms. "Isa's right, Harms. We all knew that this day could come."

Clark frowns at Harms. Harms takes his gun out of its holster. "If anyone touches him I'll blow them to pieces. There's not enough reason for closure!"

Isa looks kindly at Harms. "I will not be the cause of my men falling. There are families to consider. Duty calls for closure."

Harms shakes his head. "Tommy, Jack, I'm sorry about this. Give me your guns. Isa's coming with me."

"Nobody likes this, Harms! Are you willing to risk my life, my family, yours?" Clark pleads.

Harms is undaunted. "I'm willing to blow your head off if you try to stop me. Give me your guns, both of you."

Clark looks at Kennedy and nods. They give their guns to Harms, who unloads them and gives them back to them.

"Now help Isa up and lay him down in the back seat of my car," Harms says.

They reach down for Isa. Clark simultaneously reaches into an open toolbox and pulls out a utility knife. They lift Isa up and walk to the outside.

Kennedy and Clark lay Isa down gently onto the back seat of Harm's car. The whole time Harms is covering them from behind.

"Okay, close the door and get away from the car," Harms says.

Clark and Kennedy back up. Harms jumps into the front seat and speeds away. Clark and Kennedy watch the car race off.

Harms pulls into his garage. The garage door begins closing. "We're home Isa, we're home. I'll take care of you like you took care of us."

The garage door completely closes. Harms switches the map light on, turns, and kneels facing Isa. "Isa. Isa!"

Harms looks at the bloodstained seat and the open gash on Isa's neck. "Oh Isa!" he cries. Harms opens the car's back door, hugs Isa's head, and continues to sob.

The side door of the garage opens. Light enters the car. Harms grabs his gun.

"Drop it," the voice says.

There is complete silence. "Drop it, I said," repeats the voice.

Harms turns, gun in hand. He points it at the shadow. The shadow is pointing a gun at him. Slowly the shadow begins to lower its gun. Harm's arm remains tight and straight. Harms moves forward. The shadow's arm is at a 30-degree angle to the ground. Harms has the gun up against the shadow's forehead. Another figure comes into the doorway behind the shadow.

"It was not time for closure!" Harms says.

"It was Isa's order!"

"It was not time for closure!" Harms screams.

Harms cocks the trigger, hesitates then drops the gun to his side and fires. "It was not time for closure," he cries, "it was not time for closure."

His body falls into that of the shadow's. They hug.

"It was not time for closure," Harms repeats.

"Jack, open the garage door," Clark says, "I'll get rid of the body."

The garage door begins to open.

"Wait, wait," Kennedy says feebly. He leans into the car and snaps Isa's dog tags off his neck.

Across town, grunting and moaning are coming from a dark hotel room. A figure gets up and turns the light on in the bathroom. It's Lucia, she's bare chested but wearing underpants. She bends and snorts a line of coke. "This is all a lot of kicks, but I want to stop. I mean it."

"Come back into bed. I think that I can change your mind," the man in the bed says.

"It better be something really convincing," she quips.

"Turn the light on. I'll show you."

Lucia turns the light on. Mark Koss opens a box with a diamond necklace in it. She slides next to him. He reaches down, takes a puff from his pipe, puts it in the ashtray, and fastens the necklace around her neck. "Is this convincing enough?"

Shortly after, Koss and Lucia are dressed. Mark's sitting with his head in his hands.

Lucia is glaring at him. "Men, you all like sugar but you don't like cavities."

"This is blackmail. Please, Lucia. I just gave you twenty-five thousand worth of jewelry."

"I want you to make the transaction tomorrow morning, turning over my husband's books to me."

"I can't! I won't! Gent America Media would blow sky high!"

"Then I'll show these photos on my phone to Mrs. Koss."

"But you can't. She's just itching for a reason to take half of everything I own." Koss hesitates, "I should have stuck to the fifty-dollar drug addicts," Koss mumbles to himself.

Lucia grabs him by the collar. "Listen to me! You'll do as you're told!"

"Please, Lucia, listen, I'm working on a deal. I haven't told anyone."

Lucia scans his face curiously. "What will it do for me?"

"There may be a big movie deal coming our way. That's where the real money is made. Bobby moving from Gent could foul things up."

"What will it mean for me, Marky?" Lucia asks.

"Why, it means lots and lots of money for all of us. But without my cooperation there's no deal."

Lucia stares at Koss.

Koss smiles. "The books are fine, but the big, big money's in the movies, honey!"

Chapter 12

Tables Turned

Outside Herman's condo, Ted's in a car on the phone. "You think that the mother is Gael Veenstra and that the father is an Ethiopian named Ahmed Selassie? This is good," Ted says sarcastically.

Lucia opens the door and enters. "God. I can't stand him anymore. Why did I marry him?"

Ted smiles at Lucia. "Say the word and he'll end up like Tony. You'll have to cry more convincing tears, though. That shouldn't be hard for you."

"Where are we going?" Lucia asks.

Ted turns the vehicle into traffic. "The usual."

"Ted, give me the coke."

"Hold on, honey, don't rush things."

"Ted, give me the coke. I'm stressed. He has no money anywhere." She shakes her head in disbelief. "Last week I hocked some jewelry. Now, just give me the coke. You can talk later."

"You know, if your husband was out of the picture, things would be smoother. His books would pop up, they'd be bestsellers. Then maybe a movie deal. You're the only heir." Ted smiles from temple to temple. "It would have to be done carefully, of course."

"Give me the coke!"

"Stop being so obnoxious . . . and be careful not to snort his insurance payments," Ted laughs and tugs at her head. "Show me some of what you learned in the orphanage."

Lucia's head goes down on his lap. She sniffles. If he's not mistaking, she's crying. Nah, that would be impossible.

Bob is standing in Koss's office.

"No literary relationship is easy, Bobby," Koss says. "Things will start to get good for us. I'm onto a movie deal. Don't abandon me now. We'll both be richer than you could ever imagine. We're in this together."

Koss looks and smiles at Bob. Bob's face is emptier than a divorced man's checking account.

"Right, Bobby?"

Bob's look is hollower than a doughnut hole.

"Don't do anything stupid. Okay? All you have to do is to put your name on three more books. Find them, Bobby, and we're home free."

Koss reaches and Bob shakes his hand.

Later that evening Lucia is bare and standing next to a bed.

A man's figure is on the bed. "You're fucked up!" he says.

"No, it's you that's fucked up!"

"Where did you scam the name Lucia from?"

"It's no scam," she growls. Lucia throws her shoe at the man in the bed. "My name was Lucy. The orphanage sent me to live with an Italian family in Bensonhurst when I was nine. It was the best four years of my life."

She wipes tears from her eyes.

She sits on the chair. "All I wanted was someone to love me. The Russos loved me. Then they took me away from them!"

"That's when you started with Tony. When you were nine!"

Lucia sniffles, "Yes, no, I was eleven or twelve."

Lucia throws her other shoe at him.

"But I loved him. I always loved him!"

"And, did he ever love you?"

"He loved a hundred girls."

"Is that why he died?"

Bob gets out of the bed and stands over her. "Look," he says, "our money problems are over. Koss is making a deal. We'll have more money than we know what to do with. We'll have a new start. I'll take care of you."

Lucia looks at Bobby.

"Bobby . . . I stopped believing! I already sold everything we have. You'll never forgive me once you know who I am and how I get by."

"I want this to work," Bob says desperately.

"Work? Do you know what I do for work? The only job I've ever been good at?"

"What are you trying to tell me?"

Lucia looks at him. She's not sure if she should laugh or cry, "You'll hate me for telling you."

"Lucia, have you ever told the truth in your whole life?"

"You'll hate me. You'll hate me forever," she forewarns.

"You mean your clients? Nothing would surprise me!"

Silence rushes into the room like a dam break.

Lucia nods, "Okay," she says softly, "Koss, Basle."

Tears well up in Bob's eyes. He gets up, goes into the closet, and comes out with a suitcase.

"I told you you'd hate me! You're like everyone else, see, you're running out too!"

"You're sick! But you won't get anything else from me."

"Bobby, you wouldn't. I'm sorry Bobby. I'm sorry," she pleads.

Bob moves to leave. "Yeah, you're sorry because you don't have any other choices. For people like you, Gael, Koss, and Basle, *honesty's the best policy when all else fails.*"

"Oh, really? Who are you trying to kid? Is that what you tell the fans of your books?"

Bob winces and walks out.

The following day in the Gent America Media conference room, Jennifer is checking the immaculately cleaned room. Lou walks in.

"Has Bob arrived?" Jennifer asks him.

"Bob the shit head?"

Jennifer doesn't answer. Bob walks in. Lou walks out.

Slowly the room fills up with Koss and individuals who no one in the company knows. Jennifer sits next to Koss. After twenty minutes, Koss asks Jennifer to leave. She quietly closes the conference room door behind her and walks to her cubicle.

Lou sticks his head inside her kingdom. "How's it going in there?"

"I'm no expert but from what I gather, I'd say that GAM stock is looking higher."

"I'd never have believed it." Lou shakes his head. "That phony piece of worm discard pulled it off. Movies. You could shoot me."

"Lou, with the love that most folks here have for you, I wouldn't say that too loud."

Lou smiles, "Still in love with that jerk, are we?"

"The man I was in love with is not a jerk." She hesitates. "Maybe he never existed at all."

Lou watches Jennifer. After twenty seconds, he leaves thinking. *You can only have so much fun watching a puppy suffering.*

A few hours later, Bob is sitting with Gael in her condo.

"This thing is out of control," Bob says.

"Bob, I don't know what's so important that it can't wait for tomorrow morning."

There's a knock at the door. Bob looks at Gael, "He's here."

"Who's here?

Bob opens the door. Ted walks in. Bob socks him. Ted rubs his jaw and grabs for his gun.

"I know, Ted. I don't think you'll be firing that gun here, and if you don't put it away, I'll stick it up your ass," Bob threatens.

Ted puts the gun in its holster. "What are you talking about? You know what?"

"About you and Lucia."

Gael grimaces.

"I deserved that . . ." Ted says, "but deserve it or not, the next time you swing at me I'm gonna take you out."

"I don't think so." Bob pauses and stares them both down. "I can't think of two more detestable people in the world, but you're the only ones who can help me."

Gael seems impressed with Bob's newfound testicles.

Bob continues. "Koss has a movie deal. I need the books. After that I'm out of this town and you're out of my life."

Ted shoots several lethal glances at Gael, but apparently, she's wearing lethal-glance-proof armor.

Bob is wondering what Ted is trying to communicate now.

Bob continues, "A nun has the books, and she wants to sell them to me, but her price is far higher than I can reach."

"What's higher than you can reach?"

"A two-million-dollar donation. I can't reach that," Bob says.

"Why is this important to me?" Ted asks.

"It's important because Koss is making a deal that will make us all rich. GAM stock will double, triple."

"Where's the author at?" Gael smiles. "The real author."

Bob shoots hostile glances at Gael, but her lethal, glance-proof-armor, obviously also blocks hostility. Still, he feels invigorated and in control for the first time since he found the book on the bus. He has nothing to lose. His feet touch the bottom. He springs to the top of the water.

"I'm not sure," Bob says. "He may be dead for all I know . . . and that's how you will be, Ted, if you ever touch my wife again."

"He's not dead," Gael says.

At the same time, in Kennedy's basement, Harm's, Kennedy, and Clark are huddled.

"It's finally all over," Kennedy says.

"In the end, Isa got his way. We're all still free." Harms says.

Kennedy nods. "Is there anything that we have to know or do to clean things up?"

"No," Clark says, "everything's been taken care of."

"Where's his body?" Harms asks.

"It's best if you don't know," Clark answers.

"Say," Kennedy says smiling, "this doesn't mean that we won't see each other or anything. . . . After all, Isa died, not our friendship."

Later, Bob is back at his apartment. He opens the door. Gael and Ted enter.

Bob nods. "I went and spoke to the good sister. She's certain that Isa's dead."

"And her proof?" Ted asks.

Bob tosses the dog tags at Ted. Ted looks at it and reads out loud, "Sgt. Ahmed Selassie."

"Give me those," Gael demands.

Ted hands the dog tags to Gael. "I have something to do," he says, and walks out.

Gael stares. She's entranced. She stares at the floor. "Ahmed wrote *Standard Deviations*, *Square Pegs in Circles*, and *Gracious Ignorance*." Gael continues staring at the floor. "He gave them to you because of Lucia. . . . Oh my God, Lucia."

"What? What are you talking about?" Bob hesitates before continuing. "How do you know?"

Gael continues to speak in tongues. "I know. And I also know that he's not dead."

Bob's losing his sanity. This is all too much for him. "How do you know that? Damn it, Gael! How do you know?"

"He moved books from the Star Bright Hotel last night."

"Could it have been anyone else?" Bob meekly asks.

"How far do you trust Ted?" Gael asks.

"How far could I throw this building?"

Later that night in Ted's apartment, all is dark except for the light coming from his computer screen. Ted is on a Wikipedia screen reading about Haile Selassie, the Ethiopian emperor who people like Bob Marley worshipped as a god.

From behind, someone with rubber gloved hands wraps a rope around his neck. Ted convulses.

"Sorry Teddy, it's time to go," a voice says.

Ted struggles, but he's pushed further against his desk. He doesn't have a chance. His body slumps, and two silenced shots are heard.

Shortly after, a pair of hands with tissue in them erases the screen, clears the history, and logs out.

After a minute, Teddy's screen goes black and the computer says, "Goodbye Teddy."

Chapter 13

Tables Spun Again

The following day the police arrest Bob. He is standing in a lineup at the station. On the other side of a one-way glass plate is an elderly woman, standing in the company of Kennedy and Clark.

"Number three, ma'am? Take your time."

"I don't know," the woman says.

Clark speaks into a microphone. "Number three, turn to the right and give us a profile."

Bob turns to the side.

"Is that him, ma'am?" Clark prods.

"I'm . . . I'm not sure."

Clark blows out impatience mixed with scents of cigar and whiskey.

The woman looks at the man in the lineup and then back at Clark. "Will he know that I picked him?"

"If that's him, you won't have to worry. He'll be locked away for life," Kennedy says.

The woman looks kindly at Kennedy and then Clark. "Yes, that's the man that I saw entering Mr. Basle's apartment last night."

"Are you 100 percent sure?" Clark asks.

"Yes, I am," she responds.

"Let's book him," Kennedy says.

Bob spends the night in lockup. He's in way over his head. In fact, he's so far down that they're going to have to question him from a submarine.

Early the next day while Bob's laying on the metal cot dreaming about sleep, the lockup guard yells, "Herman out!"

The turnkey opens the cell door. Bob steps out. He's handcuffed and brought to another room, where Gael and Arnold Schuman are sitting with attorney Shelby Warren, a sharply dressed man Bob has never seen before.

Bob breaks down crying on the table. "I didn't do it. I didn't do it. I didn't do it."

Arnie puts his arm on Bob's shoulder. "We know that you didn't do it. Calm yourself. In an hour, you'll be out of here. You remember Shelby Warren?"

It would have been difficult for Bob to remember Shelby Warren since they've never met.

"I've hired him to help you," Arnie continues. "This is an obstacle that will iron itself out."

Shortly after, at the police station, Lucia is seated in front of Detective Holt.

"Ma'am, just a few more questions," Holt says.

Lucia smiles. "Yes, of course."

"Did you know that Ted Basle worked for your husband?"

"No. I read in the paper about Basle. But I can't believe that my husband would have anything to do with someone like him."

"I see," Holt says as he jots notes on a piece of paper.

"So, you've never personally met Mr. Basle?"

"No, of course not."

Holt rolls his eyes and nods. "Mrs. Herman, you're being recorded."

"Yes, I know, you told me."

Later that day, Bob is sitting in Arnie Schuman's office. Arnie is standing and looking out the window.

"Shelby Warren got you bailed. You need to find money. We need to give him at least fifty thousand for his retainer."

"I don't have fifty cents," Bob says.

"Call your parents, your wife's parents. Everything's at risk here, everything," Schuman says coldly.

Later that evening there's a knock at Gael's apartment. Gael stares at the door.

"Who is it?"

"Police."

Gael opens the door. Detective Kennedy flashes his badge and walks in.

Gael suspiciously watches him. "Yes?"

"Ma'am, I'd like to have a word with you. May I?"

"Exactly who are you? You waved that thing too fast for me to get anything."

Kennedy shows her his badge. He smiles firmly, "Detective Jack Kennedy."

"I assume that this is about official police business, Detective?"

"I'm glad that you asked, because actually, it's not."

Gael looks at Kennedy like someone might look at the guts of a fish clumped on a Manhattan sidewalk on a hot summer day. Kennedy appreciates her sentiment. He smiles again, this time showing his pearly yellows. "I have something that you may want."

"Oh," Gael pauses, "I doubt that."

"Don't. I have the contents of locker 117," he whispers.

Gael tries to disguise her surprise. Her mind is scurrying faster than a mouse from an alley cat.

"I'm not going to go into detail here," Kennedy says. "I doubt that the place is bugged, but you are known to have a guest or two."

Gael stares at him. *How dare he?*

"I'm not judging you, ma'am, you're not married." Kennedy pauses, "I'll be waiting for you at the entrance to the Children's Zoo in Central Park in one hour."

Gael stares.

"I'll let myself out, Miss Veenstra."

Gael undresses and takes a shower. She dries, puts on her underwear and robe, and takes the gun out of her purse.

An hour and fifteen minutes later, Kennedy's in front of the Children's Entrance of the Central Park Zoo. He's trying not to seem like he's pacing, but he is. His palms are sweaty, and he can smell a familiar odor sneaking out of the top of his shirt.

He used to *always* use the chemical poison to cover his essence but the hell with Procter and Gamble and all the other substance-poisoning conglomerates. He was conducting his own personal boycott. It's not always easy. The chemical concoctions the corporations put in our food makes for some pretty revolting scents.

He's startled when Gael walks up from behind. He points in the direction of a bench. They walk together and sit.

"I like sunny days," Kennedy says. "Everything's so clear."

"Oh?" Gael queries.

"Did you bring your checkbook, ma'am?"

"No, I didn't."

"Oh. . . . Then why did you come?"

Gael chuckles. "You're very confident. May I ask why? I really don't see how it's warranted."

"Let's just say that I'm confident that you'd help a close relative."

"I don't have a close relative."

"Don't you?"

"It's obvious that you don't know me," Gael rebutted.

"Abigael Veenstra, I know things that you thought you forgot."

Gael smiles brightly, bringing the tulips that the nation of her forefathers is so well known for. "I like the park, Detective, the sun, but you really don't convince me; and quite frankly, I find you a bit confused."

Kennedy doesn't particularly like conversing with ladies and the good Lord knows he's an expert, picking up hundreds, if not thousands, of prostitutes. He may have booked ten of them; the rest he used as cum dumpsters. It worked for everyone.

Thoughts like this brought him around to reality, self-assurance. He flashes his teeth, which look like the before of a bad whitening commercial. "Let's just say that my confidence is rooted in the suspicion, no, let me say, in the conviction that I'm sure a mother will do whatever she can to help a daughter."

"Kind of an antiquated belief. I suppose that you haven't heard of filial cannibalism."

Kennedy shakes his head. Over-educated whores always annoyed him. "We're talking about your daughter, not animal kingdom."

"I didn't know I had one."

"No, not legally, maybe. But Lucia Herman is the child that you gave up for adoption, twenty-three years ago. She's in trouble, big trouble, and her loving husband, who's in a world of woe, needs the books that I have."

"I don't know what you're talking about."

"If you insist," Kennedy clasps his hands together. "Miss Veenstra, Isa's name is Ahmed Selassie. He's now deceased. But Lucia, who the St. Anthony orphanage called Lucy, who then became Mrs. Robert Herman, is your daughter—yours and Ahmed's, that is."

Kennedy smiles, he's impressed with himself. "Ethiopian, Muslim, mixed children were not the rage a few decades ago."

Gael hears Kennedy but her mind is someplace else. Ahmed destroyed any docile thought that she had about the opposite sex. She worshipped him from when he got his head smashed on his desk by Mr. Thomas. If he'd have only tried harder to be a man, Lucia would have been theirs. Instead, he, like all men of the cloth, buried himself in ceremony. There's not much a man can say that she hasn't heard and far less that any man could do to injure her. She's starting to appreciate the sunny day.

"Your daughter had a deal with good Sister Brenda, who double-crossed her like she double- crossed your son-in-law."

Kennedy is truly enthralled—with himself, that is. He continues, "You see the good sister and your daughter knew each other from Saint Anthony orphanage, years ago. She's a dilly, your offspring. Besides being a whore and a liar, she has a nasty coke addiction."

Kennedy smiles widely, proudly demonstrating that he had a bacon-and-egg bagel for breakfast. "And Sister Brenda, she's just a whore."

Gael is watching an ugly black crow pick at gum stuck to the sidewalk. Every time someone approaches he retreats, but he's back at it in an instant, similar to the kind detective. Courtesy, professionalism, and respect.

"Can we talk now, Abigael? I mean, we're both grown-ups, and I'm quite a reasonable man."

"Evidently," she quips sardonically.

"Look Miss Veenstra, I'm almost certain that you killed Ted trying to protect Lucia. You buy the books from me, and I'll give you a bonus. . . . I'll keep my mouth shut."

The crow pulls and the gum is released from the pavement.

"Detective, I think that our amusing little chat is over."

She stands and walks away. Kennedy follows her. "Miss Veenstra."

She ignores him.

Later that evening Gael is standing and Bob is sitting at his condo.

"You can't give up. She's your wife."

"She's a heartbreaking prank. And since when does any of that matter to you?"

"Bob, you've got to stand up for yourself, for her, for the both of you."

Bob is analyzing a hardly visible crack on the ceiling.

He's startled by the conviction in Gael's voice. "*Stand up for the both of you,*" she repeats.

Bob mockingly stands. "Okay, I'm standing." He runs his hand through his hair. "I should have left the damn book on the bus."

"We all should have done a lot of things differently, but it's too late for that. You must do what you can, to better your lives now."

"Lucia can't get any better at what she does. She plays men like they're musical instruments. . . . And she's had more trumpets, flutes, and trombones in her mouth than the New York Philharmonic."

Bob laughs hysterically, stumbling through the maze his life has been since he found the book on the bus. "Do the humane thing, Gael. . . . Give me your gun. Let me finish myself. . . . Without the books, I'm dead anyway."

"You'll have the books and you'll put your life back together . . . with Lucia."

"You're nuts. . . . Isa would never give up his books. I know him! You don't know him!"

"I have three books, and I'll be getting the rest."

"You're crazy!" Bob stares at Gael. "No, you're insane!" Bob drifts. "You don't know Isa," he says quietly.

Gael opens her purse and takes out a letter. "I know Isa."

Bob's not sure what his screen directive is. To change the tone a bit, he snaps the letter from her and reads it over and over. "Hey, this sounds like Isa's writing, who was he writing love letters to?"

"To me . . ."

Bob turns the page over.

Love, Ahmed.

Bob looks down, expecting the floor to part and him to fall into the opening. He shakes his head. Gael grabs him.

"Take control of your life," she says. "Reach inside for your dignity, your honor."

Bob looks at Gael. Tears are welling in his eyes. "If you get me the books, I can begin to get them ready for Koss. I still am a good editor."

"And Lucia?" Gael asks.

"What about her?"

"I want Lucia to own 50 percent of the books and the rights," Gael says.

The closet door opens. Lucia walks out, holding a gun. "That won't do. I want 100 percent." Lucia smiles snidely. "Mark Koss is picking the books up now."

"Lucia," Bob says.

"Shut up, Bob. The books are rightfully mine. My deceased father wrote them."

Bob's somewhere deep in the forest. *Isa is Lucia's father?* He's captivated. *What next?*

"I got all my brains from you, Mother," Lucia says.

Whoa, whoa, let me off the ride. Bob looks at Lucia. It's the first spotting of a real space alien.

Lucia continues. "It's working out better than I planned. First, I thought that I'd have to kill Bob to get the rights. Then I thought it better to kill Isa. I tried to kill him in the park, but failed. My partner finished the job."

Bob's getting motion sickness.

Lucia smiles and continues. "Detective Kennedy is my partner, Mommy. Now if you could just tie each other up for me, he will be here shortly."

Gael begins to cry. "Lucia, oh Lucia, what have they done to you?"

"It's a little late to ask. You don't care anyway. Your tears are as phony as your boobs. You were more sincere when I met you leaving Bob's apartment."

Lucia's eyes begin tearing.

"But I had no idea that you were my . . ."

"Don't say it. If you say it, I'll shoot," she points the gun at Gael's face. "I swear I'll shoot," she says in earnest.

Bob is slowly weaving through the bush; Ahmed is Lucia's father, Gael is her mother.

Gael looks from Lucia to Bob. She stares in his eyes. Bob smirks. *I bedded a mother and daughter. Ahh, today it's really no biggie, it's almost bourgeois.*

Gael's confused. What is he smirking about?

Bob continues panning for nuggets. *It's wonderful, what letting Hollywood dictate the moral molding of a country will do,* Bob thought. *He could probably get a positive plug on Yahoo, Google, and CNN News if he also had relations with Ahmed and Ahmed got a "so-called" sex change operation.*

Bob walks in front of Gael. "If you're going to shoot, shoot me. This whole travesty is my doing." Bob inches closer to Lucia.

"Don't push your luck," Lucia snipes.

Bob continues moving toward Lucia. She cocks the trigger.

"I mean it!" Lucia shoots and hits Bob in the left arm. Bob's body coils back. It actually hurt less than he would have imagined. He straightens and steps toward Lucia.

"Give me the gun," Bob says.

Tears are falling from Lucia's eyes. "Get back. I swear."

Bob grabs Lucia. She falls into him and drops the gun. "No one will take care of me. No one loves me."

"It's not true, honey," Gael says. "Lucia. I'll make it all better. Your mother will . . ."

Lucia quickly grabs the gun and points it toward Gael.

"Don't ever say that again. Get away from me or I'll shoot! Both of you, get away from me!" Lucia warns.

On the Far West Side, on an empty street in front of a warehouse Detective Clark is standing next to his car. Another squad pulls up.

Detective Kennedy jumps out. "What's wrong?" Kennedy asks.

"My car's on the fritz. While I'm waiting, I thought we'd pass some time together," Clark says.

"While we're waiting?" Kennedy reaches into his car and grabs the microphone. "This is Detective Kennedy! Get someone down here on Staley and Webb in front of the old Getz factory now!" he screams.

Clark grins. "You're too predictable, Jack, like the break-in at Isa's center. Greed was always your downfall. It's closure, Jack."

Kennedy turns around and goes for his gun. Clark shoots twice. Kennedy falls, gun in hand. Detective Clark drops his tape-covered pistol and drives away.

Not far away, Detective Holt's car turns onto an empty street. He parks and turns around and unlocks Koss's cuffs.

"You've made the mistake of your career," Koss growls. "Do you know what you are doing? I know the mayor personally and . . ."

Holt interrupts him. "You're being undesirably discharged, for the second time."

"What are you talking about?" Koss said with an air of arrogance that would choke Jamie Dimon.

"In Iraq, our boys found paper in their first-aid canisters because you sold the bandages to Al Qaeda. Our boys went without armor because you sold them to ISIS. You were a Halliburton stooge, Captain Kosel."

"You've got the wrong man, officer. My name is Koss."

"Yes, now it is. You paid to legally change it to Koss, like you paid to get your undesirable discharge changed into a general." Holt smiles. "I give it to you. It took a lot of nerve joining the VFW in Brooklyn. But I guess a large donation gets you into most anyplace."

Koss is now understanding the seriousness of the situation. He tries to smile.

"Money can't buy honor," Holt says, "and people like you are the reason that twenty-eight military personnel take their own lives, each and every day."

"Officer, you're insane, you don't know who I am. I support the Patrolmen's Benevolent Association, the VFW, and fallen soldiers."

Holt continues to smile.

"I'll have your badge! Do you know who I am!?"

"I'll tell you who you are. Captain Ginsel plea-bargained and got you off the hook with an undesirable discharge, Captain Kosel. Would you like to at least apologize before you die?

"Apologize? Before I die?"

"Mr. Koss, those are defective cuffs. That's how you got them off. Take this twenty-two that you had between your legs. It's yours, I took it from your office. It's the one that you killed Scumbag Basle with."

"Wait . . . wait . . ."

"Take the gun!" Holt screams.

Koss grabs the gun.

"Captain Kosel, would you rather spend the rest of your life in prison or die?"

Tears ran down Koss's face.

"I know what I'd rather do," Holt says mockingly.

Koss turns the gun on Holt and pulls the trigger.

"It's not loaded!" Koss screams.

Holt shoots him twice. "I didn't know that."

Holt picks up Koss's head. Koss's eyes open slightly. Detective Holt winks. "Your second *undesirable* discharge came from a thirty-eight special. . . . It was for our boys in Iraq."

There's a knock at the Herman condo. Lucia opens the door at the same time she's shakily holding the gun on Gael. Bob is unconscious and bleeding from the shoulder.

"Give me the gun," Detective Clark says.

Some days later in Gael Veenstra's apartment, Lucia, Bob, Isa, and Gael are seated eating.

"Every man lives his life for something. . . . Even Ted Basle . . . if it wasn't for his PI work and greed we'd never be here. . . . Life is filled with necessary evils," Isa says.

Isa looks across the table at Gael. "Take care of our daughter."

"Of course," Gael nods.

"And I'll keep studying," Bob says.

Isa stands and puts his hands on Bob's shoulders. "You'll be fine, son. . . . Remember, writing and life are long roads. Experience is our teacher, and if we live and write from our hearts we can't miss, no matter how little we have in our pockets. . . . Even if it's nothing, no matter who reads our work. . . . Even if it's nobody."

"Isa, you once told me that there was something that I must do for you. What was it?"

Isa looks at Lucia. "Take care of my daughter. . . . Men of honor take care of their families."

Bob hugs Isa. Clark, Holt, Gallo, and Harms are waiting.

"My brothers are calling."

Lucia runs toward him. "But Isa!"

Isa smiles. Lucia stares at him, she smiles. "Dad, where will you go?"

He hugs her. "I'll never be far away."

"I love you," Lucia hugs her father with all her might.

"Honey, life will be filled with dragons and shepherds, challenges and triumphs." He resembles Abbaa Gudaa and Uncle Caleb and smiles in a fatherly way.

Lucia is a changed woman. The many fallen tears over the last days have purified the stream. Her womanly beauty is far more ravishing than Jimmy Choo or Ralph Lauren could ever counterfeit. She studies Isa's eyes and sees all the way to Harar.

She's at peace.

"Our intentions are our personal gateway to heaven," he says.

Lucia's eyes flood with tears of elated enlightenment. Gael hugs her daughter.

Isa rises and moves toward the door. He nods. "Dreams replace regrets." He looks at Bob. "You are a man, my son, and no matter what society's mad scientists try to concoct, after their zany experiments are done, *men* and *women's distinction* unites society."

Isa continues, "Honor is the thread of humanity, and without it, civilization unravels." He nods again. "Lack of honor and lack of truth is at the base of today's malcontent. We should not blend thoughts and sexes forcing them into a gigantic politically correct zombie-fest. We should accentuate them."

Isa looks at his squad. "Men, take care of my family like you've always taken care of me. I'm going to go to the land of my forefathers. The weather there should be a little gentler on my bones."

Isa shows the healing cut on his throat. "Clark, I know you have good aim with the cigar but you came a little too close for comfort with that box cutter."

The group laughs.

For the first time in a long time, Cat sees nothing funny.

"Oh," Isa turns, "I forgot something."

He takes a picture out of his pocket and hands it to Lucia.

It's a picture of him and his squad in Iraq.

"Keep this, my daughter, and remember chivalry."

CHIVALRY:
A SCREENPLAY

CHIVALRY: Written by Patrick Girondi

Based on Chivalry the Novel

Four bodies are partially charred and hanging from a bridge. Their uniforms are U.S. Army.

March 31, 2004 Falluja, Iraq fades to March 31, 2010

A U.S. Army squadron is turning down a street. The bridge from the first scene is in the background.

Two Iraqi women, carrying long black objects are walking toward the men from a hundred yards away.

The groups move closer to one another.

> SGT. AHMED SELASSIE
> Iisqat al'aslihat alkhasat bik!

The squadron stops and draws their weapons. The women continue to advance.

> SGT. AHMED SELASSIE
> Iisqat al'aslihat alkhasat bik!

One of the women points the black object toward the troops.

> SGT. AHMED SELASSIE
> No!!!

The squadron fires, and shots are heard over the screams.

The women fall to the ground. The group arrives. They are joined by another U.S. Army group, which is peppered with people dressed in civilian clothes.

The groups stare down at the dead women. The black objects were two ebony walking sticks.

EXT. MILITARY POLICE/ARMY HEADQUARTERS, BAGHDAD, SUNNY SUMMER DAY 2010

SERGEANT AHMED SELASSIE, mid 30s, black, average height, slim and convinced, walks up to the drab and tan barracks. CORPORAL HURT, 20s, stands at attention at the entrance.

> SGT. AHMED SELASSIE
> Sergeant Selassie to see Colonel Drummond.

> CORPORAL HURT
> I'll let him know that you're here.

INT. ARMY HEADQUARTERS OFFICES OF COLONEL DRUMMOND

Sergeant Selassie walks into typical Army deco- rated room and salutes. COLONEL DRUMMOND, white, 50ish man with a crew cut, is sitting at his desk. He returns the salute.

> COLONEL DRUMMOND
> At ease Sergeant. (pause) If you're here to ask for slack or a deal you're in the wrong place. You should be talking with your attorney, not me. . . . Do any of your soldiers have any relatives that are senators or congressmen?

> SGT. AHMED SELASSIE
> Not that I know of, Sir.

> COLONEL DRUMMOND
> Of course not. If they did, they wouldn't be here. Or if they were here, they'd be commissioned officers sitting behind some safe desk. Politicians . . . the taxpayer foots the bill for their vulgarity, and the poor fight

the wars they start to promote
capitalism.

The Colonel tries to smile. Ahmed remains unmoved.

> COLONEL DRUMMOND
> Sergeant, I, like most of your
> platoon, am from New York State.
> Do you realize that this situation
> is painful for me as well?

> SGT. AHMED SELASSIE
> Yes sir.

> COLONEL DRUMMOND
> Military police platoons as yours
> are here to protect civilians, not
> kill them. Are you sticking to
> your story, Sergeant?

> SGT. AHMED SELASSIE
> Yes, Sir.

> COLONEL DRUMMOND
> Do you like Kansas, Sergeant?

> SGT. AHMED SELASSIE
> Kansas, Sir?

> COLONEL DRUMMOND
> That's right, Kansas, as in
> Leavenworth Prison, Kansas.

> SGT. AHMED SELASSIE
> Never been there, Sir.

> COLONEL DRUMMOND
> Well, that's where you and
> your whole platoon will be
> going for a long, long time
> if you don't change your story,
> Sergeant. . . . It didn't go well

for us here. To many, we're the
war criminals, not the goddamn
Iraqis! Your platoon killed two
women!

                SGT. AHMED SELASSIE
We thought that they were going to
fire on us, Sir.

                COLONEL DRUMMOND
Save it for the judge. One of your
men is testifying against all of
you.

                SGT. AHMED SELASSIE
He was always an outsider, Sir.

                COLONEL DRUMMOND
It doesn't matter to the court.

                SGT. AHMED SELASSIE
And if we change our story?

                COLONEL DRUMMOND
If you admit to killing the
civilians and throw yourself on
the mercy of the court, they may
be more lenient. But you'll still
go away.

Colonel Drummond takes a deep breath.

                COLONEL DRUMMOND
I can't help you. I'm sorry.

                SGT. AHMED SELASSIE
(Quietly) Yes, Sir.

                COLONEL DRUMMOND
You and Cowdar didn't shoot.
But you were in charge. You're

responsible. . . . They'll fry you,
Selassie. They'll fry all of you.
And the Army can't help you. It's
a shame that the politicians who
decided to make this war aren't
held accountable for the carnal
slaughter. . . . But every war's
the same. The age of chivalry died
when the king stopped riding out
with the troops.

                SGT. AHMED SELASSIE
        Yes, Sir.

Corporal Hurt knocks.

                COLONEL DRUMMOND
        What is it?

                CORPORAL HURT
        Sir, Captain Ginsel is here.

                COLONEL DRUMMOND
        Show him in.

Sgt. Ahmed Selassie salutes. Drummond hesitates
and salutes. Selassie walks out.

Captain Ginsel walks in.

                COLONEL DRUMMOND
        Captain. Your client, KOSEL, that
        other captain asshole, was selling
        our boys' supplies to Al Qaeda.

                CAPTAIN GINSEL
        Sir, let's get this straight. He
        was allocating the products to
        civilians.

Colonel Drummond stands and slams his hand on the
desk.

                    COLONEL DRUMMOND
Captain, let's get this straight.
You and Kosel are scum. Goddamn
it! Who do you think *they* were
selling it to? Our boys went into
their first-aid kits and found
paper instead of bandages!

                    CAPTAIN GINSEL
Sir, with all respect,
my job as attorney is to
defend . . . you don't have the
proof . . . and . . .

                    COLONEL DRUMMOND
And he is the nephew of Senator
Feinvine. Why don't you have the
balls to just say it?

                    CAPTAIN GINSEL
Sir, I don't like these political
interferences any more than
you. . . . We'll take an
undesirable discharge without
mention of the case.

Colonel Drummond looks down at his desk. He nods
his head and slowly looks up . . .

                    COLONEL DRUMMOND
Captain, that man who just left
and his whole squadron are going
away for a very long time. They
got spooked, and they killed two
Iraqi women. They didn't mean
to. They were scared and thought
that they were under attack. Your
client intentionally shortchanged
our soldiers and sold U.S. Army
supplies to the enemy.

                    CAPTAIN GINSEL
        Sir, you can't prove that. . . .

                    COLONEL DRUMMOND
        I don't need to. I know it. You
        know it. The whole goddamn army
        knows it. But it's not about
        guilt, is it? It's about political
        contacts. . . . Today's presidents
        are yesterday's tyrants. . . . No,
        they're worse. They're wolves in
        a democratic sheepskin. They're
        hypocrites like you and that
        client of yours. You're all
        mercenaries of
        Halliburton, McDonald's,
        ExxonMobil, and Chevron! Get out
        of here, Captain.

                    CAPTAIN GINSEL
        Yes, sir.

Captain Ginsel salutes. The Colonel hesitates and
disgustedly waves him away.

TAN BARRACKS BLENDING INTO THE SKY

INT. BARRACKS

Fifteen uniformed men are sitting in the barracks.

Corporal kennedy, a blond-haired corporal with a us
flag tattooed on his right forearm, is standing in
the middle of them.

                    CORPORAL KENNEDY
        We're all going away! That pussy
        Cowdar is going to rat on us all!

A short black soldier with glasses, CORPORAL HARMS,
stands up.

                    CORPORAL HARMS
          But we're innocent. We thought
          that those women were going to
          shoot. We thought that they were
          armed and probably booby trapped.

                    CORPORAL KENNEDY
          Do you see what I mean, you geek?
          Which is it, armed, booby trapped?

A tall, thin, black soldier with a slight mustache,
CORPORAL HOLT, stands.

                    CORPORAL HOLT
          Lay off the brother, man. It
          ain't gonna do us no good to fight
          amongst ourselves.

                    CORPORAL KENNEDY
          It ain't gonna do us any good to
          fight anything. That's my point. We
          got to run. The war's over. The
          only thing waiting for us back in
          the good ole USA is jail. And when
          are you gonna shave that silly
          French mustache? You look like a
          goddamn faggot.

A short bald man with a hooked nose, CORPORAL
GALLO, stands.

                    CORPORAL GALLO
          Hey man, I'm going back to
          Brooklyn.

A stubby short guy with red hair, CORPORAL CLARK,
aims his cigar and flicks it into the sink ten yards
away.

CIGAR LANDING DEAD CENTER IN SINK

> CORPORAL CLARK
> Before any of us get back to New
> York, we'll spend a minimum of
> fifteen years in a military prison.

> CORPORAL KENNEDY
> Like the fat lady . . . when she
> sings, the game's over.

> CORPORAL HARMS
> But we thought they were armed!
> They could have been! It's not our
> fault! They butchered hundreds of
> us like that! The courts have to
> know that already, right?

> CORPORAL KENNEDY
> Who's with me?

Sergeant Selassie walks in. An Arab soldier,
CORPORAL HASSAN KAMAR stands.

> CORPORAL KAMAR
> Isa. What did Drummond say? Will
> he help us? Isa.

> CORPORAL KENNEDY
> Damn you, Arab, stop calling him
> Isa. His name's Selassie, Ahmed
> Selassie

> CORPORAL KAMAR
> He saved my sand nigger ass twenty
> times. He's Isa to me.

> CORPORAL KENNEDY
> That's sacrilegious, man. Isa's
> Jesus in Arabic! Goddamn you!
> I told you a thousand times!

                    CORPORAL KAMAR
          Jesus is my guy, too. He's number
          two after Muhammad.

                    CORPORAL KENNEDY
          Well, he's number one to me!

                    CORPORAL CLARK
          Leave it alone, Kennedy.

Kennedy reluctantly listens to his friend.

                    CORPORAL KAMAR
          Isa. Will they cut us a deal? Will
          the Army back us?

Sgt. Ahmed Selassie stares at Kamar and then looks
down.

                    CORPORAL KENNEDY
          Jesus, I fucking told you! The
          Army's gonna turn their backs on
          us and watch them hang us out to
          dry.

                    CORPORAL KAMAR
          Isa?

                    SGT. AHMED SELASSIE
          If we admit to killing those
          women, they might go easy on us.

                    CORPORAL KENNEDY
          No, fuck that!

                    CORPORAL HARMS
          Well wait, what's "easy"?

Ahmed finds it hard to respond.

CORPORAL CLARK
Easy means having to fight every
day. Except you won't be fighting
the sand niggers.

CORPORAL KENNEDY
Yeah, fighting to keep American
dick out of your ass in prison.

CORPORAL GALLO
Seems like we're already doing
that right here in Iraq. Except
for you, Harms, you're not fighting
it too hard, are you?

Harms charges Gallo. A table is knocked over; an
ashtray falls to the ground and cracks. Clark blocks
Harms and pushes him back.

CORPORAL HARMS
Fuck you, Gallo! This is your
fucking fault!

Gallo stands for confrontation.

CORPORAL HARMS
You fired the first fucking shot!
I saw you, you fucking prick!

Gallo charges at Harms. Harms comes forward again
and Clark pushes him harder. Harms falls. Kennedy
grabs Gallo and holds him back.

CORPORAL HOLT
We were all fucking there! We all
did it! It doesn't matter who fired
first, they're not going to fucking
care. (quieter) Nobody cares.

Corporal Holt sits down in a trance. Kennedy and
Clark are forcing Harms and Gallo to calm down.

CORPORAL KAMAR
We didn't all do it. Cowdar didn't
fire a shot . . . and Isa.

Heavy breathing and thinking fill the silent room.

SGT. AHMED SELASSIE
We have to change our situation.

EXT. IRAQ MILITARY POLICE BARRACKS DARK

SUMMER 2010

PROTECTIVE CUSTODY

A man's shadow is approaching the barracks with a
gun in his hand. He approaches the soldier guarding the entrance.

SHADOW
Soldier, put that rifle down. I'm
not here for you.

The soldier puts the rifle down. The shadow takes
cuffs out. He cuffs the soldier to an iron pole. He
takes tape from his pocket and puts it across the
soldier's mouth.

SHADOW
Stay cool and stay alive.

The soldier nods. The shadow quietly opens the door
and tiptoes in. There's a glaring cigarette in the
room. There's some noise, and the cigarette rises
with the shadow of the man who's smoking it.

SHADOW
Corporal Cowdar?

COWDAR's shadow flicks the cigarette away and
moves onto the ground. Selassie's shadow moves in

his direction. Headlights from a passing vehicle reveal the shadow holding the man face down by the hair.

THE FACE OF SGT. AHMED SELASSIE

> SGT. AHMED SELASSIE (SHADOW)
> You will die so that others can
> live. Make your peace and prepare
> to meet your Maker.

Two shots are heard. Cowdar's head thumps on the floor. Light from a passing vehicle shows flowing blood.

TEN YEARS LATER 2020 FADE TO:

INT. OFFICES OF GENT AMERICA MEDIA, PRESENT FRIDAY EVENING

THE SIGN "GAM" IN A STEEL AND GLASS RECEPTION AREA. AN OFFICE.

A party is going on. People are standing with drinks in their hands, talking and laughing. Waiters with white vests and gloves are holding appetizer trays.

A blonde man in his 30s, bob herman, quietly sitting alone

Mark koss, a 70-year-old man with bushy mustache and

Bifocals lowers a pipe from his mouth.

> MARK KOSS
> I own this place and I say when
> it's time . . .

From behind Koss a 60ish, burly, gray-haired TED BASLE arrives and whispers in Koss's ear.

Koss listens intently, then appears surprised. Koss whispers something into Ted's ear. Ted nods and moves away.

Bob Herman watches the Koss-Ted communication. Koss regains his composure.

> MARK KOSS (CONT'D)
> Yes . . . and when I say it's time
> to eat.

Koss glares at the guests. One by one they begin to laugh. When the majority are laughing Koss speaks.

> MARK KOSS (CONT'D)
> It's time to eat!

Everyone laughs again. The group files into two glass doors.

INT. CONFERENCE ROOM OF GENT AMERICA MEDIA SHORTLY AFTER

About fifty people are seated at conference table and scattered smaller tables. Waiters are serving club sandwiches. An attractive, older redheaded woman, gael, and pretty younger blonde woman, Jennifer, are conversing. Bob herman is to the left of the redhead.

> JENNIFER
> (laughing) Gael, you're crazy.

> GAEL
> He almost faints with all that blood
> rushing to fill that thing! It's a
> pleasure that I'll never get the
> privilege to experience . . . that's
> what's crazy.

Jennifer notices Bob next to Gael, eavesdropping.

                    JENNIFER
          Hi Bob.

Gael turns her head into Bob Herman's gaze. She
leans in closer to him and whispers. . . .

                    GAEL
          Gay men. They're hung, you know?
          (whispered) Penis enlargers.

                    BOB HERMAN
          Yes . . . No! I mean I don't know.
          Not personally. I've never . . .
          I don't know. . .

                    GAEL
          Oh? Well if you decide to broaden
          your horizons, let me know. I like
          to watch.

Gael winks at Bob. Bob looks away, embarrassed.
Gael looks to a not-amused Jennifer and laughs. The
laugh trails off to a truly disappointed expression
on Gael.

                    GAEL (CONT'D)
          Men, they've become such stumbling
          wusses.

Mark Koss has heard their conversation from across
the table and stands.

                    MARK KOSS
          Gael, leave that young rooster be.
          He's turned corporate sales
          around. A toast to Bob.

Everyone looks at Bob and raises their glasses.

                    BOB HERMAN
          No . . . no Sir. That's Bob
          Phillips. . . . I'm Bob Herman.
          I'm the Special Projects Manager.

                    MARK KOSS
          Yes, of course you are.

Everyone tentatively drinks to an uncomfortable
silence.

                 MARK KOSS (CONT'D)
          Well eat and drink up, this
          party's costing me a fortune.

Everyone laughs on cue. Bob tightly grins and sips
his drink. The party billows out around Bob until
he is no longer in sight.

INT. EMPTY BUS LATER THAT EVENING

Bob drops change into the change box and heads
back. Vagrant types pepper the seats.

A brown bag wrapped with rubber bands sits in an
empty seat. It's torn open at the top from wear.
Papers can be seen inside.

Bob sits and watches the world outside the window.

                    HOMELESS MAN
          Do you want to help a brother?

                    BOB HERMAN
          What?

                    HOMELESS MAN
          Do you want to help a brother?

                    BOB HERMAN
          Uh, I don't know . . . I
          mean . . . what do you mean?

                    HOMELESS MAN
What do you mean what do I mean,
man? Do you want to help a brother
or not?

                    BOB HERMAN
I'm not sure what . . . do you
mean money?

                    HOMELESS MAN
Oh man . . . you got a dollar?

                    BOB HERMAN
Yes, but I . . .

The two look at each other in silence. Bob averts
his eyes first.

                    HOMELESS MAN
You mean yes you got a dollar
but no you don't want to help a
brother. . . . Man, you wishy-
washy.

Bob looks at his feet as the bus stops. When he
looks up, the man is getting off the bus. Bob
glances over at the brown package. He loosens his
tie and faces the brown bag. He looks away. He
looks back. He looks to the driver, who is oblivious to him. He looks out the window again, pauses,
and looks back at the bag.

INT. BOB'S STUDIO APARTMENT SHORTLY AFTER.

HIS JACKET, TIE, AND SHIRT CREATE A TRAIL FROM THE
FRONT DOOR TO THE BEDROOM.

BEDROOM

TINY, CLUTTERED. THE UNMADE BED TAKES UP ALMOST ALL
OF THE AVAILABLE SPACE.

Bob's on the bed, a cat on his bare chest. The brown bag is open on the bedside table revealing pages of a manuscript.

He's reading. The cat licks his face. His eyes turn from wonderment to frustration. He tosses the pages on the floor and pushes the rest of the manuscript off the bed, frightening the cat away. He shuts off the light and turns on his side.

> BOB HERMAN
> Goddamn good writers.

INT. OFFICES OF GAM NEXT DAY

Bob's office is tiny and neat.

He's at his desk nibbling on a carrot, staring sideways at a floppy disk labeled "Bob's Stories."

People are filing out of the office. A graying 45-year-old man pops his head into Bob's office.

> LOU MELL
> Lunch, Bobby . . . ? Bob Herman,
> earth to Bob . . . Herman!

> BOB HERMAN
> (startled) Sorry . . . What?

> LOU MELL
> Come on Bob, why don't you come to
> lunch anymore?

> BOB HERMAN
> No thanks, I'm good.

> LOU MELL
> Bob, I want to ask you a question,
> buddy.

                    BOB HERMAN
          Sure, Lou.

                    LOU MELL
          You're not jealous because I got
          picked for editing, are you?

PAUSE.

                    BOB HERMAN
          No, no of course not, Lou. You
          deserved it more than me.

Bob forces a smile.

                    LOU MELL
          Good to hear, good to
          hear . . . and you're right. Well,
          enjoy your carrot.

Lou turns to leave then stops.

                    LOU MELL
          How's your writing going? Got
          anything for the new editor to
          edit yet?

                    BOB HERMAN
          I'm working on it.

                    LOU MELL
          Good to hear, good to hear. What's
          it about?

Lou perches himself on bob's desk, towering over
him.

                    BOB HERMAN
          Oh, well . . . you know the
          usual . . . stuff.

                    LOU MELL
Must be good. Can I see some of
it?

                    BOB HERMAN
No, it's not ready and I may never
show it to anyone . . . the best
manuscripts never get read. . . .

                    LOU MELL
Listen Bob, you win some, you lose
some. I'm sure Koss will give you
another chance at being published.
Dickens tried a hundred times
before someone published him. I
mean, you've been working on stuff
for years. You must have something
worth reading.

                    BOB HERMAN
Yeah.

                    LOU MELL
All right, have a good lunch,
buddy. And don't worry . . . I
saw Koss read your last story. He
threw it in the trash after less
than a minute. Can't go anywhere
but up, right?

                    BOB HERMAN
Right, thanks. Have a good lunch.

Bob gives the finger to Lou's back. The phone rings,
Bob answers it.

                    BOB HERMAN
Bob Herman, Project Manager.

Out of the corner of Bob's eye, he notices Ted Basle
slipping into another colleague's office.

INT. CROWDED BUS A FEW EVENINGS LATER

Bob is reading the manuscript.

>   BOB HERMAN
>   This should be published.

LUCIA is standing behind him: petite, mulatto,
beautiful.

>   LUCIA
>   A writer, huh?

Bob jerks. The pages fall to the ground. Together
they gather the pieces. Lucia starts to read a line
from the manuscript.

>   LUCIA (CONT'D)
>   "We can never be truly happy until
>   we've been truly sad."

They look up at each other and smile.

>   LUCIA (CONT'D)
>   Sounds like a gold mine.

>   BOB HERMAN
>   Yeah, no kidding.

>   LUCIA
>   Oh, modest, huh?

>   BOB HERMAN
>   I didn't mean . . . it's not
>   really.

>   LUCIA
>   I like confidence in a man. Hungry?

>   BOB HERMAN
>   Um, yes. Yes, I'm hungry.

INT. CHINESE RESTAURANT

Bob and Lucia are standing to leave a semi-crowded
small restaurant.

> BOB HERMAN
> Can I walk you home?

> LUCIA
> Sure.

Pause.

> LUCIA (CONT'D)
> I don't usually pick men up on the
> bus like this.

> BOB HERMAN
> Is that what you did? Pick me up?

> LUCIA
> Sort of, I guess.

> BOB HERMAN
> How is it that someone like you is
> not . . .

> LUCIA
> Not occupied? Well, my mother is
> Italian. My parents adore each
> other. I'm looking for someone
> special but there aren't a lot of
> "death do us part" guys around
> anymore.

> BOB HERMAN
> I see.

> LUCIA
> My only guy was Italian
> too. . . . But it ended sadly.

Tony. He said he'd take care of
me. What a laugh. Latin men . . .

                    BOB HERMAN
          Oh. I'm sorry.

                    LUCIA
          Don't be. He's the boxer, Tony
          Russo. . . .

Bob shakes his head.

                    LUCIA (CONT'D)
          I hate boxing. You're not a boxer,
          are you?

                    BOB HERMAN
          No, No. Too pretty for that.

                    LUCIA
          Yes, you are.

Pause.

                    BOB HERMAN
          Thanks for dinner.

                    LUCIA
          It was the least I could do after
          that mess I made on the bus.

                    BOB HERMAN
          It's okay. I enjoyed the mess.
          Anyway, next time dinner's on me.
          You choose the place.

                    LUCIA
          So, Gent America Media?
          That's a pretty big publishing
          company. . . .

                        BOB HERMAN
            You know your stuff.

                        LUCIA
            I hear things here and there. I'd
            love to read your book.

                        BOB HERMAN
            Why?

She moves in closer.

                        LUCIA
            I don't know, I guess something
            about you makes me think it would
            be good.

Bob looks at her and hesitates.

                        BOB HERMAN
            You can't . . . it's not
            done . . . it's not good.

                        LUCIA
            Oh, come on. A big company like
            that wouldn't hire a bad writer.

                        BOB HERMAN
            Actually . . .

                        LUCIA
            Is this your only copy?

Bob nods his head.

                        LUCIA (CONT'D)
            Well . . . why don't you give me
            your number? I'll call you and
            maybe I can read it at your place.

                    BOB HERMAN
        My place?

Lucia takes out a pen and paper.

                  BOB HERMAN(CONT'D)
        Uh, you want my number?

                      LUCIA
        That will suffice for now.

She hands the paper and pen to him, and he writes
down his number in small, meek digits. They walk
past a bookstore. Bob stops and stares at a sign
that shows Bob with Lucia on a billboard.

"FAMOUS AUTHOR BOB HERMAN ACCOMPANIED BY HIS BEAU-
TIFUL WIFE WILL AUTOGRAPH HIS BEST SELLER TODAY"

Lucia walks ahead.

                      LUCIA
        Bob?

                    BOB HERMAN
        Coming.

Bob smirks, shakes his head, and looks back at the
poster that is actually an ad for a series of self-
help books. TIRED OF GOING NOWHERE?

INT. BUS LATER THAT NIGHT

Bob's on the left of a sleeping drunk. The bus is
empty. He clears his throat.

                  BOB HERMAN (low)
        Excuse me. . . . Excuse me.

Bob touches the shoulder of the drunk, who slightly opens his eyes. Bob doesn't notice and looks away, turns back, and is startled.

                    DRUNK
          What do you want?

                    BOB HERMAN
          I found a brown paper bag with a
          manuscript in it. Is it yours?

                    DRUNK
          Mine. . . ? Yes, son, it's mine.

                    BOB HERMAN
          Oh, wonderful. . . . It's a
          wonderful piece. I was wondering.
          . . . if you would like to . . .
          Uh, my name's Bob, I work at a
          publishing company. I think that
          with some, just a few changes,
          the book could go places. We could
          publish it together. You could
          coauthor.

                    DRUNK
          Coauthor?

                    BOB HERMAN
          Author . . . Well, that's not
          important now. The important thing
          is that I've found you. Are you
          interested in being partners, a
          writing team?

                    DRUNK
          Sure. I think that it would be
          fun.

                    BOB HERMAN
          Do you need a place to stay?

                    DRUNK
          Truthfully. I do. Do you have fifty
          for a room?

                    BOB HERMAN
          Sure.

Bob reaches into his pocket. He hands the drunk
a business card and three twenties. Bob looks out
the window.

                    BOB HERMAN
          Ahh damn, my stop's coming. Take
          this. Call me first thing in the
          morning.

Bob smiles, turns, and turns back.

                    BOB HERMAN (CONT'D)
          What's your name?

                    DRUNK
          Name?

                    BOB HERMAN
          Yes, what is your name?

The drunk shrugs.

                    DRUNK
          Why it's Ernest.

                    BOB HERMAN
          Good. Ernest . . . Ernest what?

                    DRUNK
          Hemingway.

The drunk cracks up in laughter. Bob struggles to stand up for himself. His stop comes. The drunk leaves the bus, and Bob freezes in humiliation.

INT. BUS LATER THAT NIGHT

The bus is at a stoplight. Bob is the only passenger.

> BUS DRIVER
> Hey, I like the company, but
> you're better off going home.
> I don't get much traffic on the
> bus at this hour. Tell you what,
> I'll have lost and found give you
> a ring tomorrow. If someone's
> looking for it, they'll tell
> you. If not, after 60 days, it's
> rightfully yours. Got a card?

BOB'S EYES. He watches the stoplight turn to green.

INT. OFFICES OF GENT AMERICA MEDIA

Lou is sitting on Bob's desk, laughing. His umbrella is dripping on the floor.

> LOU MELL
> Boy oh boy, I just had to tell
> someone about her. Who'd have
> thought that a little ole editor
> could score something like that on
> a whim?

> BOB HERMAN
> Seriously, Lou. I need to make the
> right choice.

> LOU MELL
> Calm down, calm down. Give them to
> me again, I'll focus.

                    BOB HERMAN
Candidate number one has
fifteen years in CBS Corporate
Headquarters.

                    LOU MELL
Mm Hm. Okay. Then . . .

                    BOB HERMAN
Candidate number two has a
master's in communication and has
published.

Lou nods his head approvingly.

                BOB HERMAN (CONT'D)
Candidate number three has great
references, she'll work for 20
percent less than the other two.

                    LOU MELL
Who'd you say this was for?

                    BOB HERMAN
Marketing, Dan and Scott.

                    LOU MELL
Well, that's easy then.

Bob smiles.

                LOU MELL (CONT'D)
Pick the one with the biggest
tits.

Jennifer interrupts them.

                    JENNIFER
Bob, got the bus company on
line 4.

                    BOB HERMAN
          The bus company? Oh. Thanks Lou.

Lou winks.

                     LOU MELL
          Anytime. Bus company? You know,
          Bob, the bus doesn't give frequent
          rider miles.

Jennifer lingers.

                    BOB HERMAN
          I got it, Jennifer.
          Thanks . . . thanks, Lou.

Jennifer leaves. Lou watches Jennifer as she leaves.

                     LOU MELL
          Have you ever poked Jennifer? You
          know she wants you.

                    BOB HERMAN
          Let me get this.

                     LOU MELL
          The bus company can wait. Have you
          done her or not?

              BOB HERMAN (impatiently)
          No.

                     LOU MELL
          Why the hell not? I'd do her.

                    BOB HERMAN
          That's the difference between you
          and me. For you they just have to
          breathe. I have to be attracted.

Lou shakes his head.

LOU MELL
When the fruit's ripe . . .

Lou walks away. Bob hesitates, then presses line 4.

BOB HERMAN
Bob Herman.

He turns and speaks into the phone more quietly.

BOB HERMAN
Yes, it was a brown paper bag
with papers of some kind in
it. . . . No one asked for it?

Jennifer walks back to his desk.

BOB HERMAN(quickly)
Okay, thanks, bye.

Hangs up.

JENNIFER
Bob . . . some of us are going for
a drink this evening after work. .
. . Would you like to join me, us?

BOB HERMAN
Tonight? No, got plans tonight.

Bob rushes out and forgets the manuscript on his
desk.

FADE TO:

INT. AIRPORT BAGHDAD US MILITARY HANGAR SUMMER 2010

Corporals Kennedy, Clark, Harms, Holt, and Kamar
are standing in the half-lit hangar.

CORPORAL HOLT
If we get caught, we're history.
This whole story will blow up in
our faces. Aiding a murderer could
carry hard time. They'll figure out
that we were all in on it when Isa
iced Cowdar. Then we're history.

CORPORAL KAMAR
If it wasn't for Isa . . .

CORPORAL KENNEDY
Isa? You damn Arab! Isa is Jesus.

CORPORAL HARMS
Yeah Isa. Think about it,
Kennedy. . . . Jesus gave His life
for his principles, equated to the
sins of others, so that they may
live. . .

CORPORAL HOLT
Then on the third day he was
resurrected. . . .

CORPORAL KAMAR
He did it for us. I'd die for him.

CORPORAL CLARK
You may have to.

CORPORAL KENNEDY
Isa.

CORPORAL CLARK
That's who he is from now
on. . . . We'll get him home.

CORPORAL HARMS
He should be here any
minute. . . .

The hangar floor is filled with black body bags.

                    CORPORAL CLARK
Empty that bag. We'll ditch the
body. That's Isa's seat home.

                    CORPORAL HOLT
How do we know they'll put him on
the plane and not to freeze to
death in the hold?

                    CORPORAL CLARK
The decomposed go in the hold.
These are the fresh arrivals.

Kennedy and Gallo unload the body from a bag. The
body is mangled. Kamar, Clark, Harms, and Holt are
with Isa.

                    CORPORAL HOLT
Stay cool, brother.

They all hug.

                    CORPORAL CLARK
Remember Gallo's cousin at JFK.
Don't budge until you hear 'And on
the third day he arose according
to the scriptures.'

Isa gets into the body bag.

                    CORPORAL CLARK (CONT'D)
And Isa . . . when it's our turn,
we'll not let you down.

                         ISA
I know.

Harms is openly crying.

                    CORPORAL HARMS
          Goodbye, brother. . . .

Harms hands Isa a water bottle and K-ration.

                 CORPORAL HARMS (CONT'D)
          Don't forget to drink, brother.

Isa nods.

                         ISA
          Goodbye.

Clark zips up the body bag.

FADE TO:

INT. IL MULINO RESTAURANT MANHATTAN PRESENT

Bob is sitting at a booth in the exclusive restaurant rolling a spoon in his hand.

He glances to the left and right. He gets up and
walks to the host. The host is looking at his reservation pad. He glances at Bob, looks down, and
then calmly looks up.

                         HOST
          Yes sir, may I help you?

                      BOB HERMAN
          Yes. Are you sure . . . I mean my
          date was supposed to be here an
          hour ago.

Bob fidgets.

                         HOST
          Sir. I assure you that there is
          no way to get by me. Your name is
          Herman isn't it?

                    BOB HERMAN
Yes. Yes it is.

                      HOST
Well Mr. Herman, just relax. As
soon as she arrives, I'll seat her.

Bob turns to leave. As he does, he spots Lucia.

LUCIA NONCHALANTLY ENTERING RESTAURANT

                    BOB HERMAN
You're late. You look beautiful.

                      LUCIA
I know. I'm sorry. I got tied up.
I was shooting some pictures for
my portfolio.

                    BOB HERMAN
Your portfolio?

                      LUCIA
Yes. I met a guy who says that I'm
a natural to be a model.

                    BOB HERMAN
Oh . . . Good . . . Let's sit
down.

They sit. Bob feels out of place in the fancy
restaurant.

                    BOB HERMAN
So you've been here before?

                      LUCIA
Here? No. It just looks so
beautiful, I've always wanted to
come. I guess I just had to wait
for the right person to bring me.

> BOB HERMAN
> I'm glad you waited.
> So . . . modeling? I thought
> you said that you worked as a
> secretary. Two jobs?

> LUCIA
> I have to look out for myself.
> I mean, who else will? Who else
> ever has?

> BOB HERMAN
> Well, there's me.

A huge, beautiful smile from Lucia.

> BOB HERMAN (CONT'D)
> Although I think that you'd make
> a beautiful model. You'd make a
> beautiful anything.

They open the menu. There are no prices listed. Bob
is obviously nervous about that.

> LUCIA
> I'm going to call you Bobby from
> now on. Would that be all right?
> Bobby?

Bob swoons.

> LUCIA (CONT'D)
> Jesus, I'm starved.

EXT. RESTAURANT

THEY'RE LEAVING THE RESTAURANT. LUCIA OVERHEARS
THE WAITER AND THE HOST COMMENTING.

> WAITER
> Don't do me any favors. He had the
> table the whole night and left me
> three dollars.

                    HOST
        Last of the big spenders.

Lucia and Bob continue to walk.

                    LUCIA
        Got any wine at home? I think now
        would be a good time to take a
        look at your book.

                 BOB HERMAN
        Uh, no. But . . .

                    LUCIA
        What is it? Don't you want to have
        me over?

                 BOB HERMAN
        Yes, it's just that . . . I don't
        know.

                    LUCIA
        I know what this is. I'm on
        to you. You're going through a
        confidence crisis. But you're
        a writer. I read it in your
        eyes the first time that I saw
        you. . . . You see Bobby, men
        never catch women that don't want
        to be caught. I want to be caught
        by a writer, a blond, handsome
        writer. Is that you, Bobby?

She moves in closer.

                 BOB HERMAN
        Yes, it is . . . I mean, yes, I am.

                    LUCIA
        Yes, you are . . . Now, let's go
        back to your place.

She kisses Bob's cheek.

EXT. BUS STOP

They stand in silence waiting for a late bus.

> LUCIA
> I'd figure a guy on the brink of
> being published by such a big
> company would at least have a car
> or an Uber account, Bobby.

> BOB HERMAN
> A car? Uber? I'm planning on
> getting one soon. All or nothing,
> that's me. I wait till I can
> have the best of something, no
> compromising.

> LUCIA
> My kind of man.

The bus pulls up, and they get in.

EXT. BOB'S APARTMENT

Lucia is already unimpressed. Bob opens the door,
lets Lucia in first, then runs to pick up the clothes
and mess. Lucia doesn't look happy.

She sits on the couch.

> LUCIA
> So, is this just your writing
> studio or . . .

> BOB HERMAN
> This? No, I mean, I like to live
> modestly.

> LUCIA
> I guess.

Bob goes into the kitchen.

                        BOB HERMAN
          So, I don't have any wine, but I've
          got some apple juice.

The cat tries to rub on Lucia's leg. She grimaces
and pushes him away. Her cell phone rings.

                         LUCIA
            Hello? Hey . . . um, no. False
            alarm. (she turns from Bob,
            whispers) Yeah, yeah, I know.

When she hangs up, Bob hands her an apple juice.
He awkwardly leans in to kiss her.

                     LUCIA (CONT'D)
          Bob. Don't.

                        BOB HERMAN
          I'm sorry. What's wrong?

He takes her hand.

                         LUCIA
            Don't do that. Bob, don't do that.

She pulls her hand back.

                        BOB HERMAN
             Lucia.

She takes a deep breath.

                         LUCIA
          Bob, that was Tony.

                        BOB HERMAN
          Tony? Your ex?

                         LUCIA
             Yeah . . .

                    BOB HERMAN
Oh? I thought . . . What did you
tell him?

                    LUCIA
You heard. I didn't tell him
anything.

                    BOB HERMAN
I thought that it was a closed
chapter?

                    LUCIA
A lost life is more like it.
I gave him everything. He was
my first, my only. . . . In the
end, he beat me and cheated
and . . . I'm just, I don't want
to be a fool again. What if you're
not what you seem? It's possible,
you know. I thought he was a good
man and he was . . .

                    BOB HERMAN
I am what you think! I am!

                    LUCIA
I'm just, I know this doesn't make
any sense to you . . . it doesn't
make any sense to me . . . maybe
I'm feeling a little emotional and
confused right now. I think
I should just go home.

She gets up and goes to the door.

                    BOB HERMAN
Wait . . .

                    LUCIA
I'm sorry, I should just go.

                    BOB HERMAN
        Why? What's wrong?

                     LUCIA
        I'll call you . . .

                    BOB HERMAN
        I love you.

The door closes on his words.

INT. OFFICES OF GENT AMERICA MEDIA MORNING

Bob slumps through the hallway to his office with
his head hung.

BOB'S OFFICE

A small crowd is at Bob's desk. Koss has pages in
his hand. He quietly passes one to Gael.

                    MARK KOSS
        Humph. I knew that this Phillips
        had something.

                     GAEL
        This is Herman. Phillips is the
        head of corporate sales.

                    MARK KOSS
        Technicalities.

Bob clears his throat. The group looks.

                    BOB HERMAN

Why are you all in my office?

                    MARK KOSS
        Herman. This is good, Herman.

Bob gently takes the papers from Mark.

                    BOB HERMAN
          It's nothing really.

                    MARK KOSS
          I like it. I like how it flows. Lou
          said you were piddling with the
          writing again, but I had no idea
          how far you've come. Still needs
          a little work, though. The voice
          isn't quite you. A bit forced.
          Needs more . . . honesty. Have an
          edited copy on my desk by next
          Monday. You got one week, Herman.
          Don't let me down.

Koss leaves. The rest follow. GAEL stops.

                    GAEL
          Hmm. You of all people. Who would
          have thought? Don't let us down,
          Bobby.

She brushes her chest against his as she leaves.

                    JENNIFER
          I'm sorry Bob, I didn't mean
          to snoop, but I saw it and was
          curious, then Gael came and one
          thing led to another . . .

BOB STARES.

                    JENNIFER (CONT'D)
          It's really good, Bob. I'm happy
          for you.

She kisses him on the cheek.

BLACKOUT

MONTAGE

BOB'S APARTMENT

Bob trying to call Lucia, no answer.

Bob going to her apartment and knocking, no answer.

The manuscript on one side of the room, Bob on the other.

Bob standing over the manuscript. Staring blankly at the manuscript. Looks at Cat.

> BOB HERMAN
> What should I do?

The cat blinks and stares at him.

> BOB HERMAN (CONT'D)
> I know, I need to find her.

Picks up manuscript.

Bob at the computer. His face changes from frustrated to happy to exhausted.

TRANSITION TO:

INT. MARK KOSS'S OFFICE

Bob is standing at Koss's desk. Koss is sitting. On his desk is a manuscript: *Standard Deviations* by Bob Herman. He gets up and walks around to the front of his desk.

> MARK KOSS
> Well son, I gave you a
> week and here it is. I like
> that . . . Bobby, it's gold.

Bob smiles and nods. Koss kisses Bob on the cheek.

                    MARK KOSS
          You've always been like a son to
          me. I knew from the moment that
          I hired you.

                    BOB HERMAN
          Gael hired me, sir.

                    MARK KOSS
          Technicalities.

Koss smiles.

                    MARK KOSS (CONT'D)
          Sit down. I'll get Arnie Schuman on
          the phone. He's the best agent in
          the country, he'll take care of you.

Bob sits. Koss takes the phone into his hands.

                    MARK KOSS
          Arnie, Mark Koss. I got one. I'll
          sponsor . . . How many bestsellers
          did Selton write this year . . . ?
          This kid will double that . . .
          Herman. Robert Herman

                    BOB HERMAN
          Bobby . . . I'd like to go by
          "Bobby."

                    MARK KOSS
          Bobby Herman. He's one of mine.

Koss sets the phone down and winks at Bobby.

                    MARK KOSS (CONT'D)
          You've arrived. You'll become a
          pillar around here. A piece of
          this place will belong to you
          someday. . . . I can feel it.

Bob stares.

All images are original paintings for *Chivalry* by Megan Euker,
Acrylic on Board, 10" x 12", 2023
Photo credit: Jay Knickerbocker

Ahmed

Abby

Ahmed's Squad

"The *rat-a-tat-tat* sound of gunfire was heard."

Bus in New York

Bob Herman

Lucia

GAM Office

Gael

Arnie Schuman

Ahmed Writing

Tony's Funeral

Ahmed (Isa)

Sister Brenda

Lucia

"The age of chivalry died when the king stopped riding out with his troops."

                    MARK KOSS
     Don't you have anything to say,
     Bobby? Anything to ask?

Ted Basle passes the doorway.

                    BOB HERMAN
     Who is that man?

Mark smiles, takes Bob by the shoulder.

                    MARK KOSS
     Do you like baseball, Bob?

                    BOB HERMAN
     Baseball?

Pause.

                    BOB HERMAN
     Well, kind of . . .

                    MARK KOSS
     Well in the old days teams didn't
     have ghezzillions to buy forty
     players for a roster. Each team
     had a guy that could do it all.
     He got the job done. . . . When
     the center fielder was having a
     bad day or the catcher or the
     shortstop . . . they called in
     the utility man. And somehow,
     someway, smoothly, not so smoothly,
     ethically, unethically he got
     the job done. Ted Basle is Gent's
     utility man. . . . He gets the
     job done. . . . Sometimes we all
     need utility men Bob. . . . The
     president of the United States has
     a whole department of them.

                    BOB HERMAN
          Never heard of them.

                    MARK KOSS
          Sure you have. . . . The CIA.

Koss winks.

                    MARK KOSS (CONT'D)
          Don't worry, Bobby, we take care
          of our own here, and if you ever
          need a utility man, it's carte
          blanche.

He reaches into his drawer and gives Ted's business
card to Bob.

                    BOB HERMAN
          Utility man.

                    MARK KOSS
          That's right. All right Bobby,
          get back to work. And start your
          next big baby. You're not a famous
          writer . . . yet.

INT. OFFICES OF GENT AMERICA MEDIA LATER, EVENING

Bob is whistling and collecting his things to go
home. Jennifer arrives.

                    JENNIFER
          Bob . . . How did it go with Koss?

                    BOB HERMAN
          He's going to publish it.

                    JENNIFER
          I'm so happy for you! Do you need
          someone to celebrate with?

>   BOB HERMAN
>   No . . . Thanks Jen. I have plans.

>   JENNIFER (quietly)
>   You're a busy guy.

Bob leaves.

INT. BUS LATER

Bob is riding. He stares at his name on the manuscript with a far-gone grin. As people walk on
the bus, Bob hides the manuscript, especially from
anyone looking homeless. His stop comes and goes,
and he continues on toward Chinatown.

EXT. LUCIA'S APARTMENT

BOB excitedly rings her buzzer. No answer. He rings
and rings and rings.

>   LUCIA
>   Bob?

Bob turns to see Lucia approaching her door with
groceries.

>   BOB HERMAN
>   Lucia! Why haven't you returned my
>   calls?

She seems harder than she was before.

>   LUCIA
>   What are you doing here?

>   BOB HERMAN
>   I've missed you so much, you look
>   beautiful. Where have you been?

Lucia looks around and pulls him in the door.

INT. LUCIA'S STUDIO APARTMENT

A tiny gypsy-like space full of trinkets: beads
hanging from the ceiling separating the living
space. The bed is a mattress on the floor surrounded
by white hanging beads.

Bob takes some strands of beads in his hands.

> BOB HERMAN
> These aren't plastic. . . . They're
> stones.

> LUCIA
> Of course they're not plastic.
> Won't find anything plastic here
> accept for maybe the liner bag of
> the garbage.

> BOB HERMAN
> They're some kind of mineral
> stone.

> LUCIA
> That's right, Bobby. They're
> Brazilian.

> BOB HERMAN
> Wow.

Lucia is unpacking her groceries. Bob walks to a
shelf on the right side of the bed. There are jade
pieces of a Buddha and elephants. There's a piece
of paper next to them.

CHRISTIES AUCTION CERTIFICATE OF AUTHENTICITY

Bob looks to the right and notices cocaine dust and
a cutter on a small mirror. Lucia is putting away
groceries at a leisurely pace. It seems as if she's
done this speech a thousand times:

                    LUCIA
Bob, you don't know me. You don't
know who I am, what I've done.

                  BOB HERMAN
Stop it. Stop it. Damn. . . .
I don't care. I know you. I don't
care. Can't we start fresh?

                    LUCIA
A fresh start for a coke fiend?

Bob hesitates.

                  BOB HERMAN
        Yes.

                    LUCIA
A fresh start from murder? From
murdering a baby?

                  BOB HERMAN
What? What baby?

                    LUCIA

        Tony's . . . and mine.

                  BOB HERMAN
        What!

                    LUCIA
I was seven months
pregnant. . . . Too late for an
abortion. Tony took me to the
gym locker room. His doctor was
waiting. They sedated me. They
forced the baby to be born and
they left it to die. Die there in
the locker room! I woke and there
it was. Red and tiny and blue and
beautiful. It was still faintly

breathing. I thought I was alone.
I tried to take it and run to a
hospital. Tony's doctor blocked
me. The baby fell. It moved. The
doctor injected a syringe into its
chest. The baby jerked. . . .

> BOB HERMAN
> And what did they do with it?

> LUCIA
> Him! Him! It was a beautiful boy!
> *Don't call him an it*! . . . They
> took him into the bathroom. I
> heard the toilet flush, once and
> twice and again and . . . leave me
> alone, Bobby. I ruin everything
> I touch.

She takes his face in her hands, walks him toward
the door.

> LUCIA (CONT'D)
> Oh Bobby, I want to be with
> you, I just wish he were
> dead! I know that's awful, but
> sometimes I think it's the only
> way. . . . Leave me alone. Don't
> call me. Don't think about me. It's
> for your own good. . . . Do you
> understand? He won't let us and
> I don't want to ruin you. . . . Do
> you want to be ruined? Maybe call
> me sometime down the road, Bobby.

She shuts the door leaving him standing in the
hallway. He knocks on the door. Nothing.

> BOB (meekly)
> Lucia?

LUCIA on the inside takes the jade piece lovingly in her hands. She places it besides several other jade pieces.

> BOB HERMAN (whispered)
> But Lucia . . .

With palms flat, Bob gently bumps his forehead against the door. He hesitates, turns, and slowly walks away.

EXT. STREET

BOB walks down the street back to the bus stop.

A dark-skinned man in his 40s, ISA, is watching him. A squad car is parked up the street. The driver, Clark, is a white, stubby 50ish male with red hair, smoking a cigar, and passenger Kennedy is a 50ish white male. They're watching both Isa and Bob.

> DETECTIVE KENNEDY
> Anything to worry about?

> DETECTIVE CLARK
> I hope not. If Isa's ever
> discovered we're all as good as
> gone. The whole cover-up will be
> on our laps.

> DETECTIVE KENNEDY
> We'll do a check on this guy just
> to be safe. . . . And if there's a
> problem, remember Isa's command.
> He iced COWDAR so all of us could
> live. If they get onto Isa, there's
> closure.

> DETECTIVE CLARK
> You mean we ice Isa.

Clark flicks his cigar out the window at a street sign.

CIGAR HITS SIGN DEAD CENTER

                    DETECTIVE CLARK
          I still got it.

Squad car heads in Bob's direction.

INT. BOB HERMAN'S APARTMENT THAT EVENING

Bob is pacing, disheveled, looking at the phone. He
sits on the edge of the bed with Ted Basle's card
in his hand. He picks it up and dials.

SPLIT SCENE. BOB IN HIS BED, TED IN A ROBE IN HIS
DEN.

                    TED BASLE
          Hey ya Bobby!

                    BOB HERMAN
          Uhuh, I'm sorry, wrong number.

He hangs up. The phone rings.

                    BOB HERMAN
          Hello? Oh hi, Dad . . . good,
          good . . . I had called to tell
          you that I'm finally going to be
          published . . . yep . . . Dad, I
          know that I owe you lots . . . as
          soon as the royalty check comes,
          I'll get it to you . . . Yes, I'm
          definitely getting published . . . a
          lot, I don't remember the exact
          amount . . . well, because I have
          an agent that takes care of those
          details . . . no, I won't gamble
          it . . . well, because I didn't

> want to jinx it . . . I haven't
> gambled for a while now . . . do
> you want a copy . . . ?
> sort of, a few hundred pages,
> I guess . . . yeah I could give
> you a summary . . .
> what about Mom . . . ? uhhuh
> . . . uhhuh . . . Yeah
> okay . . . bye.

Dial tone. Bob's father has hung up.

                    BOB HERMAN
          Love you.

FADE TO: MONTHS LATER

MONTAGE: RAVES OF *STANDARD DEVIATIONS*, THE BOOK IS
EVERYWHERE, IN EVERYONE'S HANDS.

INT. FOUR SEASONS WEEKS LATER

SIGN: ROBERT HERMAN'S AUTOGRAPHING PARTY

Bob's seated in front of a stack of books. The line
of people waiting for an autograph does not seem
to be cheering him up. Bob's picture is on the back
cover.

A 60ish man with white kinky hair, Arnie, walks
from behind and rests his hand on Bob's shoulder.

                    ARNIE SCHUMAN
          The *Times* says that you're the find
          of the century.

Bob grooms his hair back, smiles, turns, and opens
a book, pen in hand. Mark Koss approaches, smacking
him on the back.

>   MARK KOSS
>   Hi Bobby my boy. I'm waiting for
>   your second jewel. Is it coming?

Bob smiles.

>   BOB HERMAN
>   Yes, Sir. Just polishing it up.

>   MARK KOSS
>   Looking forward to it, kid.

BOB'S HAND SIGNING HIS NAME. PULL OUT TO REVEAL BOB
SIGNING HIS NAME ON A CHECK

INT. BOB'S APARTMENT

>   BOB HERMAN
>   And that takes care of that.

Cat hops on desk. The computer is on, screen is
blank.

>   BOB HERMAN
>   No more credit collector calls.
>   Nothing but blue skies ahead. All
>   I have to do is write another
>   amazing book.

He stares at blank screen, hesitates, and writes a
few lines.

He takes a deep breath.

>   BOB HERMAN (CONT'D)
>   It's okay. I have plenty of time.
>   Anyway, I think I deserve a little
>   celebration.

INT. RACE TRACK

Bob's standing with two guys his age. In the background the announcer is calling the race.

> ANNOUNCER
> And it's Blue Bonnet from
> behind . . . Blue Bonnet *by a*
> *nose* . . . hold your tickets for
> the final.

Bob looks down at his tickets.

> CHUCK
> You may have published a
> bestseller but your luck hasn't
> changed here . . .

> BO
> You must have lost twenty grand.

> BOB HERMAN
> I wish it was only twenty.

FADE TO:

INT. MARK KOSS'S OFFICE WEEKS LATER

Koss is on the phone.

> MARK KOSS
> Yeah, Arnie, I'll talk to
> him . . .

Mark Koss firmly hits the intercom.

> MARK KOSS (CONT'D)
> Jennifer, did you tell Bob Herman
> that I wanted him?

> JENNIFER
> Yes sir.

MARK KOSS
Well, go and get him. Now!

INT. MARK KOSS'S OFFICE SHORTLY AFTER

Mark is seated. Bob is sitting on the desk.

BOB HERMAN
Well, you see, writing books is
not like printing newspapers. I've
started, like, five more.

MARK KOSS
Bob, you hit the iron when it's
hot. Tomorrow the schleps that
bought your first book will forget
your name. Do you know what it
cost me to get you on the *New York
Times* bestseller list? Bring me
what you got. *I'll get a ghost.*

BOB HERMAN
But . . .

MARK KOSS
Bob, this firm stuck its neck out
to help you. . . . Every Gent
shareholder is counting on you.
It means a lot to the bottom
line. . . . Do you like being a
writer, Bobby?

BOB HERMAN
Yes. . . . Yes, I do.

MARK KOSS
Bring me what you got.

Bob nods.

MARK KOSS
Good boy, Bobby.

Bob gets up and leaves.

INT. BUS LATER THAT EVENING

BOB looks up and down the aisle. He notices a stack of newspapers. He shuffles through them.

INT. BOB'S APARTMENT

Bob, sitting with his back to us, runs his fingers through his hair. He punches the tab key with his finger. He punches it harder and harder. Finally he shuts the computer off.

Suddenly he stands. An idea. He goes to file cabinet and pulls out an old manuscript.

INT. MARK KOSS'S OFFICE NEXT DAY

Koss is on the phone, holding the old manuscript.

>   MARK KOSS
>   Arnie. I can't figure it out. It's
>   all garbage. Just garbage. I mean
>   it's infantile. . . . Yes it came
>   from Herman!

INT. OFFICES OF GENT AMERICA MEDIA FRIDAY AFTERNOON

Gael and Jennifer are by the espresso machine.

>   GAEL
>   I think Herman bought *Standard
>   Deviations*.

>   JENNIFER
>   What? Uh-uh, Bob wouldn't buy a
>   manuscript. It's not possible.

>   GAEL
>   Not possible? Where have you
>   been? They all buy scripts. It's

the author's *name* that sells the
book, not the content. Besides,
I've seen other things that he's
written. He doesn't have it.

                    JENNIFER
          That's loathsome. . .

Bob's entering. Gael's leaving still looking at
Jennifer.

                      GAEL
          Anyway, he'd better buy or find or
          write something soon if he wants
          to stay in this office. Koss didn't
          like him from the start. . . .

Gael impudently looks at Bob and walks out. Bob
pours a cup of coffee. There's a moment of silence.

                    JENNIFER
          Bob, did you write *Standard
          Deviations*?

                    BOB HERMAN
          What kind of a question is that?

                    JENNIFER
          There are rumors. . . . Are you
          the author?

                    BOB HERMAN
          Jennifer. I've written another one
          that will convince them all. Koss
          is reading it right now.

Jennifer smiles.

                    JENNIFER
          Good, Bob.

Bob pours some of the scalding cup of liquid into his mouth. He stands there with his mouth half open sucking air in.

Koss comes in.

                    KOSS
          Excuse us, Jennifer.

Jennifer leaves.

                    MARK KOSS
          Bobby, what are you trying to
          pull? First you give me a piece
          of gold and then you give me a
          piece of shit. Look, I understand
          that the second novel is harder
          than the first, but you've got to
          rise to your potential man. Do you
          understand me?

Bob nods.

                    MARK KOSS
          We want you to do well. You want
          you to do well. Do it.

Mark leaves Bob, who uncomfortably swallows the hot brew.

EXT. STREET LATER

That evening, dark and drizzly.

Bob is walking. A bus is passing. Lucia's on the bus.

                    BOB HERMAN
          Lucia! Lucia!

Bob runs after the bus. He tires. Isa walks out of the shadows behind Bob. Isa looks at Lucia. She looks back. He looks at Bob, who wipes his mouth and crouches down to catch his breath. Bob looks at Isa.

> BOB HERMAN
> Do you want something?

Isa smiles.

> ISA
> We all want something.

Bob looks around. The street is empty.

> BOB HERMAN
> Where did you come from?

> ISA
> Come from?

> BOB HERMAN
> Yes. Where did you come from?

> ISA
> Well my people were from Ethiopia.
> I grew up here. My family is
> related to Haile Selassie . . . .

> BOB HERMAN
> Oh . . . is he some sort of black
> hero?

> ISA
> Black? I'm not much darker than
> you. Ethiopians are African, Arab,
> and Asian. People who categorize
> others as Crayola colors are
> infantile. Don't you think?

                    BOB HERMAN
          Oh? Think? You're here now, I
          mean in this country. That pretty
          much makes you black. If you're
          interested in the truth.

                      ISA
          Only when we reside with the truth
          can we understand when we are
          living a lie.

                    BOB HERMAN
          OK, have a good night.

Bob starts to walk away.

                      ISA
          What do you want with the girl on
          the bus?

Bob stops. His eyes quiz Isa.

                      ISA
          She's certainly a beautiful woman.

                    BOB HERMAN
          Yes. Yes. I have to go now.

Isa smiles.

                      ISA

          In a hurry?

                    BOB HERMAN
          Look . . . I don't know you nor do
          I . . .

                      ISA
          Yes . . . But someday I'll ask you
          to do something for me.

Isa turns to leave. He crosses the street. A brown bag with rubber bands around it is in Isa's arm. A car passes, blocking the street.

                    BOB HERMAN
          Wait! Wait!

Isa's gone. Bob runs down the street and into a dead-end alley.

                    BOB HERMAN
          No! Where did you go? Please!

He catches his breath. Newspapers move. and two homeless people rise from the rubble.

                    HOMELESS MAN
          Hey, I'm right here. How's about
          helping me out with some change?

                    HOMELESS MAN 2
          I'm right here, help me out too.

Bob backs out of the alleyway and quickly turns the corner nervously looking back. Two men approach him from behind. Bob ducks into a bar.

INT. BINO'S

Bob enters the small, dimly lit bar.

Hanging autographed photos of fighters line the wall, and the last one is signed Tony Russo. Bob looks closely at the photo, then around. A few guys sit at the end. They do not look like Tony. Bob steps to the bar and orders.

                    BOB HERMAN
          Double shot of Chivas.

The bartender silently serves him.

                    BOB HERMAN
          Another, please.

                    BARTENDER
          What, are you in a race?

Bob tightly smiles.

                    BOB HERMAN
          Please just pour me another.

LATER

Bob is heading back from the bathroom. He's unsteady.

                    BARTENDER
          Hey Tony! What's up, my guy?

Bob focuses.

THE PICTURE OF TONY RUSSO, TONY'S FACE

Bob moves back to his spot as the bartender approaches.

                    BARTENDER
          Refill?

Bob looks over at Tony.

                    BARTENDER
          Refill?

                    BOB HERMAN
          Yeah. Yeah man, refill.

The bartender pours the drink. Bob downs it. The bartender begins to walk away.

                    BOB HERMAN
          Wait. Is that Tony Russo?

The bartender stares.

                         BARTENDER
          Why? He go with your girl or
          something? If he did I don't want
          no trouble here. I'll lose my
          license.

                         BOB HERMAN
          Another please.

                         BARTENDER
          Hey, it's your stomach.

The bartender pours a drink. Bob downs it, nervously pushes his hand into his pocket, and walks
toward Tony.

                         BARTENDER
          Hey Tony, this guy . . . Tony!

Tony looks at bartender then Bob.

BOB'S HAND IN HIS POCKET
SHAKING AND POINTED TOWARD TONY

                         TONY
          Madonna!

Tony raises his hands.

                         TONY (CONT'D)
          Whatever you got I don't want any
          of it. I ain't bothering nobody.

Bob seems momentarily confused, looks from side to
side, and nervously pushes his hand further into
his pocket.

                         TONY
          Please. Please. If Mikey O. sent
          you, I can fix everything. I swear.

Bob jerks his head to grab composure. He hesitates.

                    BOB HERMAN
        I'm a friend of Lucia.

                      TONY
        Oh, yeah, Lucia.

                    BOB HERMAN
        Leave her in peace. Got it?

                      TONY
        In peace. I got it.

                    BOB HERMAN
        If you don't, I'll be back to
        straighten things out.

                      TONY
        Sure. Sure, in peace, don't worry.

Bob glances down at his jacket pocket and pushes
his hand in toward Tony's gut.

                    BOB HERMAN
        You better get it . . . or you'll
        really get it.

Bob lowers his arm and walks out of the bar.

                    BARTENDER
        Who was that guy, Tony?

                      TONY
        I don't know, but he had me
        spooked.

EXT. BINO'S

Bob trots outside and down the street. He stops,
gasping for breath, glances back defiantly at Bino's.
No one is outside.

His hand comes out of his pocket revealing a cell phone. He walks steadily to the bus stop and catches a bus just in time.

INT. BUS

Seated, Bob relaxes, smiles, then chuckles out loud.

INT. LUCIA'S APARTMENT LATER

An elderly well-groomed man heads out of Lucia's apartment. Tony passes him. The man looks away.

> TONY
> I thought you said you dropped that dirtbag.

> LUCIA
> Which one?

> TONY
> I'm not the one you play with, Lucia. Some young yuppie-looking blond guy.

> LUCIA
> Oh, I'm sorry, baby. You mean the wannabe writer. I did drop him.

> TONY
> Well he just came into Bino's and threatened me with a gun.

> LUCIA (amused)
> *What?*

Lucia laughs.

                    TONY
          Oh is that funny?

                    LUCIA
          He wouldn't hurt a fly, couldn't
          hurt a fly. (sort of disappointed)

                    TONY
          Why's he still sniffing around here
          if he ain't paying no bills here?

                    LUCIA
          Probably the same reason you are.

He presses her up against the wall. He reaches his
hand down to her crotch.

                    TONY
          This is why I'm here. And I'm the
          only one who gets it for free. You
          know the rules. If you can't get
          nothing from them, you dump 'em.
          And don't get me angry or . . .

                    LUCIA (CHOKING)
          He just don't understand.

                    TONY
          Do you want me to explain it to
          him?

                    LUCIA (RECOVERING)
          No, Tony. . . . He thinks that I'm
          a nice girl.

                    TONY
          You are a nice girl, baby. You're
          my nice girl. You ain't goin' sweet
          on him, are you?

Lucia is still looking away.

                              TONY
                   Not going soft, are you?

Tony sees:

PICTURE OF BOB'S PHOTO ON HIS BOOK ON HER DESK

                              TONY
                   I thought you said he didn't have
                   nothin'? You're not falling for
                   this fag, are you?

                              LUCIA
                   I was trying to tell you, that
                   book is a bestseller.

                              TONY
                   I don't believe it. That guy?

                              LUCIA
                   I know. Did you bring my candy?

Tony kisses her hard then picks her up against the
wall wrapping her legs around himself.

                              TONY
                   We're a team, baby, don't forget
                   it.

CAMERA FOCUSES ON A PICTURE OF THE BLESSED MOTHER
CRYING Noise and grunting as they begin to make
love.

FADE TO:

BOB'S SLEEPING FACE

INT. BOB'S APARTMENT LATER THAT NIGHT

Bob's sleeping face up, holding the book. There's
a knock.

Someone's at the door. Bob jerks, looks at the digital clock. 4:03.

Bob walks to the door. Another loud knock. He looks
through the peephole, but it's covered.

Bob opens the door, leaving the chain latched.

> BOB HERMAN
> Gael?

> GAEL
> I want to talk.

> BOB HERMAN
> At four a.m.?

> GAEL
> I do some of my best talking in
> the morning. Let me in.

> BOB HERMAN
> Are you on something?

> GAEL
> If so, all the better for you.

> BOB HERMAN
> I'm not interested, Gael.

He closes the door. She stops it with her hand.

> GAEL
> Is this the way you treat your
> partner?

> BOB HERMAN
> Partner?

                    GAEL
I know you didn't write *Standard
Deviations*. . . . You don't even
know what "standard deviations"
means.

He tries to close the door, but she stops it.

                    GAEL
You've produced only crap since
you plagiarized the book, I take
it that you have trouble.

                 BOB HERMAN
How are you so sure?

                    GAEL
Call it woman's intuition. Point
is, I can help you.

Gael gestures to the chain on the door. Bob opens,
Gael walks in and closes door.

                 BOB HERMAN
Make it fast.

Gael lights a cigarette.

                 BOB HERMAN
Don't smoke. . . . Please don't
smoke.

Gael blows a cloud of smoke in his face.

                    GAEL
It's all too much for you, Bobby.
Your life needs a woman's touch.
Without it, you'll spiral down and
crash. I'm here to catch you. I
knew from the beginning that you

                    didn't write that book. I'll help
                    you. . . . And you'll help me.

                              BOB HERMAN
                    How will you help me?

                                GAEL
                    I'll be your manager.

                              BOB HERMAN
                    Koss got me a manager, Schuman.

                                GAEL
                    Schuman's a literary agent. You
                    need a situations manager, someone
                    to hold you on top. And you'll pay
                    support. It will be the best move
                    you ever made.

Bob gets an ashtray and places it on a chair for
Gael.

                           GAEL (CONT'D)
                    That's it, Bobby. . . . Koss will
                    be happy about the arrangement.
                    I know the ropes. He knows
                    that he can always count on
                    me to bring home the victory.
                    After all, we all want the same
                    thing. . . . Your success.

                              BOB HERMAN
                    Get real, Gael.

                                GAEL
                    Oh I'm for real, Bob.

Gael gently grabs his shoulder and reaches her
right hand down to her purse. She pulls out a small
pistol.

                    BOB HERMAN
          Jesus! Is that real?!

                    GAEL
          Did you see me light my cigarette
          with it? Get into the bedroom,
          Bob. If we're going to be
          partners, you've got to get used
          to taking orders.

Bob looks at the gun.

                    BOB HERMAN
          Are you crazy?

                    GAEL
          No, but I'm very, very resourceful.
          You'll come to appreciate that
          part of me. . . . Move.

Bob turns and goes into the bedroom. Gael follows
him.

FADE TO:

DIGITAL CLOCK 5:30

Grunting coming from the bedroom. Gael rolls off
of Bob.

                    GAEL
          To be honest, I expected less.

                    BOB HERMAN
          Me too.

                    GAEL
          So what is it? You paid some guy
          for his book. Pay him for another.

Bob hesitates.

                    GAEL
        Spill it.

                    BOB HERMAN
        It goes like this . . .

FADE TO:

INT. HALL OUTSIDE OF BOB'S APARTMENT LATER THAT
MORNING

Gael closes the door behind her, turns, and is face-
to-face with Lucia. Lucia is noticeably stunned.

                    GAEL
        Don't expect a lot. He's probably a
        little tired.

Gael opens the door for Lucia, revealing Bob half-
dressed.

                    BOB HERMAN
        Gael, you forgot your . . .

Bob's eyes meet Lucia's. Lucia runs down the hall
stairs.

                    BOB HERMAN
        Lucia!

Bob's holding a silver lighter in his hand. Gael
grabs it.

                    GAEL
        It really wasn't important.
        I only smoke before I fornicate.
        She's cute, partner, real
        cute . . . don't make Mamma
        jealous.

Bob runs down the stairs and out into the street,
just missing Lucia driving off in a cab.

                        BOB HERMAN
          Shit.

GAEL EXITS IN THE BACKGROUND.

INT. CAB

The driver is a middle-aged black man.

                        CABDRIVER
          You look distressed, can I do
          anything for you?

                        LUCIA
          Yes, keep your eyes on the road.

                        CABDRIVER
          That guy who came out after
          you . . . is that your man?

Lucia stares out the window.

                        LUCIA
          I don't know what he
          is. . . . I don't know who I am.
          I don't know what I want. . . .
          I don't know why I went there.

                        CABDRIVER
          Seems to me you want him. . . .

The cab pulls in front of Lucia's place. She rummages through her purse; it's full of money.

                        LUCIA
          I forgot my wallet. How much is
          it?

                        CABDRIVER
          It's $19.50.

Lucia smiles.

                    LUCIA
        I'll run up to the apartment, or
        would you like to have me in your
        debt?

The cabdriver smiles.

                    CABDRIVER
        Mmmm. Mmm. I'd love to have you in
        my debt.

The cabdriver reaches to the backseat and hands a
card to Lucy.

                    CABDRIVER
        This is my number. I'll be your
        personal chauffeur.

Lucia takes the card and smiles.

                    LUCIA
        Oh I like that idea. I'll call.

Lucia exits and walks up to her building. The cab
pulls away.

INT. OFFICES OF GENT AMERICA MEDIA MONDAY MORNING

BOB is on the phone listening to LUCIA'S answering
machine.

                    BOB HERMAN
        Lucia, I'm so sorry. I don't know
        how many times I need to tell
        your answering machine. Please,
        I have to talk to you. I know
        I wasn't good enough for you
        before. . . . I saw it in your
        eyes when I brought you to my
        apartment. . . . Please, I can
        explain. . . . I'm a published
        author now. . . . I'm good enough

now, you'll see . . . please, call
me . . . I'll do anything. I love
you.

Bob hangs up. Frustrated, he rises and walks by
Lou's desk.

                    LOU MELL
          Asshole.

Koss passes, pats Bob on the back. Bob glances back
confused.

                    MARK KOSS
          That's my boy, Bobby.

Bob turns into coffee room, GAEL is stirring an
espresso.

                    BOB HERMAN
          What's going on here?

                    GAEL
          Koss knows that you're my project
          now.

                    BOB HERMAN
          What's Lou's problem?

                    GAEL
          He knows too.

                    BOB HERMAN
          So?

                    GAEL
          Bobby. I get my bell rung once,
          twice a month. . . . Now that
          you're my project, Lou's afraid
          that he won't be ringing it
          anymore. . . . You know when Lou
          and I leave for our workouts?

                    BOB HERMAN
        Yeah.

                      GAEL
        We work out.

Bob leaves. Jennifer walks by, and Gael winks at
her.

                      GAEL
        He's been allocated to me,
        honey. . . . I honestly don't know
        what you see in him. . . . He's
        about as manly as a pink
        dress. . . . But when pushed, he
        can perform. I'll give him that.

Jennifer leaves.

EXT. STREET MONTAGE:

ISA WALKING DOWN THE STREET. IN A CAR NEARBY, TED
BASLE WATCHES HIM.

ISA WALKING SOMEWHERE ELSE. TED TAKES PICTURES
FROM HIS CAR.

ISA APPROACHING A SOUP KITCHEN. TED PARKED WATCH-
ING.

ISA ENTERS.

INT. SQUAD CAR SAME TIME

Detective Kennedy is in the passenger seat. Detective Clark is in the driver seat scratching his
bare arm.

FADED TATTOO OF US FLAG

They are watching Ted Basle.

>   DETECTIVE KENNEDY
>   Shit. Now who's this asshole?

>   DETECTIVE CLARK
>   We've got a problem.

INT. OFFICES OF GENT AMERICA MEDIA

Gael's office. Gael is working on the computer and filing her nails.

GOOGLE HOME PAGE. GAEL HITS SEARCH.

Ted comes in and dumps pictures of Isa on Gael'S desk.

>   GAEL
>   Got him?

>   TED BASLE
>   Got him. I still need a name.

>   GAEL
>   How hard can it be to identify a
>   street person?

Gael studies the pictures. Is that recognition in her eyes?

>   TED BASLE
>   Thousands of them die every year
>   without ever being identified. He
>   may be joining them. Ugly, huh?

>   GAEL
>   I don't pay you for your opinions.

She continues to look at the photo.

                    TED BASLE
                   (squinting)
          Sorry. . . . I think you're hiding
          something from me.

                    GAEL
          You know what I think? I think
          that you're too smart for your own
          good.

Gael reaches in her purse. She takes out a stack
of hundred-dollar bills. She counts fifty of them.

                    GAEL
          I won't give you another dime
          without his name.

                    TED BASLE
          Why are you so tough with me?

                    GAEL
          There can only be one king of the
          forest.

                    TED BASLE
          Men . . . we don't stand a chance.

INT. BUS NIGHT

Bob is standing, staring blankly out the window.

                    VOICE
          Don't turn around. Get off at the
          next stop.

Bob goes to turn.

                    VOICE
          Don't. Get off and go into the
          Euro Café at the next stop.

Bob gets off and straightens up his collar. Isa follows him into a coffee shop.

INT. COFFEE SHOP

They sit in a corner booth.

> BOB HERMAN
> You're the writer of *Standard Deviations*, aren't you?

> ISA
> I arranged the words into their form, but we are all the writer of *Standard Deviations*. There are things you don't understand.

> BOB HERMAN
> Boy, don't I know it. It's great to finally meet you, sir. Thank you, I can't tell you how import . . .

Bob extends his hand, Isa doesn't accept. Bob clears his throat.

> BOB HERMAN (CONT'D)
> I wanted to find you. I looked everywhere, then people read your book and one thing led to another . . . it all happened so fast . . . I meant no disrespect.

Isa remains silent.

> BOB HERMAN (CONT'D)
> I saw you carried another manuscript the other night. I'd like to buy it.

> ISA
> My words are precious to me. . . . But sell words? No.

                    BOB HERMAN
But you can get off of the
streets.
You can live in a nice house
and . . .

                    ISA
No.

                    BOB HERMAN
What's your name?

                    ISA
My name is not your concern.

                    BOB HERMAN
This means everything to me!

                    ISA
Silly things often occupy a lot of
space in small lives.

Bob smooths his hair back.

                    BOB HERMAN
I'm begging you. You don't
understand.

                    ISA
Don't I? I've been observing
you. . . .

                    BOB HERMAN
What do you mean?

                    ISA
You and the people you've hired
must stop looking for me.

                    BOB HERMAN
     So you've watched me struggle all
     along knowing that all you had to
     do to help me was show your face?

                    ISA
     You've made a big mistake.

                    BOB HERMAN
     Coauthor the book with me. You can
     be rich.

                    ISA
     You must stop looking for me.

Isa rises.

                    BOB HERMAN
     Give me another book and I will.

                    ISA
     There's something you must do.

                    BOB HERMAN
     Anything.

                    ISA
     You must start being a man of
     honor.

                    BOB HERMAN
     But . . .

                    ISA
     Do not follow me.

Isa leaves.

                    BOB HERMAN
     Honor?

Bob takes out his cell phone and dials.

                    BOB HERMAN
          Gael, Bob. I found him, but the
          weirdo won't have any part of it.

INT. TED BASLE'S CAR

Gael is in the passenger seat. Both she and Ted are
watching Isa leave the coffee shop.

Gael speaks into the phone.

                    GAEL
          Don't sweat it, sweetheart.

She nods at Ted, then hangs up the phone.

INT. EURO CAFÉ

                    BOB HERMAN
          Gael? Gael?

Frustrated, he hangs up and sits, staring at the
wall.

EXT. EURO CAFÉ

Gael gets out of the car. Ted drives off to follow
Isa.

INT. EURO CAFÉ

Gael sits down next to Bob.

                    GAEL
          So that was our laureate?

                    BOB HERMAN
          Where the hell did you come from?

                    GAEL
          We'll get him. He's got a tail.

> BOB HERMAN
> A tail? Jesus, maybe you should
> just let me handle this, Gael.

> GAEL
> Like you have up until now? Time's
> money. . . . You don't get it, do
> you?

> BOB HERMAN
> I can't convince him. How will
> you?

Gael smiles.

> BOB HERMAN
> He's not that easy.

> GAEL
> Neither am I. . . . Besides,
> Africans are overrated. Latinos
> are where it's at. Give me a young
> Italian, Brazilian, or Greek any
> day.

Gael gets up and leaves. She turns.

> GAEL
> You've turned over our savior. Take
> the day off, Bobby. You've earned
> your thirty pieces of silver.

INT. BOB'S APARTMENT LATER THAT EVENING

Bob is on the phone. Lucia's answering machine
picks up again.

> BOB HERMAN
> I have to stop calling you, but
> I can't. Why won't you just call
> me back? We have something, damn
> it! I'm sorry, I didn't mean to

yell . . . just, I need to find
you. I need you . . .

He trails off and hangs up. Next to the phone is
Ted's card. He dials the phone, then hangs up.
After a moment, he dials again.

INT. TOAD HALL BAR

Bob and Ted are sitting with coffee in front of
them.

> TED BASLE
> You read my mind, Bobby.

> BOB HERMAN
> What do you mean, I read your
> mind?

> TED BASLE
> Well, Bobby . . . let me put it
> this way. Mark Koss is on top of
> the wall, if you know what I mean.

> BOB HERMAN
> What, like Humpty Dumpty?

> TED BASLE
> Precisely. And I'm the guy that
> makes sure that Humpty Dumpty
> doesn't take a fall cause all
> d' king's horses and d' king's
> men couldn't put Humpty together
> again. . . . And because I occupy
> this position you could say that
> I'm the most important man in
> Gent. I was going to call you
> because you've become an important
> resource. Gent stock is counting
> on you. I'm a large shareholder so
> I am counting on you. . . . Now
> how can I be of service?

Bob clears his throat.

> **BOB HERMAN**
> Ted, a writer's emotional
> stability is everything. If I lack
> confidence or stability, then it's
> transferred to my work. I've fallen
> for this girl, but something's
> not right. She's got wild stories
> and expensive clothes, and I
> just don't want to be taken for a
> ride. . . . You know what I mean.

> **TED BASLE**
> Bobby, this is Ted you're talking
> to. You're no writer, everyone
> knows that now. But that doesn't
> mean that I don't want to keep our
> man happy. Name? Address?

> **BOB HERMAN**
> Lucia, 234 East Second. I don't
> have her last name.

> **TED BASLE**
> Sure Bobby. What kind of
> information? Medical? Criminal?
> Scholastic?

> **BOB HERMAN**
> Yes . . . yes, all of it.

Bobby looks humbly at Ted.

> **TED BASLE**
> You got it, Bobby. I'll get you
> info on her lawyer and doctor
> and lawsuits and credit cards and
> exes. You'll have it all.

> **BOB HERMAN**
> Thanks Ted.

Bob reaches to shake Ted's hand. Ted smiles, squeez-
ing Bob's hand tightly.

> TED BASLE
> I'm your friend, Bob. At Gent we're
> all one big happy family. The most
> important part of Gent is the
> bottom line. You see Bob, I guard
> the bottom line. Someone messes
> with you, they mess with the
> bottom line . . . they're messing
> with me.

Bobby tries to move his hand from Ted's grip. Ted
holds tight. Bob stares at Ted.

> TED BASLE (GENTLY)
> Anyone who messes with the
> bottom line is messing with
> me . . . anyone. Got that?

> BOB HERMAN
> Yes. Thanks, Ted. I really
> appreciate it. Listen, don't tell
> anyone about this, okay?

> TED BASLE
> You just go home, Bobby. Leave it
> up to me.

Ted leaves Bob alone and uncomfortable.

INT. BOB'S APARTMENT LATER THAT EVENING

Bob's at his laptop with a pencil in his ear looking industrious. There's a knock. He jots something
down. He makes a frustrated face and walks toward
the door.

> BOB HERMAN
> Who is it?

                        VOICE
            Police.

Bob walks back to his desk, clears the page on his
laptop, and goes back to open the door.

                     BOB HERMAN
            What can I do for you?

                     POLICEMAN
            Are you Robert Herman?

                     BOB HERMAN
            Yes.

                     POLICEMAN
            Can you please come to the station
            with us, Mr. Herman?

                     BOB HERMAN
            Why?

                     POLICEMAN
            Sir, please get your jacket. I'll
            explain on the way.

INT. POLICE STATION

Detectives Harms and Clark are talking near file
cabinets. In the background. Bob Herman is sitting
at a desk.

                     DETECTIVE HARMS
            We've got to hold this guy. He's
            onto Isa.

                     DETECTIVE CLARK
            I told you to avoid using his
            name.

DETECTIVE HARMS
If this thing blows up, it will
be front page news. We'll all go
away for a very long time. Isa
(whispered) shot COWDAR for us
all, and we were all a part of
it. . . .

Harms stares at Clark. Clark drags long on a cigar.
A woman in uniform passes.

POLICEWOMAN
Hey Clark, put that out. No
smoking in the building. You men
think that you're above the law.

The woman turns the corner.

DETECTIVE CLARK(UNDER HIS BREATH)
Yeah and two women officers got
shot with their own guns this
year . . . cunt.

DETECTIVE HARMS
You've got to book Herman.

DETECTIVE CLARK
If I booked everyone that had
reason to kill Russo, we'd be
filling out paper for a month.

Harms looks toward Bob, who is oblivious to what's
going on.

DETECTIVE CLARK
We either need to get him to
confess to assaulting Russo, or
to lie about knowing him, then we
can book him.

INT. POLICE STATION

Bob's sitting in front of Detective Clark. Another
detective is in the corner of the room.

                    DETECTIVE CLARK
          Standard Deviations, isn't it, Mr.
          Herman? I loved it.

                    BOB HERMAN
          Thank you. Will you please tell me
          why I'm here?

                    DETECTIVE CLARK
          You don't know?

               BOB HERMAN (UNCONVINCING)
          I'm not one to be trifled with.

                    DETECTIVE CLARK
          Of course, Mr. Herman. I'm sure
          you're not.

                    BOB HERMAN
          I still don't know why I'm
          here. . . . Now what is this
          about? I want to call my attorney!

                    DETECTIVE CLARK
          Do you own a gun, Mr. Herman?

                    BOB HERMAN
          A gun? No, of course not.

                    DETECTIVE CLARK
          Will you give us permission to
          search your apartment?

                    BOB HERMAN
          My apartment? Why? I want to call
          my attorney.

                    DETECTIVE CLARK
          If you'd like. I think we could
          settle this quickly though, if
          you'd just cooperate.

                    BOB HERMAN
          No, no. . . . I want my phone
          call.

INT. POLICE STATION INTERROGATION ROOM

Arnie Schuman and Ted Basle are standing behind
Bob. Clark is sitting and Kennedy is standing
behind Clark.

                    DETECTIVE CLARK
          Do you know why anyone would want
          to kill Tony Russo?

          BOB HERMAN (SURPRISED AT THE NEWS)
          Tony Russo? I don't even know him.

                    DETECTIVE CLARK
          Book him.

Detective Clark stands up. Kennedy approaches Bob.

                    ARNIE SCHUMAN
          Wait just a . . .

Bob interrupts.

                    BOB HERMAN
          Wait. Arnie. Wait. I met him once.

                    DETECTIVE CLARK
          Did you point a gun at Russo in
          Bino's Bar?

                    BOB HERMAN
No. I told you, I don't own a gun.
He's a scumbag. He was messing
with a girl I know. I walked
over to ask him to leave her
alone. . . . I pointed at him with
my cell phone in my pocket. He may
have thought it was a gun.

                  DETECTIVE CLARK
Did you tell him it wasn't a gun?

                    BOB HERMAN
I was surrounded by five of his
friends. Would you have told him
it wasn't a gun? He's really dead?

                 DETECTIVE KENNEDY
Should I book him?

                  DETECTIVE CLARK
Not yet. Would you like some
water, coffee?

                  ARNIE SCHUMAN
What kind of game are we playing
here detective?

Ted Basle eyeing Clark and Kennedy. Clark looks at
Ted.

                  DETECTIVE CLARK
May I ask who you are, Sir?

                  ARNIE SCHUMAN
He is my assistant.

Looking at Ted.

                  DETECTIVE CLARK
Are you an attorney?

                    ARNIE SCHUMAN
          No.

                    DETECTIVE CLARK
          A paralegal?

                    ARNIE SCHUMAN
          No.

                    DETECTIVE CLARK
          A relative?

                    ARNIE SCHUMAN
          Detective, who are you
          interrogating here? It is late. If
          you're going to book my client I
          wish that you would. Otherwise I'm
          going to have to insist that you
          release him.

INT. POLICE STATION DARK

Bob is walking out with Arnie and Ted. Clark and
Kennedy are in the background.

EXT. CEMETERY NEXT DAY

Tony Russo's casket is being lowered into the
ground. Many old Italian women in black howl and
cry. Bob approaches the cemetery and stops to watch
the funeral from a distance. He spots Lucia. She
watches the casket lower with little expression on
her face.

A hooded man walks up to Bob. It is Isa.

                    ISA
          I thought you'd show up here. I
          have what you want.

Isa shoves the book into his stomach.

> ISA
> If you're an honorable man, you
> and your people will leave me
> alone. If not you'll risk the world
> finding out who the real author is
> and more. . . . Too much more for
> you to understand.

> BOB HERMAN
> I will, I will. Thank you. Wait,
> let me give you something.

Bob reaches into his pocket for money.

> ISA
> These are the clothes of a free
> man. You will not enslave me with
> your money or fame. I am free!

Isa leaves.

Bob walks away from the funeral and takes out his
phone.

> BOB HERMAN
> Gael. I have the second
> book. . . . He was at the
> funeral. . . a friend well, a
> friend of a friend, it doesn't
> matter. . . . I don't know . . . I
> know! . . . But Gael, he said that
> if we don't stop following him he'd
> let the world know who the real
> author was.

Bob puts the phone in his pocket and happily walks
through the cemetery toward Lucia. He encounters
the Bino's bartender.

> BARTENDER
> Hey. I wouldn't go up there.

                    BOB HERMAN
Oh?

                    BARTENDER
Were you his friend?

                    BOB HERMAN
No.

                    BARTENDER
A little respect then.

The teary-eyed bartender looks away and then back
to Bob.

                    BARTENDER (CONT'D)
He might have been a jagoff. But
he was our jagoff . . . okay?

Bob gently nods and moves to the parked cars on
the road.

Ted Basle watches him from a car. Bob indiscriminately opens the package and reads page 26:

                    BOB HERMAN
The general replied. "Because the
Gulf War was about democracy as
much as the invasion of Iraq was
about terrorism as much as Vietnam
was about fighting communism as
much as the Civil War was about
ending slavery."

Bob continues to page through the manuscript. He
pictures Iraq vividly in his head. Time passes. He
looks up. He's alone. He turns to the beginning.

                    BOB HERMAN
I devote this book to all of the
hopeless romantics who fought
in conflicts created by political
invention.

INT. BOB'S APARTMENT EARLY EVENING

BOB'S asleep, pages in hand. Phone rings. He fumbles to answer.

> BOB HERMAN
> Hello . . . Jennifer . . . what
> time is it . . . ? I
> overslept. . . . What's wrong
> . . . ? You want to come here? Do
> you know where I live . . . ? All
> right, if it's really important.

Bob stands up, walks into the bathroom, and turns on water.

INT. OFFICES OF GENT AMERICA MEDIA, JENNIFER'S OFFICE SAME TIME

Gael walks in. Jennifer is sitting at her desk. She hangs the phone up and looks guiltily to the side.

> GAEL
> Should I know who that was?

Jennifer looks at her strangely.

> JENNIFER
> Koss may allow you to run
> everything in this company. But
> you don't run my personal life.

> GAEL
> Not yet. . . . Lover boy's done
> with book 2.

> JENNIFER
> Oh? So soon?

> GAEL
> Genius . . . is that what you most
> adore about him?

                    JENNIFER
No, the thing that attracts me
to him is that he's nothing like
you. . . . Get your ride, Gael,
and leave him alone.

                    GAEL
I'm going to keep riding him until
he's out of gas. You might try
yourself . . . oh, that's right,
you offered but he doesn't want
you on his pony.

                    JENNIFER
He doesn't know me, and he'd have
nothing to do with you if he
wasn't forced into it.

                    GAEL
Don't bet on it. A trapped manhood
can be very cooperative . . . and
virile.

                    JENNIFER
Well, leave him out of your trap.

                    GAEL
Oh . . . and if I don't?

Jennifer stands.

                    JENNIFER
Gael. Look into my eyes.

Gael remains immobile.

                    JENNIFER
What do you see?

                    GAEL
I see a half-witted little
lovestruck maiden.

                    JENNIFER
          Little half-witted lovestruck
          maidens giggle into the eyes of
          peril.

Jennifer walks defiantly past.

                    GAEL
          Not if the eyes they look into are
          those of the Big Bad Wolf.

                    JENNIFER
          You're not a wolf, and *canis
          simensis* only eat rats.

INT. BOB'S APARTMENT

JENNIFER and BOB are having coffee.

                    JENNIFER
          But why would you sleep with
          someone that you don't love?

                    BOB HERMAN
          Jennifer . . . I'm a
          man . . . sometimes a scared man
          but all the same a man. You may
          not have noticed, but men aren't
          always real particular.

                    JENNIFER
          In the end, you're just putty
          in Koss and Gael's hands. Bob,
          you need to find someone else to
          publish your work.

                    BOB HERMAN
          I can't.

                    JENNIFER
          Of course you can. *Standard
          Deviations* made it to the top ten.
          You're one of the top authors in
          the country.

                    BOB HERMAN
          It's not that simple.

Bob looks away.

                    JENNIFER
          Bob, I'm going to ask you this
          again. Did you write that book?

Jennifer stares into his eyes. Bob looks away. He
turns back.

                    BOB HERMAN
          Jennifer. Have you ever been in love?

                    JENNIFER
          Love? Yes.

                    BOB HERMAN
          I'm in love. Love makes people do
          stupid things.

Jennifer stands.

                    BOB HERMAN (CONT'D)
          Where are you going?

                    JENNIFER
          Back to work. We're all not authors.
          I just came to tell you to watch
          your back around Gael and Koss. And
          as far as love's concerned . . . if
          it finds you worthy it will guide
          its own course.

She leaves.

INT. OFFICES OF GENT AMERICA MEDIA FOLLOWING DAY
LATE EVENING

MANUSCRIPT ON BOB'S DESK

BOB'S sitting with a desk lamp on. He rises and
exits. The offices are empty. He heads to the elevator.

INT. LOBBY GENT AMERICA MEDIA BUILDING

BOB'S walking out.

> GUARD
> Good night, Mr. Herman.

> BOB HERMAN
> Good night Donny.

Bob goes through the revolving door. The guard
Donny is on his cell.

> DONNY
> He just left. . . . No, ma'am. He's
> by himself.

INT. RESTAURANT NEXT DAY

Gael is sitting at a table.

> TED BASLE
> Hey Gael.

> GAEL
> Sit down and lower your voice.
> I pay you for discretion.

Ted sits down and taps an unlit cigar on the table.

> GAEL
> Well?

Ted takes out another picture.

> TED BASLE
> He's called Isa.

Gael stares at the picture.

> GAEL
> Is he?

> TED BASLE
> That's all I got. There's nothing
> on him anywhere. He sleeps at a
> soup kitchen run by a nun. . . .

Detective Clark is in the background sipping coffee
at the restaurant bar.

He gets on his cell phone.

> DETECTIVE CLARK
> Meeting, thirty. I've got Isa's
> tail.

INT. DETECTIVE KENNEDY'S HOME BASEMENT SHORTLY AFTER

Detectives Harms, Holt, Kennedy, and Clark are
together.

> DETECTIVE CLARK
> The tail is professional, or sort
> of professional.

> DETECTIVE HOLT
> What happened to the author?

> DETECTIVE CLARK
> He's nothing to worry about. Isa
> would never tell him anything. Do
> you remember a guy on the force
> in the 80s named Basle?

DETECTIVE HARMS
Ted Basle . . . he was on the take
for drugs . . . never went away
but was booted off the force.

DETECTIVE CLARK
He's a PI now. He's Isa's tail.

DETECTIVE HARMS
For who?

DETECTIVE CLARK
Hard to tell. A woman, Gael
Veenstra, works for Gent America
Media. He does some work for Gent.
She's got her own story.

He chuckles. The men listen on the edge of their
seats.

DETECTIVE CLARK
It seems that Isa and Gael may
have a shared past . . . and
something that links them to the
future.

INT. FOUR SEASONS SOME WEEKS LATER. THE LOBBY IS
PACKED.

BILLBOARD "ROBERT HERMAN *SQUARE PEGS IN CIRCLES*,
BOOK SIGNING"

Bob is unenthusiastically signing books. Koss,
Arnie, and Gael are standing behind him. Arnie
whispers to KOSS.

ARNIE SCHUMAN
(whispered)
Square Pegs in Circles will sell
twice as many copies as *Standard
Deviations*.

                          MARK KOSS
            How nice.

Bob looks up, his eyes focused. Lucia's in the line
with a book in her hand. Bob stands, ignores those
ahead of Lucia, and approaches her.

                         BOB HERMAN
            Lucia.

                          LUCIA
            Hello Bobby.

                         BOB HERMAN
            I've been . . . I miss you so
            much.

Lucia embraces him dramatically.

                          LUCIA
            I miss you too, Bobby. I miss you
            too. Can we go somewhere to be
            alone?

                         BOB HERMAN

            Sure, Sure, of course. Um . . .

He glances at Koss and Schuman, who are speaking
to people.

                         BOB HERMAN

            Oh, forget it. They'll understand.

They leave, arm in arm.

INT. RESTAURANT, CANDLELIGHT. BOB AND LUCIA ARE
SITTING ACROSS FROM EACH OTHER.

                    LUCIA
      . . . and then Tony was killed,
      and I had no one to turn to.

                  BOB HERMAN
      How could you have ever been drawn
      to him?

                    LUCIA
      I was desperate for security. I
      still desperately need security.

                  BOB HERMAN
      Lucia, I love you, I have since
      the day we met, but I don't want
      to just be a replacement for Tony.

                    LUCIA
      Bob, Tony never existed. . . .

                  BOB HERMAN
      My life's been filled with
      disappointment. I've mostly
      disappointed myself, everyone
      around me. We'll start over,
      Lucia. We'll be an unstoppable
      team.

They kiss.

INT. OFFICES OF GENT AMERICA MEDIA THE FOLLOWING
DAY

Koss is staring out the window. Gael is in front
of him.

                  MARK KOSS
      That ungrateful punk. I never
      did like him. He ran off to the
      Bahamas with his book advance.

I'll never get the three books
he's on contract for. If I could
get what I've invested I'd flip him
to someone in a heartbeat. . . .

Koss slams his fist on the desk.

                    MARK KOSS
If he doesn't produce this firm is
in jeopardy. I'm fucked.

                    GAEL
What if we get ahold of the books
and cut out the middleman?

                    MARK KOSS
Cut out Bobby?

                    GAEL
All he is to us at this point is
a name. We could pay him, and go
straight to the source for the
books.

                    MARK KOSS
Cut out Bobby, huh? You don't
think it's too soon?

                    GAEL
Never.

                    MARK KOSS
And he'd let us?

                    GAEL
Definitely.

                    MARK KOSS
Really?

INT. RECEPTION HALL A WEEK LATER

Bob and Lucia are kissing at their wedding reception. They stop, and Lucia feeds cake to Bob. Mark Koss stands up.

> MARK KOSS
>
> I took this boy under my wing. He is now a man. I wish him and his bride a long and happy life. And many, many more bestsellers!

> LUCIA
>
> Hear, hear.

Mark raises the glass. The banquet of eighty people toast.

INT. RECEPTION HALL SHORTLY AFTER

Gael walks to Lucia.

> GAEL
>
> All my best, Mrs. Herman.

Lucia stares.

> LUCIA
>
> The name's Lucia.

> GAEL
>
> Come now honey. I only stole him from you for a little while. A real lady doesn't hold a grudge.

Walking away, Lucia steps on Gael's foot.

> GAEL
>
> Ah! Bitch.

INT. GENT OFFICES WEEKS LATER

Bob's sloppily dressed, sitting at his desk. Lou Mell passes.

                    LOU MELL
          Must be nice to do nothing and get
          paid for it.

Bob runs his hand over his head. He looks toward the computer. He turns it on. He stands up and walks out. He walks to Jennifer's desk.

                    BOB HERMAN
          Jennifer, get me a copy of
          Standard Deviations.

                    JENNIFER
          Standard Deviations?

                    BOB HERMAN
          You heard me, a copy of *Standard
          Deviations*. Maybe if I study,
          really study it. Something will
          come to me.

                    JENNIFER
          Like what?

                    BOB HERMAN
          Get me *Standard Deviations*!

Jennifer stands.

                    JENNIFER
          They're in the back.

Mark Koss enters.

MARK KOSS
How's the third one coming, Bobby?

INT. BOB AND LUCIA'S CONDO

BOB HERMAN
Let's not talk about money. What's
for dinner?

LUCIA
I didn't marry you to cook. We're
eating out.

Bob walks into the room holding a stack of receipts.

BOB HERMAN
These are yours, all yours! You're
spending money faster than the
mint can make it! We're broke!

LUCIA
Cool it. Get an advance.

BOB HERMAN
I already got my
advance. . . . And an advance on
my advance.

LUCIA
Go to your parents.

BOB HERMAN
I was supposed to pay them back
out of the advance. . . . The
advance that paid for our wedding
and our trips and your clothes
and . . . they don't have a dime
left to give me.

LUCIA
Well you better think of
something.

                    BOB HERMAN
I'm tired of thinking! My head
hurts from thinking. Why don't
you just go to your parents?! They
didn't come to the wedding, the
least they could do is send us a
gift!

                    LUCIA
I can't ask them to send us money.

                    BOB HERMAN
Why?

                    LUCIA
You promised to take care of me!
I should have known better! Well
believe me I will take care of me
if you don't!

                    BOB HERMAN
What does that mean? What does
that mean?!

Lucia smirks. Bobby glares, runs his hand through
his hair and walks out.

EXT. STREET ON THE WAY TO THE SOUP KITCHEN

ISA'S walking, holding a bag.

EXT. DARK BUS STATION

Isa walks in, goes to locker 117, puts coins in
slot, places bag in locker, and exits the bus station. Outside waiting in a car are Ted and Gael.

                    GAEL
Old man Koss has no idea what he'd
be without me.

                         TED BASLE
               Maybe you should start working for
               yourself.

Isa comes in sight.

                           GAEL
               There he is. Go and get him.

Ted opens the door and takes his gun from his holster. He rushes behind Isa.

                         TED BASLE
               Just a moment, fellow. NYPD.

Isa continues to walk.

Holt and Harms are in an unmarked squad car.

                      DETECTIVE HARMS
               Shit. What do we do?

                      DETECTIVE HOLT
               Just hold on, brother. . . . Call
               Clark.

Gael opens the car door.

                           GAEL
               Shit.

Gael quietly comes behind Ted and Isa.

                         TED BASLE
               Turn around or I'll shoot.

Isa continues to walk. The manuscript falls out of
his hands. He stops to pick it up.

                           ISA
               Shoot.

Isa picks the manuscript up. As he stands he glances at Gael.

FADE OUT.

INT. GREGORY'S COFFEE ON PARK LATER

Bob is sloppily groomed and sitting with Ted Basle.

> BOB HERMAN
> Look Ted. I'll give you anything
> if you find this guy.

Ted looks to the side and smirks.

> TED BASLE
> All you've told me is that he's a
> light-skinned, Arab street person
> that gave you some manuscripts and
> that he hangs around Chinatown.

> BOB HERMAN
> He's some sort of philosopher.
> His great, great grandfather was
> related to an Ethiopian king named
> Selassie . . . I think.

Bob grabs Ted by the collar. Ted stares and Bob lowers his hands. Bob wipes his mouth.

> BOB HERMAN (CONT'D)
> I'll give you anything. . . .
> Anything.

> TED BASLE
> Yeah, you will until I ask for it.

> BOB HERMAN
> Try me.

                    TED BASLE
          All right.

Ted grins. Ted takes the pen from Bob and writes
on a napkin.

                    TED BASLE
          He lives at this soup kitchen.
          They call him Isa. Sounds like a
          girl's name to me.

                    BOB HERMAN
          You knew?

                    TED BASLE
          It's my business to know, and I'll
          collect when the time comes.

INT. KOSS'S OFFICE SAME TIME

Gael is standing in front of Mark's desk. He's
seated.

                    MARK KOSS
          I don't get you.

                    GAEL
          You don't need to. I'm here to
          take Herman off your hands. You
          said that all you wanted was your
          investment back.

                    MARK KOSS
          It would take the profit on his
          next three books to do that.

                    GAEL
          That's what I figured. I'll match
          what Gent has at stake, and you'll
          release Herman to me?

                    MARK KOSS
You got to let a guy make a little
profit, Gael.

                    GAEL
I will. . . . Do we have a deal?

                    MARK KOSS
You're a businesswoman. You know,
I need time to think. Come and ask
me that again in a week.

INT. SISTER BRENDA'S SOUP KITCHEN BASEMENT NIGHT

The scene is black. Fire from the water heater
gives little light to room. Someone is fumbling
with a flashlight. The light goes onto stacks of
bound papers. The person picks up three of the
bound stacks and leaves.

INT. KOSS'S OFFICE

Koss is seated. Bob Herman is standing in front of
him.

                    MARK KOSS
Bobby, I really love you and that
wife of yours. I'd hate to lose
you, but if you don't produce in a
hurry Gael and someone that she's
dealing with will take you over.

                    BOB HERMAN
Don't do it. . . . Give me some
time. Please Mr. Koss, just a
little time.

                    MARK KOSS
I'm sorry, we just don't have any
more of that.

FADE OUT.

INT. SISTER BRENDA'S SOUP KITCHEN

Bob walks in and looks around. He sees Isa sitting at a table, reading.

Bob sits.

                    ISA
          How did you find me?

                    BOB HERMAN
          I've got my ways.

                    ISA
          I'll burn the rest of the books
          before I give them to you.

                    BOB HERMAN
          Rest? How many are there?

Isa starts to get up. Bob clutches Isa's arm.

                    BOB HERMAN
          Wait, wait, please. I'll be
          ruined . . . my wife . . .

                    ISA
          Money or a lack of it cannot
          destroy what's not already ruined.
          If you crash you'll be a better
          man for it. For you and your
          girlfriend.

                    BOB HERMAN
          Isa. Please. She's my wife.

Isa stares.

                    ISA
          Your wife . . . ? Face the truth
          and make your bread another way.

                    BOB HERMAN
        It's all I know how to do.

Isa takes Bob's hand.

                       ISA
        Until now all you've done is
        plagiarize. I'm sure that you're
        capable of something else,
        something honorable.

                    BOB HERMAN
        What are you, some kind of
        prophet? Honorable! You're no
        different than the rest of us.
        Ruin me, Isa, and I'll ruin you!

                       ISA
        Get out.

                    BOB HERMAN
        I'm sorry. Please. Just one more
        book and I'll leave you alone
        forever.

                       ISA
        Get out!

Bob storms away.

SISTER BRENDA WATCHING FROM THE KITCHEN

Sister Brenda stops Bob at the door.

                  SISTER BRENDA
        Come with me to my office, Sir.

                    BOB HERMAN
        I'm sorry, Sister. I'm leaving.

                    SISTER BRENDA
          I'd like to help you.

INT. SISTER BRENDA'S OFFICE

                    SISTER BRENDA
          We're all fond of Isa. He does
          maintenance here. He's been a huge
          help, he doesn't seem to know the
          word "no."

                    BOB HERMAN
          Yes, Sister. I'm sure that he's
          wonderful.

                    SISTER BRENDA
          I overheard you talking. I know
          who you are. And I know what
          you've done.

                    BOB HERMAN
          What are you talking about?

                    SISTER BRENDA
          The Bible isn't the only book I've
          read, Mr. Herman.

She reaches down next to her desk, lifts a stack
of manuscripts, and dumps them on her desk. Bob
reaches but Sister Brenda drives a ruler hard onto
the stack.

                    SISTER BRENDA
          This soup kitchen is running out
          of money. We can't build, we can't
          fix, we can't nothing.

                    BOB HERMAN
          How much do you want for them?

INT. DETECTIVE KENNEDY'S HOME BASEMENT THAT AFTER-
NOON

Harms, Clark, and Kennedy are at a foldable card
table.

Laundry is stacked on the floor next to them.

> DETECTIVE KENNEDY
> Why would Gent Publishing care
> about Isa?

> DETECTIVE CLARK
> Herman, Gael Veenstra. They
> both work for Gent. It must have
> something to do with the company.
> But what do they want?

> DETECTIVE KENNEDY
> I guess anything's possible.

> DETECTIVE HARMS
> Who owns Gent?

> DETECTIVE KENNEDY
> A guy named Mark Koss.

> DETECTIVE HARMS
> How old is he?

> DETECTIVE KENNEDY
> 65, 70.

> DETECTIVE HARMS
> What do we know about him?

> DETECTIVE KENNEDY
> He was an officer in Iraq.

> DETECTIVE CLARK
> Are you sure?

                    DETECTIVE KENNEDY
Yeah, it's verified. He's a member
of some VFW in Brooklyn.

                    DETECTIVE CLARK
Have you talked to them yet?

                    DETECTIVE KENNEDY
Wanted to meet with you guys first.

                    DETECTIVE HARMS
Maybe that's the connection.

                    DETECTIVE CLARK
I don't like it. . . . It's too
risky. If they discover that Isa
walked out of a body bag, we're
all done. The investigation of
those two women shot will explode
again. The Iraq politicians will
demand justice and the politicians
here at the end of big industries'
strings will give them our heads
on silver platters. . . . We sell
a lot of Coca-Cola, Microsoft
software, Levi's Jeans and
McDonald's in the land that just
years ago massacred American boys.

                    DETECTIVE KENNEDY
The only thing that can save
this country from the rich is a
revolution.

                    DETECTIVE HOLT
We can do that later, brother.
For now there are more pressing
things.

The three get up and walk out. The basement door
is opened into another scene.

INT. JFK AIRPORT HANGAR SUMMER 2010 NIGHT

The door to the hangar opens. An Italian-looking man (Gallo's cousin) with a bag in his hand enters and closes the door.

There are body bags lying all over the floor of the hangar. He walks to the center. He cups his hands together.

GALLO'S COUSIN
And on the third day he arose again according to the scriptures.

Noise is heard. Gallo's cousin looks to the left.

A BODY BAG IS SITTING UP

Gallo's cousin runs, opens it. Isa's head comes out. He's all bloody.

GALLO'S COUSIN
Oh my God. Are you hurt?

ISA
No.

GALLO'S COUSIN
Why are you all bloody?

ISA
This was the bag of someone else before it was mine.

GALLO'S COUSIN
Here, let me help you up. There's a bathroom by the wall. I have an airport maintenance uniform for you. Clean up, then you'll be free.

FADE TO BLACK.

INT. SISTER BRENDA'S SOUP KITCHEN

Sister Brenda is sitting at her desk.

Crucifix above her.

A large, young, dark-skinned guy, Larry, comes to
the door.

                    LARRY
          Sister. Mr. Herman is here.

                SISTER BRENDA
          Show him in.

INT. SISTER BRENDA'S OFFICE SHORTLY AFTER

Bob is still standing in front of Sister Brenda.
She's examining something on her desk.

                SISTER BRENDA
          I had expected more.

                 BOB HERMAN
          More? I can't afford this.

                SISTER BRENDA
          Mr. Herman, we have a deal.
          I've upheld my part. Do I have
          to remind you that we are the
          rightful heirs of Isa's property?
          He was a nonpaying tenant. You see
          Mr. Herman, those manuscripts are
          rightfully our property.

                 BOB HERMAN
          Don't even think about it, Sister.
          It wouldn't be in your best
          interest.

                SISTER BRENDA
          I'll decide what's in the best
          interest of this center.

                    BOB HERMAN
        Sister. I'll double the check. But
        I need the next two books.

                    SISTER BRENDA
        It may not be the best strategy,
        to piecemeal these books. I was
        thinking about selling them in a
        block. I have another interested
        bid.

                    BOB HERMAN
        These books are worthless without
        my name on them.
        They're just manuscripts. Don't
        outsmart yourself, Sister.

Sister Brenda pushes the check back at him.

                    SISTER BRENDA
        Regardless, you'll have to do
        better than this.

Ted's car. Gael is smoking a cigarette.

                    GAEL
        If we get the books, Bob works for
        us. We'll be in the chips.

                    TED BASLE
        I like it. I like it.

Ted puts the car into gear and pulls away.

                    GAEL
        Where are we going?

                    TED BASLE
        To see the lady who holds the key.

EXT. SOUP KITCHEN

Ted and Gael walking downstairs to Ted's car.

>   TED BASLE
>   Can't argue with her logic. The
>   manuscripts aren't books without
>   Herman's name on them.

>   GAEL (STERNLY)
>   I control him.

Gael reaches for the door as Ted enters the car. Isa walks from the soup kitchen with a package. Gael stares at him.

>   TED BASLE
>   There's our author again.

Gael looks and moves in Isa's direction.

>   TED BASLE
>   Where are you going?

>   GAEL
>   To deal with him.

>   TED BASLE
>   To deal with a shit bum?

Gael runs, Ted follows and passes her. Gael runs to catch up.

>   TED BASLE (CONT'D)
>   Turn around, or I'll really shoot
>   this time.

The manuscript slips as Isa turns at the building's end. He pauses to secure it, then looks up to meet Ted's pistol and GAEL.

GAEL STARING AT ISA.

                    GAEL
          Put your gun down, Ted. Sir, we'd
          like to buy your manuscript.

Gael squints as she looks at Isa.

                    ISA
          It's not for sale.

                    GAEL
          Everything has a price.

               ISA STARING AT GAEL

                    GAEL
          Ted, leave us alone. I'll handle
          this.

Ted looks in disbelief.

                    TED BASLE
          Are you nuts? I won't leave you
          alone with this scum!

                    GAEL
          Leave. . . . Damnit, just leave!

Ted turns to leave then looks at Gael.

                    TED BASLE
          Do you want my gun?

                    GAEL
                  (calmly)
          How many do you think I need?

Ted leaves. Gael removes a pistol from her purse.
Isa stares.

                    GAEL
          Where are you going with that
          book?

                    ISA
To a place where they can be safe.

                    GAEL
They'll be safe with me.

                    ISA
I will not sell my books.

                    GAEL
A pity. . . . Locker 117 should
be pretty full. I could shoot you
now.

                    ISA
Oh.

                    GAEL
I always wondered if there would
be justice for a man who ran off
on his pregnant girlfriend. Ahmed,
Deo, Isa. How do you know what
name to answer to?

                    ISA
Abby, I wanted to be with you, but
you made the decision to abandon
our daughter.

                    GAEL
You didn't care. You lived two
blocks away. You could have
come by anytime. But you buried
yourself in your religion. You
didn't give a damn.

                    ISA
Abby . . .

                    GAEL
My parents named me Abigael. I was
Abby to you and my old friends,

but now I'm Gael. You were so
proud. . . . The nephew of a
philosopher, the relative of the
great Selassie.

                    ISA
Abby, It's a long story.

                    GAEL
Aren't they all. . . . And it's
Gael. Get it?

                    ISA
Abby, I'm sorry, but I had few
choices. You'd never understand.
The situation is complex.

                    GAEL
If you call me Abby again, I'll
shoot you right in your control
tower.

Abby points the gun at Isa's penis.

                  GAEL (CONT'D)
I knew that if I ever saw you
again, that you'd give me that
shit. I'd have recognized you
sooner without the beard. Are you
incognito?

                    ISA
You should know something.

                    GAEL
Nothing that you could tell me
could change anything.

                    ISA
I'm not so sure.

                         GAEL
          Oh Ahmed, you always liked to
          dramatize.

Isa nods.

                         ISA
          Lucia is our daughter.

Gael holds her head for a moment. She looks aside.
When she looks back tears are running down her
face.

                         GAEL
          The orphanage said she was adopted
          by people out west. Are you sure?

Isa nods gently.

                         ISA
          I want you to know that I could
          not contact you. . . . It was
          a question of honor. If I was
          found, many would have suffered. I
          recently found out about Lucia and
          have been coping. . . .

                         GAEL
          And that is honorable? You're a
          coward!

                         ISA
          Gael! A man died. I . . .

                         GAEL
          And what about me? Did you care
          that my soul died? What kind of
          honorable man abandons a daughter?
          Man of honor. . . . So you
          murdered someone in Iraq and have
          been hiding ever since . . .

Gael removes the safety and again points at his
crotch.

                    GAEL (CONT'D)
          You're a coward that no one will
          miss.

                    ISA
          My squad was in trouble.

                    GAEL
          And what about me? Did you care
          that I was in trouble? Had you
          shown more concern, had you
          insisted and demonstrated how we
          would have lived. But no, instead,
          you ran away and buried your head
          in your holy book.

Gael points the gun at his face.

                    GAEL (CONT'D)
          Man of honor. So, let me
          understand this. You murdered
          someone in Iraq and have been
          hiding ever since? Why hide?
          That's what soldiers are supposed
          to do.

                    ISA
          I murdered an American.

                    GAEL
          I am not stupid. I figured that
          out. Why else would you live
          like a dog in the shadows? How
          chivalrous.

                    ISA
          Without chivalry, life is not
          worth living.

                         GAEL
          I don't need to hear about it.

Gael is openly crying.

                         ISA
          If you speak about this, I will be
          dead before I make it to trial.

                         GAEL
          What do I care, you coward?

Gael rubs her forehead, then points the gun at
Isa's face.

                         ISA
          Life is filled with tough choices.
          If you shoot, I only ask that you
          take care of our daughter.

Gael falls down to the ground crying. Isa leaves,
and Gael collects herself and joins Ted in the car.

EXT. CENTRAL PARK NIGHT

Wind ruffling newspapers, light from a lamp's partially covering Isa as he sleeps. A shadow moves
over him and pulls out a large knife. The knife
raises. A voice is heard in the distance. The
shadow stabs Isa in the chest. Isa grunts.

                    DETECTIVE CLARK
          Isa! Isa!

Isa blocks the second thrust, and the shadow turns
and sees Clark, who fires a shot. The shadow turns
and runs away.

Clark arrives.

                    DETECTIVE CLARK
          Isa. Shit. Are you all right?

                    ISA
          Yes, but I'm cut on my chest.

Clark helps him up.

INT. DETECTIVE KENNEDY'S HOME, BASEMENT

Isa is laid on a mattress in a dimly lit room. The
three detectives are over him.

                DETECTIVE HARMS
          This is getting crazy, crazy.

                DETECTIVE CLARK
          I couldn't make him out. I shot
          hoping that he would stop so I
          could identify him. If I would
          have killed him there would be an
          investigation.

                DETECTIVE KENNEDY
          Lucky, but why were you there?

                DETECTIVE CLARK
          I followed Isa from the center
          this afternoon. It's not the first
          time that he's slept in Central
          Park. I went to check on him.

                    ISA
          It's time for closure.

                DETECTIVE HARMS
          No fuckin' way.

                    ISA
          It's time for closure.

          DETECTIVE HARMS (shaking head and
                  speaking softly)
          No, Isa.

                    DETECTIVE KENNEDY
          Isa's right, Harms. . . . We all
          knew that this day could come.

Clark frowns at Harms, who takes his gun out of its
holster, pointing it at Kennedy and Clark.

                    DETECTIVE HARMS
          If anyone touches him, I'll blow
          them to pieces. There's not enough
          evidence for closure!

                    ISA
          I will not be the cause of 10 men
          falling. There are families to
          consider. Duty calls for closure.

                    DETECTIVE HARMS
          I'm sorry about this. Give me your
          guns. Isa's coming with me.

                    DETECTIVE KENNEDY
          Nobody likes this! Are you willing
          to risk my life, my family, yours?

                    DETECTIVE HARMS
          I'm willing to blow your head off
          if you try to stop me. Give me
          your guns, both of you.

Clark looks at Kennedy and nods. They give their
guns to Harms, who unloads them and gives them
back to them.

                    DETECTIVE HARMS (CONT'D)
          Now help Isa up and lay him down
          in the back seat of my car.

They reach down for Isa. Clark simultaneously
reaches into an open toolbox next to Isa. He pulls

out a utility knife. They lift Isa up and walk out
to the car.

EXT. ALLEY BEHIND KENNEDY'S HOME

Kennedy and Clark lay Isa gently down in the back seat.
The whole time Harms is covering them from behind.
Harms jumps into the front seat and speeds away.

CLARK AND KENNEDY WATCHING THE CAR SPEED OFF

INT. DETECTIVE HARMS'S HOME, GARAGE. THE AUTOMATIC
GARAGE DOOR IS CLOSING.

                    DETECTIVE HARMS
          We're home, Isa. We're home. I'll
          take care of you. I'll take care
          of you like you took care of us.

The garage door closes. Harms switches map light
on, turns and kneels, facing Isa.

                    DETECTIVE HARMS
          Isa. Isa!

OPEN GASH ON ISA'S NECK AND THE BLOODSTAINED SEAT

                    DETECTIVE HARMS
          Oh Isa!

Harms opens the back door of the car and hugs Isa's
head.

                    DETECTIVE HARMS
          (crying) Oh Isa!

The side door of the garage opens. Light enters the
car. Harms grabs his gun.

                    VOICE
          Drop it.

Silence.

                              VOICE
          Drop it!

Harms turns with the gun in his hand. He points at
the shadow. The shadow is pointing the gun at him.

Pause.

The shadow begins to slowly lower its gun. Harms's
arm remains tight and straight. Harms moves forward,
gun in hand. The shadow's arm is at a 30-degree
angle to the ground. Harms has the gun up against
the shadow's forehead. Another figure comes into
the doorway behind the shadow.

                        DETECTIVE HARMS
          It did not call for closure!

                           SHADOW
          It was Isa's order!

                        DETECTIVE HARMS
          It did not call for closure!

Harms cocks the trigger, hesitates, then drops the
gun to his side and fires.

                        DETECTIVE HARMS
                          (crying)
          It did not call for closure.

His body falls into that of the shadow. They hug.

                        DETECTIVE HARMS
                          (crying)
          It did not call for closure.

                        DETECTIVE CLARK
          I'll get rid of the body.

The garage door begins to open.

                    DETECTIVE KENNEDY
                       (feebly)
          Wait, wait.

Kennedy leans into the car, and snaps the dog tags
off Isa's neck.

INT. HOTEL ROOM, DARK, SAME TIME

Grunting and moaning are coming from the room.
A figure gets up and turns the light on in the
bathroom.

LUCIA'S FACE

She's bare chested in underwear. She bends to snort
a line of coke.

                       LUCIA
          This is all a lot of kicks but
          I want to stop. I mean it.

                       VOICE
          Come back to bed. I think that
          I can change your mind.

                       LUCIA
          It better be something really
          convincing.

                       VOICE
          Turn the light on. I'll show you.

Lucia turns the light on. Mark Koss opens a box
with a diamond necklace in it. She slides next to
him. He reaches down, takes a puff from his pipe,
puts it in the ashtray, and fastens the necklace
around Lucia's neck.

                     MARK KOSS
          Is this convincing enough?

SHORTLY AFTER

Koss and Lucia are dressed. Mark's sitting with his
head in his hands. Lucia is glaring at him.

> LUCIA
> Men. You all like to eat sugar,
> but you don't like cavities.

> MARK KOSS
> This is blackmail. Please, Lucia.
> I just gave you 25,000 worth of
> jewelry.

> LUCIA
> I want you to sign over my
> husband's books to me.

> MARK KOSS
> I can't! I won't! Gent would blow
> sky high.

> LUCIA
> Then I'll tell Mrs. Koss.

> MARK KOSS
> But you can't. She's just itching
> for a reason to take half of
> everything I own.

Lucia walks to him and takes him by the collar.

> LUCIA
> Listen to me! You'll do as you're
> told!

> MARK KOSS
> Please Lucia, listen, I'm working
> on a deal. I haven't told anyone.

Lucia looks on with curiosity.

                    LUCIA
What will it do for me?

                  MARK KOSS
There may be a big movie deal
coming our way. Bobby moving could
foul things up.

                    LUCIA
What will it do for me?

                  MARK KOSS
Lots and lots of money.
   . . . Without my cooperation
there's no deal. . . .
The books are fine, but the big
money's in the movies.

FADE OUT.

EXT. OUTSIDE HERMAN'S CONDO

Ted's on the phone in the car.

                  TED BASLE
You think that the mother is Gael
Veenstra and that the father is a
black man named Ahmed Selassie?
(sarcastically) This is good.

Lucia opens door and enters.

                    LUCIA
God. I can't stand him anymore.
Why did I marry him?

                  TED BASLE
Say the word, and he'll end
up like Tony. You'll have
to cry real tears though.
Convincing . . . that shouldn't be
hard for you.

                         LUCIA
              Where are we going?

Ted turns the vehicle into traffic.

                      TED BASLE
              The usual.

                         LUCIA
              Ted, give me the coke.

                      TED BASLE
              Wait a minute, honey.

                         LUCIA
              Ted, give me the coke. There's
              no money anywhere. I hocked some
              jewelry last week. Give me the
              coke. Talk later.

                      TED BASLE
              You know, if your husband was out
              of the picture things would be
              smoother. His books would pop up,
              they'd be bestsellers. Then maybe
              a movie deal and you'd be the only
              heir. . . . It would have to be
              done carefully, of course.

                         LUCIA
              Give me the coke!

                      TED BASLE
              Stop being so anxious, and be
              careful. . . . You don't want to
              snort up his insurance payments.

Ted laughs and tugs at her head.

                      TED BASLE
              Show me some of what you learned
              in that orphanage.

Lucia's head goes down on his lap. She sniffles.

INT. KOSS'S OFFICE

BOB is standing in front of KOSS.

> MARK KOSS
> No literary relationship is easy,
> Bobby. . . . But I'm onto a movie
> deal. Don't abandon me now. It
> will make us both richer than
> you could imagine. We're in this
> together. Right? Don't do anything
> stupid. We'll both be richer than
> you could ever imagine.

Koss reaches for Bob's hand. Bob shakes Mark's hand.

FADE OUT.

INT. BEDROOM, LATER

Lucia is standing. A man's figure is on the bed.

> VOICE
> You're fucked up!

> LUCIA
> You're fucked up!

> VOICE
> Where did you scam that name Lucia
> from?

> LUCIA
> It was no scam!

Lucia throws her shoe.

                    LUCIA
        My name was Lucy. The orphanage
        sent me to live with an Italian
        family in Bensonhurst when I was
        nine. It was the best four years
        of my life.

She wipes tears from her eyes.

                    LUCIA
        All I wanted was someone to love
        me. The Russos loved me. Then they
        took me away!

                    VOICE
        That's when you started with Tony.
        When you were nine!

                    LUCIA
        (sniffling) Yes. No. I was eleven
        or twelve!

Lucia throws other shoe.

                    LUCIA
        But I loved him. I always loved
        him!

                    VOICE
        Did he ever love you?

                    LUCIA
        He loved a hundred girls.

                    VOICE
        Is that why he died?

Lucia looks up. The voice is Bob.

> BOB HERMAN
> Look. Our money problems are over.
> Koss is making a deal. We'll have
> more money than we know what to do
> with. We'll have a new start. I'll
> take care of you.

Lucia looks at Bobby.

> LUCIA
> Bobby. . . . I stopped believing!
> I already sold the house. You'll
> never forgive me once you know who
> I was and what I do to get by.

> BOB HERMAN
> I want this to work.

> LUCIA
> Work? Do you know what I do for
> work? The only job I've ever been
> good at?

Bob stares at Lucia.

> LUCIA
> You'll hate me.

> BOB HERMAN
> Oh my God! Why tell me? Why would
> you ever be honest?

> LUCIA
> You'll hate me. You'll hate me
> forever. I'm a salesperson.
> I sell myself . . . and like a
> salesperson, I have clients.

Silence.

                    BOB HERMAN
          Nothing would surprise me!

Silence.

                    LUCIA
                   (quietly)
          Koss, Basle.

Tears well in Bob's eyes. He gets up, goes into the
closet and comes out with a suitcase.

                    LUCIA (CONT'D)
          I told you you'd hate me! You're
          like everyone else. You're running
          out!

                    BOB HERMAN
          You're sick! But you won't get
          anything else from me.

                    LUCIA
          Bobby, you wouldn't. I'm sorry,
          Bobby. I'm sorry.

Bob moves to leave.

                    BOB HERMAN
          Yeah, you're sorry all right,
          because you don't have a choice.
          For people like you, Gael, Koss,
          and Basle, honesty's the best
          policy when all else fails.

                    LUCIA
          Oh really? Is that what you tell
          your book fans?

Bob winces and leaves.

FADE TO BLACK.

EXT. NEW YORK CITY STREET SUMMER 2011

Isa is standing on the side of the airport maintenance truck. Gallo's cousin is on the inside.

> GALLO'S COUSIN
> My cousin told me to tell you that
> you won't be alone for long. Soon
> most of them will be back in the
> Big Apple.

> ISA
> Give them my best wishes and
> warmest goodbye.

Isa walks away from the truck.

> ISA
> (singing)
> Oh, it's good to be a free man.

INT. OFFICES OF GENT AMERICA MEDIA, CONFERENCE ROOM
FOLLOWING DAY

The conference room is immaculate. JENNIFER walks
in with bottled water. LOU walks in.

> JENNIFER
> Has Bob arrived?

> LOU MELL
> Bob the puss head?

Jennifer looks at Lou. Bob walks in. Lou walks out.

INT. OFFICES OF GENT AMERICA MEDIA, HALLWAY LATER

JENNIFER quietly closes the conference room door
behind her. She walks. LOU confronts her.

> LOU MELL
> How's it going in there?

> JENNIFER
> Gent stock's looking higher.

> LOU MELL
> I'd never have believed
> it . . . the phony pulled it off.
> Movies . . . Are you still in love
> with that jerk?

> JENNIFER
> (low voice) The man I was in love
> with is not a jerk. . . . Maybe he
> never existed at all.

Lou watches Jennifer walk away.

INT. HERMAN'S CONDO SHORTLY AFTER

Bob is sitting with Gael.

> BOB HERMAN
> This thing is out of control.

> GAEL
> Bob, I don't know what's so
> important that it couldn't wait
> for tomorrow morning.

There's a knock at the door.

> BOB HERMAN
> (confidently)
> He's here.

> GAEL
> Who's here?

Bob stands and opens the door. Ted walks in. Bob
socks him. Ted rubs his jaw and grabs for his gun.

> BOB HERMAN
> I know, Ted.

> TED BASLE
> Know what?

                    BOB HERMAN
        Know about you and Lucia.

                    TED BASLE
        I deserved that. . . . But deserve
        it or not, the next time you swing
        at me, I'm gonna take you down.

                    BOB HERMAN
        I hate both of you, but you're the
        only people in the world who can
        help me. Koss has a movie deal.
        I need the books. After that, I'm
        out of this town and you're all
        out of my life.

Ted glances at Gael.

                    BOB HERMAN
        A nun has them, and she wants to
        sell them to me. . . . But her
        price is far higher than I can
        reach.

                    TED BASLE
        How do you know it's more than you
        can afford?

                    BOB HERMAN
        Because before she raised her
        price the offer was a two-million-
        dollar donation. I couldn't afford
        that.

                    TED BASLE
        Why is this important to me?

                    BOB HERMAN
        It's important because Koss is
        making a deal that will make us
        all rich. Gent stock will double,
        triple . . .

                         GAEL
          Where's the author of the
          material?

                    BOB HERMAN
                    (irritated)
          I'm not sure. He may be dead for
          all I know . . . and that's how
          you will be, Ted, if you ever
          touch my wife again.

                         GAEL
          He's not dead.

INT. DETECTIVE KENNEDY'S HOME BASEMENT SAME TIME

Harms, Kennedy, and Clark are together.

                    DETECTIVE KENNEDY
          It's finally all over.

                    DETECTIVE HARMS
          In the end Isa got his way. We're
          all still free. . . .

                    DETECTIVE KENNEDY
          Is there anything that we have to
          know or do to clean things up?

                    DETECTIVE CLARK
          No. Everything's been taken care of.

                    DETECTIVE HARMS
          Where's his body?

                    DETECTIVE CLARK
          It's best if you don't know.

                    DETECTIVE KENNEDY
          Say, this doesn't mean that
          we won't see each other or

anything. . . . Isa died, not our
friendship.

INT. HERMAN'S CONDO LATER THAT EVENING

Bob, Gael, and Ted are sitting together in the
apartment.

> BOB HERMAN
> I went and spoke to the good
> sister. She promises that Isa's
> dead.

> TED BASLE
> And her proof.

Bob tosses the dog tag at Ted. Ted looks at it.

> TED BASLE (CONT'D)
> Sgt. AHMED SELASSIE.

> GAEL
> Let me see that.

> TED BASLE
> I got something to do.

Ted exits. Gael stares at the floor.

> GAEL
> (in trance) Ahmed wrote *Standard
> Deviations* and *Square Pegs in
> Circles* and *Gracious Ignorance*.
> He gave you the books because of
> Lucia. . . . Oh my God. Lucia.

> BOB HERMAN
> How do you know?

> GAEL
> (in a trance)
> I know. And I also know that he's
> not dead.

                    BOB HERMAN
                    (anxious)
          How do you know that? Damn it,
          Gael! How do you know it?

                       GAEL
          He moved books from locker 117 in
          the Sun Bright Hotel last night.

                    BOB HERMAN
          Could it have been anyone else?

                       GAEL
          How far do you trust Ted?

                    BOB HERMAN
          About as far as I could throw this
          building.

INT. TED'S HOME THAT NIGHT

Dark but for computer screen. Ted has his back to
the camera and is working on Google. View of Wikipedia screen about Haile Selassie, the Ethiopian
emperor who people like Bob Marley worshipped as
a god.

Ted copies the page. From behind someone with rub-
ber-gloved hands wraps a rope around his neck. Ted
convulses.

                       VOICE
          Sorry, Teddy. Time to go.

Two silenced shots are heard. Ted's body slumps.

INT. TED'S HOME THAT NIGHT SHORTLY AFTER

A pair of hands erases the history, wipes down the
screen with tissue, and logs out.

                    COMPUTER
          Goodbye, Teddy.

INT. POLICE STATION NEXT DAY

Bob is standing in a lineup. On the other side of
the one-way glass Detectives Harms and Clark are
with an elderly woman.

                DETECTIVE CLARK
          Number three, ma'am.

                ELDERLY WOMAN
          I don't know.

Detective speaks into a microphone.

                  DETECTIVE
          Number three, please turn to the
          side.

Bob turns to the side.

                DETECTIVE CLARK
          Is that him, ma'am?

                ELDERLY WOMAN
          I'm . . . I'm not sure. (pauses)
          Will he know that I picked him?

                DETECTIVE CLARK
          If that's him, you won't have to
          worry. He'll be locked away for
          life.

The woman looks kindly at Kennedy and then Clark.

                ELDERLY WOMAN
          Yes, that's the man that I saw
          entering Mr. Basle's apartment
          last night.

> DETECTIVE KENNEDY
Are you 100 percent sure?

> ELDERLY WOMAN
Yes I am.

> DETECTIVE KENNEDY
Book him.

INT. LOCKUP NEXT DAY

> LOCKUP GUARD
Herman out!

A black turnkey walks over and opens the cell door. Bob Herman walks out.

INT. HOLDING ROOM MINUTES LATER

Gael, Arnold Schuman, and another white male, attorney SHELBY WARREN, are waiting for Bob. He enters and breaks down crying on the table.

> BOB HERMAN
I didn't do it. I didn't do it. I didn't do it.

> ARNIE SCHUMAN
We know that you didn't do it. Calm yourself. In an hour you'll be out of here. You remember Shelby Warren. I've hired him to help you. This is an obstacle that will iron itself out. I hope.

INT. POLICE STATION SHORTLY AFTER

Lucia is seated in front of Detective Holt.

> DETECTIVE HOLT
Ma'am, just a few more questions.

                    LUCIA
Yes, of course.

               DETECTIVE HOLT
Did you know that Ted Basle worked
for your husband?

                    LUCIA
No. I read in the paper about
Basle. I can't believe that my
husband would have anything to do
with someone like him.

               DETECTIVE HOLT
I see . . .

The officer jots on a piece of paper.

            DETECTIVE HOLT (CONT'D)
So you've never personally met Mr.
Basle?

                    LUCIA
No, of course not.

LUCIA'S SWEET FACE

INT. Arnie Schuman OFFICES LATER THAT DAY

Bob is sitting. Arnie is standing.

               ARNIE SCHUMAN
Shelby Warren got you bailed.
You need to find money. We need
to give him at least a 50,000
retainer fee. . . . Call your
parents . . . your wife's
parents? Everything's at risk
here, everything.

INT. GAEL'S APARTMENT LATER THAT EVENING

Gael is at the stove. There's a knock. Gael walks
to the door.

                    GAEL
          Who is it?

                    VOICE
          Police.

Gael opens the door. Detective Kennedy walks in.

                    GAEL
          Yes?

                    DETECTIVE KENNEDY
          Ma'am I'd like to have a word with
          you. May I?

                    GAEL
          Who are you?

Kennedy pulls out his badge.

                    DETECTIVE KENNEDY
          Detective Jack Kennedy.

                    GAEL
          I assume that this is official
          police business.

                    DETECTIVE KENNEDY
          I'm glad that you asked, because
          actually it's not. I have something
          for sale that you may want to buy.

                    GAEL
          Oh, I doubt that.

                    DETECTIVE KENNEDY
Don't. I have the contents of
locker 117. I'll be waiting for you
by the bird house in Central Park
in one hour. I'll let myself out,
Miss Veenstra.

EXT. CENTRAL PARK ONE HOUR LATER

Gael is sitting on a bench. Detective Kennedy walks
up.

                    DETECTIVE KENNEDY
I like sunny days. Everything's so
clear.

                         GAEL
Oh?

                    DETECTIVE KENNEDY
Did you bring your checkbook?

                         GAEL
No.

                    DETECTIVE KENNEDY
Oh . . . then why did you come?

                         GAEL
                      (laughing)
You're so confident. May I ask why?

                    DETECTIVE KENNEDY
Let's just say I'm confident that
you'd help a close relative.

                         GAEL
I don't have a close relative.

                    DETECTIVE KENNEDY
Don't you?

                    GAEL
You don't know me.

              DETECTIVE KENNEDY
Abigael Veenstra, I know things
about you that you think no one
knows. Things that you'd like to
forget yourself.

                    GAEL
I like the park, Detective, but
you're not so convincing. In fact
I find you a bit confused.

              DETECTIVE KENNEDY
I'm sure that you'll be convinced
to do whatever you can to help
your daughter.

                    GAEL
Oh, you know my daughter? I didn't
know I had one.

              DETECTIVE KENNEDY
Not legally maybe. But Lucia
Herman is the child that you
brought to St. Anthony's Orphanage
thirty years ago. She's in
trouble. Her husband needs the
books that I have.

                    GAEL
I don't know what you're talking
about.

              DETECTIVE KENNEDY
Miss Veenstra, Isa's name was
Ahmed Selassie. He's now deceased.
But Lucia, who the orphanage
called Lucy Stokes, who then
became Mrs. Robert Herman, is your
daughter.

Yours and Isa's, that is.
Interracial children were not the
rage that they are today. . . . Your
daughter had a deal with the good
Sister Brenda, who double-crossed
her like she double-crossed your
son-in-law. You see, the good sister
and your daughter knew each other
from the orphanage years ago. She's
a dilly, your daughter. Besides
being a whore and a liar, she has a
nasty coke addiction.

GAEL'S STARE

>   DETECTIVE KENNEDY (CONT'D)
> Can we talk now, Gael? I'm almost
> certain that you killed Ted trying
> to protect Lucia from him. You buy
> the books from me, and I'll give
> you a bonus. . . . I'll keep my
> mouth shut.

INT. HERMAN'S CONDO LATER THAT EVENING

Gael is standing. Bob is sitting.

>   GAEL
> You can't give up. She's your wife.

>   BOB HERMAN
> She's a sad joke. And since when
> does any of that matter to you?

>   GAEL
> Bob, for once in your life stand
> up. Stand up for the both of you.

Bob stands.

>   BOB HERMAN
> OK, I'm standing. I should have
> left the damn book on the bus.

                    GAEL
We all should have done a lot of
things differently. . . . But it's
too late for that. You have to do
what you can to better your lives
now.

                  BOB HERMAN
Lucia can't get any better at what
she does. She plays men like they
were musical instruments. . . .
And she's had more flutes in her
mouth than the flutist at the
Philharmonic. . . .

Bob laughs, he breaks down.

                  BOB HERMAN
Do the humane thing,
Gael. . . . Give me your gun. Let
me finish myself. . . . Without the
books I'm dead anyway.

                    GAEL
You'll have the books, and
you'll put your life back
together . . . with Lucia.

                  BOB HERMAN
You're nuts. . . . Isa would never
give up his books. I know him! You
don't know him!

                    GAEL
I have three books, and I'll be
getting the rest.

                  BOB HERMAN
You're crazy!

Gael opens her purse. She takes out a letter.

                    GAEL
         I know Isa.

Bob takes the letter.

                    BOB HERMAN
         This sounds like Isa's writing,
         who was Isa writing love letters
         to?

                    GAEL
         To me . . .

Bob turns the page over.

LOVE, AHMED

Bob looks down. He shakes his head. Gael grabs him.

                    GAEL
         Take control of your life. Reach
         inside for your dignity, your
         honor.

Bob looks at Gael. Tears are welling in his eyes.

                    BOB HERMAN
         If you get me the books, I can
         begin to get them ready for Koss.

                    GAEL
         And Lucia?

                    BOB HERMAN
         What about her?

                    GAEL
         I want Lucia to own 50 percent of
         the books and the rights.

The closet door opens. Lucia walks out. She's holding a gun.

                    LUCIA
That won't do. I want 100 percent.
Right now Mark Koss is picking the
books up from Sister Brenda.

                  BOB HERMAN
Lucia.

                    LUCIA
Shut up, Bob. The books are
rightfully mine. My deceased
father wrote them. . . . I got all
my brains from you, Mother. And
it's working out better than
I planned. First I thought that
I'd have to kill Bob here to get
the rights. Then I thought it
better to kill Isa. Now I have the
best of both worlds. I tried to
kill Isa in the park. My partner
finished the job.
Detective Kennedy is my partner,
Mommy. Now if you could just tie
each other up for me. Detective
Kennedy will be here shortly.

                    GAEL
                  (crying)
Lucia, oh Lucia, what have they
done to you?

                    LUCIA
It's too late. You don't care
anyway. Your tears are as phony as
your boobs. You were more sincere
when I met you leaving Bob's
apartment.

Lucia's eyes are tearing.

                    GAEL
But I had no idea that you were
my . . .

                    LUCIA
          Don't say it, or I swear I'll
          shoot.

Bob walks in front of GAEL.

                    BOB HERMAN
          If you're going to shoot, shoot
          me. This whole travesty is my
          doing.

Bob inches closer to Lucia.

                    LUCIA
          Don't push your luck.

Bob continues toward Lucia. Lucia cocks the trigger.

                    LUCIA
          I mean it!

Lucia shoots and hits Bob in the left arm.

                    BOB HERMAN
          Give me the gun. . . .

Tears are falling from Lucia's eyes.

                    LUCIA
          Get back. I swear.

Lucia shoots and hits Bob in the left arm again.
Bob grabs Lucia. She falls into his arms and drops
the gun.

                    LUCIA (CONT'D)
          No one will take care of me. No
          one loves me.

                    GAEL
          It's not true, honey. Lucia. I'll
          make it all better. Your mother
          will . . .

Lucia swiftly grabs the gun and points it toward Gael.

> LUCIA
> Don't ever say that again. Get
> away from me or I'll shoot!

EXT. EMPTY STREET IN FRONT OF WAREHOUSE

Detective Clark is standing next to his car. Another car pulls up. Detective Kennedy gets out of the car.

> DETECTIVE KENNEDY
> What's wrong?

> DETECTIVE CLARK
> My car's on the fritz. While I'm
> waiting I thought that we'd pass
> some time together.

> DETECTIVE KENNEDY
> While we're waiting?

Kennedy reaches into his car and grabs the microphone.

> DETECTIVE KENNEDY (CONT'D)
> This is Kennedy! Get someone down
> here on Staley and Webb in front
> of the old Getz factory now!

> DETECTIVE CLARK
> You're too predictable, Jack,
> like the break-in at Isa's
> center . . . Greed was always your
> downfall. It's closure, Jack.

Kennedy turns around and goes for his gun. Clark shoots twice. Kennedy falls, gun in hand. Detective Clark drops his tape-covered pistol and drives away.

INT. DETECTIVE HOLT'S CAR SHORTLY AFTER

Detective Holt's car turns onto an empty street. He parks and turns around and takes off Koss's cuffs.

                    MARK KOSS
          You've made the mistake of your
          career. Do you know what you are
          doing? I know the mayor personally
          and . . .

                    DETECTIVE HOLT
          You're being undesirably
          discharged for the second time.

                    MARK KOSS
          What are you talking about?

                    DETECTIVE HOLT
          In Iraq, our boys found paper in
          their first-aid canisters because
          you sold the bandages to the
          civilians. They sold them to Al
          Qaeda. You had a lot of nerve
          joining the Oakton VFW. But I
          guess a large donation gets you
          into most anyplace. . . . But
          it can't buy you honor, Captain
          Kosel.

                    MARK KOSS
          You're insane and I'll have your
          badge. Do you know who I am?

                    DETECTIVE HOLT
          I told you who you were. Captain
          Ginsel plea-bargained and got you
          off the hook with an Undesirable
          Discharge. Money can't buy honor,
          and people like you are the
          reasons that twenty-eight soldiers
          take their own lives each and

every day. Would you like to at
least apologize before you die?

MARK KOSS
Apologize? Before I die! Officer,
you're insane, you don't know who
I am. I support the Patrolmen's
Benevolent Association, the VFW,
and Fallen Soldiers.

DETECTIVE HOLT
Mr. Koss, those are defective
cuffs. That's how you got them off.
Take this twenty-two that you had
between your legs. It's yours, I
took it from your office. It's the
one that you killed scumbag Basle
with.

MARK KOSS
Wait . . . Wait . . .

DETECTIVE HOLT
Take the gun!

Koss grabs the gun.

DETECTIVE HOLT
Mr. Koss, what would you rather
do, spend the rest of your life in
prison or die?

TEARS RUNNING DOWN KOSS'S FACE

DETECTIVE HOLT
I know what I'd rather do.

Koss turns the gun on Holt and pulls the trigger.

MARK KOSS
It's not loaded!

Holt shoots Koss twice.

                    DETECTIVE HOLT
          I didn't know that.

Holt picks up Koss's head. Koss's eyes open slightly.
Detective Holt winks.

                    DETECTIVE HOLT
          Your second undesirable discharge
          came from a thirty-eight
          special. . . . It was for all our
          boys in Iraq.

INT. HERMAN'S CONDO

There's a knock. Lucia opens door. Her back's
turned, she's shakily holding the gun on Gael. Bob
is unconscious.

                    DETECTIVE CLARK
          Give me the gun.

INT. GAEL VEENSTRA'S APARTMENT SOME DAYS LATER

Lucia, Bob, Isa, and Gael are seated eating.

                    ISA
          Every man lives his life for
          something. . . . Even Ted
          Basle. . . . If it wasn't for his
          private eye work and greed we'd
          never be here. . . . Life is filled
          with necessary evils.

                    LUCIA
          No. Isa . . . Dad.

Isa looks across the table at Gael.

                    ISA
          Take care of our daughter.

                    GAEL
          Of course.

                    BOB HERMAN
            And I'll keep studying.

Isa stands. He puts his hands on Bob's shoulders.

                       ISA
            You'll be fine, son. . . .
            Remember, writing and life are
            long roads. Experience is our
            teacher and if we live and write
            from our hearts we can't miss,
            no matter how little we have in
            our pockets. . . . Even if it's
            nothing, no matter who reads
            us. . . . Even if it's nobody.

                    BOB HERMAN
            Isa, when I first met you, you told
            me that someday you would ask me
            to do something for you. What was
            it?

Isa looks at Lucia.

                       ISA
            Take care of my daughter . . . by
            being a man of honor . . . If we
            are truly men of honor we will
            take care of the ones we love.

Bob hugs Isa. Clark, Holt, Gallo, and Harms are
waiting at the door.

                       ISA
            My brothers are calling.

Lucia runs.

                      LUCIA
            But, Dad, where will you go?

He hugs her.

                    ISA
     I'll never be all that far away.

                    LUCIA
     I love you.

                    ISA
     Let me go, honey. . . . And
     remember. There is no one poorer
     than someone who cannot afford
     hope.

Lucia falls to the floor crying. Gael walks to her
and comforts her.

                    ISA (CONT'D)
     She'll be better. And someday
     her regrets will be replaced by
     dreams. She'll learn, as we all
     eventually do, that when man no
     longer guides his life with honor
     he forfeits it. Honor is the
     thread of society, and without it
     the fabric eventually unravels.

Isa rises and moves toward the detectives at the
door.

                    ISA (CONT'D)
     Men, take care of my family like
     you've always taken care of me.
     I'm going to go to the land of
     my forefathers. The weather there
     should be a little gentler on my
     bones.

The screen freezes. The smiling friends become a
picture of their platoon.

The word "Chivalry" covers the picture.

FADE TO BLACK.**

Pictured Above: Robert F. Kennedy Jr. with Patrick Girondi
Photo credit: Deborah Suchman Zeolla

Other books by Patrick Girondi, published by Skyhorse:

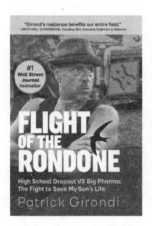

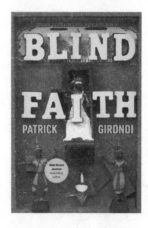

For more information on the author, visit https://patrickgirondi.com/